Heron
Fleet

Heron
Fleet

Paul
Beatty

Matador
9 Priory Business Park
Kibworth Beauchamp
Leicestershire LE8 0RX, UK
Tel: (+44) 116 279 2299
Fax: (+44) 116 279 2277
Email: books@troubador.co.uk
Web: www.troubador.co.uk/matador

ISBN 978 1780884 431

British Library Cataloguing in Publication Data.
A catalogue record for this book is available from the British Library.

Typeset in 11pt Aldine 401 BT Roman by Troubador Publishing Ltd, Leicester, UK

Matador is an imprint of Troubador Publishing Ltd

Printed and bound in the UK by TJ International, Padstow, Cornwall

To Sue, my best friend and chief encourager

Acknowledgements

I wrote Heron Fleet as part of an MA in Creative Writing at Manchester Metropolitan University. Thanks are owed to many for their help in its development: my tutors, especially Andrew Biswell, Nick Royle, Sherry Ashworth and Paul Magrs for their personal encouragement and advice, and my fellow students, particularly Alison, Dave, Iris, Lucia, Nicky, Ros and Sarah, who critiqued drafts in workshops.

The heron is a bird that has symbolism in many cultures around the world. Herons are often seen as being wise, going with the flow of life as they fly up and down waterways hunting for fish. In ancient Egypt herons were associated with Ra, the Sun God. They nested in high places from which they swooped down, reflecting creative sunlight from their huge wings. To Native Americans they are good hunters with excellent skills of judgement, wisdom and patience. In Greek mythology, herons were often considered to be messengers of the gods – although the news they brought was difficult to interpret and could be good or bad.

Chapter 1

Made iridescent by the evening light, marching over the headland towards the sea, the chain of geodesic Glasshouses looked like giant puffballs. On the top surfaces of each dome, the petal-like triangular vents, that during the day had been open to keep the plants in the houses cool, were closing to shut out the frosty night.

Francesca stood up with a groan, pushed back her straw hat and leant on her hoe. She pictured the activity in the domes. How the Gardeners would be running around, checking the temperatures, adjusting the sprinklers. How much she wanted to be with them, to share in this evening ritual, but at this time of year all the Apprentices who could be spared from other duties were directed into the fields. It was vital that seeds were sown and small plants weeded and nurtured in their early stages. If the crops did not make the most of the short growing season before the autumn storms came, the harvest might fail. But she hoped that by the time the growing season was over the Council would have made her a Gardener in her own right and she would be back with her beloved seedlings in the propagation chamber or among the squashes and zucchini in the curcubit house.

She shouldered her hoe, picked up her canvas bag and wound her way down the rows of small millet plants she had spent all day weeding. She came out on the path and turned downhill towards home. Fellow workers emerged from other fields and joined her: Jonathan, Hamied, Mary, a dozen others. At the edge of a nearly fully-grown maize crop was Anya. She kissed Francesca and then fell into the quiet procession, taking Francesca's hand in hers.

'Good day?' whispered Anya. Francesca looked at her, smiled and nodded. Anya squeezed her hand and returned her smile.

They reached the head of the combe where the path followed

the beck. Dry field margins became scrub, scrub became bushes and then they were under the trees. It was cool and green in here, where the moss clung to the rocks and water trickled. Here and there, where pools of light reached the ground through the canopy, the last bluebells flowered. Old Gatherers were fond of saying that they could remember woods where there were carpets of bluebells but Francesca didn't really give credence to these tales. In her experience the only places that bluebells could be seen were in the dark, cool places like the combe, and so it must have been for generations.

Too soon the trees thinned out and Francesca got her first view of the suspension bridge and beyond it the Gathering Hall. The sight of the Hall always gladdened her. It was the biggest building for miles around and as far as she knew the biggest building in all Albion. To the apex of the roof was about twenty metres. Its height was emphasised by the flat meadows that surrounded it. The squat shapes of roundhouses seemed to cuddle up to it. To Francesca it looked like a mother lapwing sheltering chicks, under her wings, from rain.

There was nothing in the scene to disturb her, nothing to undermine the sense of security that seeing the Gathering Hall always gave her, nothing at all. Then she spotted the thin veil of high cloud that radiated from the evening sun. She let go of Anya's hand and shaded her eyes to get a better view.

'What's the matter?' said Anya. 'What have you spotted?' Francesca pointed in the direction of the cloud. 'Don't worry,' said Anya. She stroked Francesca's arm, 'It's not typhoon cloud. There hasn't been a typhoon in over ten years. We'll not starve this year.'

Francesca smiled again and they started to pick their way down the steep steps cut into the river-cliff that led to the bridge.

Once on the bridge the group had more room and fell into a swinging, happy gait. Jonathan crept up behind Anya and tried to trip her up with his hoe. Anya turned and grabbed it. Then there was a playful struggle as she tried to disarm him while he attempted to get away. Finally, he broke free and dashed away towards the Gathering Hall. But if he thought he was in the clear he had underestimated Anya's tenacity. She dropped her rake and bag, and pelted after him. When she caught up she jumped on his back and hung on.

'So you think you can get away with goading me that easily?' she said grappling with him again for control of the hoe.

'Sorry! Sorry! I give in!' he laughed.

'Giving in is just not good enough!' she shouted. 'A forfeit! A forfeit is what I want!' The bridge was swaying with their struggle. She had him backed up towards the rope rail. Deftly she twisted the hoe, broke his grasp and with one end tripped him. 'A quick swim will cool your cheek!'

Off balance, Jonathan was at her mercy. One more push and over he went accompanied by the cheers of his fellow Apprentices. They rushed to the side of the bridge and looked over. He was just surfacing and flailed around splashing and spluttering.

'You fool!' he shouted at Anya, between catching mouthfuls of river water, 'I can't swim!'

'Is that true, Hamied? Can he swim?'

'No,' said Hamied flatly. 'He never learned when we were in the crèche. He was always too frightened of the water.'

'Shit!' said Anya and dived in after him. Francesca watched as she curled her body over the rail, breaking her landing with outstretched arms, to make sure she didn't hit the bottom. Two strokes and she had her right arm across Jonathan's chest and his head well above the water. Almost immediately, he stopped struggling and allowed her to take control. Then she sculled him to the bank near to the end of the bridge. The group met them there and helped them out.

By the time Francesca arrived, having collected up both Jonathan's and Anya's tools, Jonathan had his head down gasping and coughing, his hands on his knees. Hamied was patting him on the back and asking if he was alright. Anya looked balanced between fear at what she had nearly done and elation at her own audacity; she stood tall and there was a brightness in her blue eyes. Francesca dropped Jonathan's equipment near him and then took Anya's gear over to her.

'Are you OK?'

'I think so,' Anya replied. 'Let's go home. The excitement's over.' She picked up her bag and hoe and they walked up the bank towards the Gathering Hall. Gradually, the others followed. They passed through the Eastern Gate in the bank-and-ditch, and were counted in by the Gatekeeper.

★ ★ ★ ★

The evening meal bell had rung a little while earlier. Couples were emerging from the roundhouses and strolling towards the Gathering Hall. Occasionally a couple would stop and kiss. It was a blissful time in the sunset light with the prospect of high summer food to satisfy a day's hunger, worked up in the fields.

Francesca spotted Jonathan and Hamied, hand in hand. There were Mary and Jo, Isaac and Nathan, all of whom had been in crèche with her.

'Hi, Francesca.' It was Ruth. 'Where's Anya?'

'She hadn't finished drying her smock before the bell sounded. She said she'd catch me up.'

'Oh, after her swim in the river. She always was too impetuous. Well, that's lucky for me.' Ruth took Francesca's arm. 'It's a long time since you and I went in for evening meal together.' They walked on.

'How's Carole getting on in the kitchens?' asked Francesca.

'She likes it. The work's a bit hot this time of year and there's the downside of never being around at evening meal but that's life.'

Downside indeed, thought Francesca. Everyone knew that if one member of a partnership was assigned to the kitchens and the other not, then chances were that the partnership would split up. The cooks worked different hours to anyone else. They had to eat after everyone else had finished and were always in each other's company. Most cooks paired off with other cooks or those working the solar-ovens. That was one of the facts of community life. Ruth was likely to have a heartbreak coming in the future, to add to the disappointment Francesca had dealt her when she had broken their partnership to pair with Anya. Francesca still felt guilty about that.

4

They had come to the wide east doorway of the Gathering Hall. The children were on both sides with the Crèche Mothers. They clapped as the couples came in. Francesca remembered the summer evenings when, as a child, she had clapped in the workers at the end of the day. She could still hear in her head the voice of Bryony, her Crèche Mother, 'Clap hard Francesca. Their work will feed us all in the coming winter.' And how she had clapped, as hard as she could, for even then the thought of there being no harvest had frightened her.

Looking at the small children now, she tried to remember how it had been when she was small. One thing struck her, she couldn't remember as many couples then as there were this evening. *When you're little, places look bigger. Perhaps it's the same for numbers of people,* she thought. *But even so, I don't remember this many then.* She tried hard to count how many roundhouses there had been then on the Apprentice side of the Gathering Hall but try as she might she couldn't remember. All she was left with was an impression that when she was a girl there had been fewer.

The Gathering Hall, for all its size, was simply built, nowhere near as complex as the greenhouses. Ten roof joists set into the ground at about forty-five degrees were joined in a simple tent shape at the top to a beam that ran down the length of the hall. Outer sidewalls were made of cob. If you looked closely, you could see pieces of straw poking out of the red-clay mixture. These walls were several feet thick and served to keep the weather out but had no windows. Light came from the two gable-ends. As Ruth and Francesca went in, the sunlight was streaming through the west window in front of them. Its mixture of coloured and clear glass drew the shape of a setting sun over the centre of the High Table. Patterns of colours from the window covered the floor and the tables. In the centre of the hall, where in winter the great fire would be, was a group of singers, accompanied by two lutes. They were a group of mixed ages: Gatherers, Apprentices and children. They were singing one of the Founding Songs.

Through blasted Albion they came,
The first, the founding twenty souls,
They found this vale where plants still grew,
They gathered here and settled.

'Won't you sing for us tonight, Francesca?' It was Mary from behind her.

'Yes, do,' said Ruth enthusiastically. 'You know you've got the best voice in the community.' Several other Apprentices backed up her request.

'Are you sure, Ruth?'

'Yes of course I am. It's a long time since I've heard you sing.'

They unlinked arms and Ruth kissed Francesca gently on the cheek. 'There, go with my blessing. Coming in with you has been like old times.' Francesca smiled and strolled over to the singing group. Soon her rich voice could be heard above the others:

They ploughed and sowed and fished the bay,
Survived the storms and winter's cold,
They made a living year to year,
On the bank of the Heron Fleet.

All the Apprentices had come in by now and the children were skipping in through the door, laughing and playing. But as soon as they came inside they stopped to listen. Francesca saw Anya a little way in front. She noted her stillness, the slight inclination of her head and the sparkle in her eyes. Most of all she saw the peace on Anya's face. Francesca's voice rang clear and true.

They raised the Hall, built bank and ditch,
They set the Rule and made their Pact.
We live their way and prosper still,
In the way of the people who Gather.

Immediately a combination of emotion and relief grabbed her stomach. *She does love me*, she thought.

As the song ended a bell rang at the western end of the hall.

The Council were ready to enter. The Crèche Mothers shepherded the children to their tables and the singing group dispersed. Anya caught up with Francesca and together they went to their place with the other members of their roundhouse.

The bell rang again. Anyone not already standing got to their feet as the Council filed in to High Table. There had been twenty Founders and so, in the Heron Fleet way, the Council always had twenty elected members. The present Head of the Council was Peter. He now stood at the centre of the table, holding The Redbook, which recorded the Rule of the community. He stood ready to incant:

Reaping and sowing,
sowing and reaping,
this is the world we have.
All we know is the cycle of life.
Power to the greenwood.
Power to the field.
Power to our gathered food.

When he had finished, he closed the book and passed it to the councillor on his right. Then he picked up a flattened brown loaf from a dish in front of him. He raised it and pulled it apart. That was the signal to sit. Hardbread, brown and dusty with flour, started to pass from hand to hand. Each broke off chunks as their neighbour held the loaf out to them.

Francesca held out a loaf for Anya. 'Power to the bread,' she said solemnly.

'Power to the gathered food,' replied Anya. Then she touched her mouth and forehead with her right hand in one fluid gesture.

Still hot from the solar ovens, an earthenware tagine was placed in front of them, along with two bowls, one of green and the other of black olives. Anya took the cloth that came with the tagine and carefully lifted its inverted cone top. A breath of steamy air was released bringing a smell of cracked wheat, fresh mint and lamb.

Francesca always got a thrill out of evening meals in the

growing season, for only in the long June and July days was there regular meat. This was indeed the high time of year, a compensation for the exhausting dawn-to-dusk toil in the fields, the desperate race to plant, grow and bring in the crops before the growing season ended in thunder, lightning and torrential rain. There would even be elderflower champagne on Founders' Days.

'Tuck in,' said Anya. 'You deserve this more than most, for all that beautiful singing.'

★ ★ ★ ★

The meal was almost over, the tagines empty and only a few of the olives and the remnants of the hardbread remained. Groups from individual roundhouses were clearing up, people were mingling. It would soon be time for sleep. But it was a glorious evening and Francesca had noticed that even the Council members had left High Table and were passing from group to group.

'Well, recovered from your dip in the river?' said Jeremy. He was the youngest of Francesca's and Anya's roundhouse, only two years out of the Crèche. He was not in a partnership yet, at least he and Caleb had not declared themselves to the Council, but judging from the soft sounds that came from Caleb's cubicle in the night, that was only a formality.

Caleb made an exaggerated show of looking round.

'OK, Jerry. You're safe to remind her. No hoes she can prod you with, as far as I can see.' The others laughed.

'Very funny,' said Anya. She turned to Jeremy. 'Since you asked so kindly young man, I am fully recovered, thank you.'

'I wonder if the same is true for Jonathan?' said Susan, who, with her partner Christine, completed their group.

'As it happens, I've checked,' said a voice from above their heads. 'He's none the worse for the experience, although he's a little crestfallen.'

It was Peter and immediately they began to rise but he stopped them with a calm gesture. 'Don't get up. I don't what to disturb your conversation but I do need a word with Anya about this afternoon.' He nodded in the direction of a nearby empty table.

'Shall we go over there?' he said softly. Anya followed him.

'Wow, that looks like trouble. The Head of the Council doesn't talk to an Apprentice without a good reason,' said Susan.

Francesca watched. They had sat down. Peter was speaking to Anya seriously, moving his hands for emphasis. Occasionally, Anya nodded in response. When the conversation was over, Peter laid his hand on her shoulder and then he left. Anya came back to the group.

'Well?' said Jeremy, impatient that Anya had not immediately told them what had been said. 'What did he say?'

'He said he'd been told what had happened by one of Gatekeepers. He'd found out that Jonathan couldn't swim. He told me off for being so foolish and said that I should make amends,' she sighed. 'Since I'm such a good swimmer he thinks I should teach Jonathan to swim as a way of saying sorry. He said it would be a service to the community as well, since we could not afford to have any of the Apprentices unable to swim if the river flooded.'

'And what did you say?' said Christine.

'What do you think I said? Yes, of course. After all, you don't refuse a direct request from the Head of the Council, do you?'

'Shame, though,' said Caleb. 'That will eat up any spare time you have after work. You'd better hope he's a quick learner.'

Chapter 2

I watched the prow of the boat nose its way up the river on the late afternoon breeze. The sail was reefed to about a third of its capacity and despite the slow speed there was still enough way through the water to make her responsive to small movements of the tiller. The quiet was broken only by the warning cries of occasional water birds who flew off, disturbed by the boat's bow-wave. A few metres away a cormorant took to the wing and skimmed the surface of the river with its powerful stabbing wingbeat. Then it landed on a nearby quay.

Once, a long time ago, the buildings, wharfs and jetties all along the bank would have constituted an extensive complex of docks. Thousands of people would have unloaded the goods brought by the boats that would have tied up here. Now the jetties were derelict and breaking up, the wharfs more rubble than safe anchorage and the buildings eyeless and empty shells. All that was left of the boats were occasional half-submerged ribs of metal or wood clawing clear of the mud. No serviceable craft were evident, nor were there any people to be seen.

Ahead, the channel opened out into a rectangular basin, sealed at the far end by a set of leaking lock gates. These were spanned by a rusting, semi-circular metal bridge. But the dock walls were in better condition than many I had already passed coming upstream. The water in the basin was black and still, giving every indication of being deep and largely clear of obstructions. To the right of the lock gates a set of servicable stone steps came down into the water. I eased the boat forward and swung the tiller at the last moment so that she came parallel with them. As forward motion was lost, the tiller went light and I let it go to swing impotently. I dropped the rear anchor over the side and ran down to the prow to drop the second one. As I passed the mast I unhooked the rig draw-rope so that the sail collapsed in an orderly fashion. With no way of catching the wind, and anchors secured at each end, she was going nowhere.

The next step was to put out some bait. Taking my time I pushed the gangplank out onto the steps and transferred some of my wares from the hold to the bank: bolts of coloured cloth, tinned food, woollen goods and salted meat. Then I collected wood from the nearest ruined warehouse and lit a fire. When it was going well I put on a kettle to boil and while it was heating erected a spit. Then I sat and waited. Any people there might be would eye me up from the cover of the buildings.

Gradually it fell dark and the fire turned to a bed of hot, burning embers; time to put the spit to work. I brought a haunch of fresh venison up from the boat and mounted it over the fire. In a few minutes the skin of the meat began to brown and fat dripped sending up occasional flares of oily flames and jets of smoke. The meat smelled wonderfully appetising.

Time was running out for the Scavenger Gangs. The last three I had found were starving and I suspected at least one of having gone cannibal. If there was still a group in this city, God knew when they could have last smelled fresh meat cooking.

Just in case they got the impression that I might be easy to kill and rob, I brought my weapons from the boat and sat in the firelight to ensure that any watchers would be able see them. I oiled the crossbow and fettled some new bolts, casting some new heads from my supplies of lead and feathering half a dozen prepared shafts. Most symbolic of all, I cleaned my long spear, making sure the metal tip reflected the firelight.

No one really knew how or when it had happened, probably soon after supplies of firearms had run out, but in practically every Scavenger Gang, the spear had become the symbol of power and authority.

The moon rose. It was near midnight and I was beginning to believe I was on my own, when a single mother with a child in her arms came out from the shadows of a building on the other side of the dock and slowly made her way across the bridge. When she got to the firelight I could see that she was thin and the bones on her neck pushed painfully against stretched, pallid skin.

11

Both she and the child had the listless, vacant expression of the starving. Wordlessly she held out her hand. I cut a slice of meat from the haunch and gave it to her. She shredded it with her teeth and the child grabbed at what it could get with flailing, bony hands

Then they were all around me. They all had the same thin skin and empty eyes. I fed them all, and when the haunch was consumed, gave them salted meat, hardbread and dried fruit. Finally, the guards arrived. They were well fed, though that did not stop them taking my food. When that was gone, they dispersed the crowd and issued the invitation I had been waiting for.

'Follow us Ostlander. Boss want see yen.'

'What about my boat?'

'We set sentry.'

'Can I bring my bow?'

'No weapons.'

I locked the cabin and hold, putting inside most of the goods left on the bank. Then I followed them towards the city, taking only a few samples of my wares.

★ ★ ★ ★

The road from the basin soon joined a broader thoroughfare. Some of the buildings that lined this route had collapsed and we had to climb over or go round the wreckage. Some were still standing but their windows were empty, and in places metal bars stuck out of crumbling concrete pillars. In some places all that was left were piles of charred brick and half-burnt timbers, the result of fires left to run their course.

After about a kilometre our path began to climb gently. Then we reached a high masonry wall dominated by the bulk of a large, elaborate structure. The sun was rising and I could catch reflections which suggested that at least some of its high windows still had glass. The path crossed the wall and climbed up to a courtyard in front of impressive main doors. There was a small latch-gate with a guard who stepped aside as we approached.

The interior was gloomy, lit only by the occasional torch

burning in a wall-mounted metal bracket. Despite this, as soon as my eyes adjusted, it was surprising how much detail I could make out. My impression from the outside had been correct. There was still glass in the upper parts of the windows, some of it coloured in intricate designs. Some had figures and scenes painted on it. In the lower parts of the windows, some attempts had been made to replace broken panes, once someone had had time for something more than crude, basic survival.

My 'guard of honour' led me across the hall between twin lines of stone pillars that supported the roof. Set into the main wall opposite was an impressive doorway and stone steps that went up into a large, well-lit, circular room. This room had a tree-like central pillar whose branches became its roof-beams. The room had been designed as a meeting place and this chief, whoever he was, had the sense to use it as such.

'Bide here,' said one of the guards. 'He know yen coming.'

I sat in one of the stone seats arranged around the edge of the room. Each had a niche behind it so that a person could sit back and get some shelter from any draught. I wrapped myself in my cloak and waited.

I could remember what it had been like when I was a boy in a Scavenger Gang. How many desperate days had I spent picking through the rubble of a city not so different to this? I had been good at scavenging and seemed to have an instinct for finding food where others could not. But what I found was not confined to food. I turned up metal and plastic objects. When I broke them open some had mazes of metal lines inside, with small black and silver objects stuck to them. Others had cogs and things that appeared once to have revolved. In the end it was one of those things that changed everything for me.

One day I came across a white plastic box with a silver rod in its top. I had pulled this rod out, shaken the box and then poked at the small plates set into its front. When I pressed a bright orange plate, a small red light had appeared and a hissing sound came from the box. It didn't last long, fading away slowly and finally disappearing. In frustration I smashed it against a stone and went on scavenging.

13

But try as I might I couldn't get the picture of that box out of my head. I knew it had been made by the City builders but what was it? I began questioning the older scavengers to see if they knew anything about such things but what they told me sounded like fairy stories and made no sense. Then one day I found several sheets of paper held together with small metal clips so that you could turn the sheets over and go from one to the next.

Paper was commonplace in the ruins, we prized it for starting fires. Some of the paper we found had faded markings on it but these sheets were different. There were coloured pictures of men and women on them. I tucked the papers away in my coat before anyone could notice and take them from me.

When I got back to the camp I went to see the oldest scavenger. The look in his eyes when I showed him the paper is engraved in my memory.

'What it?'

'Writin', Tobias, writin'. If you could read these marks they'd tell you about the people in the pictures.'

'Can you read?'

'No. Me only know letter-sounds. Yem small marks am letters. There an *ay*, there a *bee*, and there an *eff*,' he traced them with his finger. 'Each one has its own sound.'

'Why yen in groups?'

'Yem words. Speak letter-sounds in group, yen hear the word speak.'

'You teach me letter-sounds?' He looked dubious. 'I'll share my scavengin wi yen.' The old man had not needed any more inducement.

'Raise yen feet Ostlander!' shouted a harsh voice. I opened my eyes. It was a guard with a spear pointed at my throat. 'On yem feet,' he repeated. 'Nonuther chance.'

I got up unsteadily. 'Sorry, I nodded off,' I said.

'Make it no habit,' said a much softer, more calculating, voice.

On the other side of the room a group of four people had appeared. The speaker was a tall young man dressed in a leather jacket and boots. Around his neck there was a clean white scarf. He wore a blue shirt. Both caught the light from the torches. I'd never seen it before but knew they must be silk. A Scavenger Gang leader with a taste in silk was a novelty, a Scavenger Gang chief who recognised silk even more so.

To the right of the man was a tall woman dressed similarly in good quality leathers. Her face was sharp, proud and beautiful, hair long and golden against the black of her jacket. Memory connects directly with the circulation and the nerves. The heart leaps and the guts churn before the mind has focused on why.

Behind her were two guards. At first I dismissed them. No surprises there, I thought. They were of the same demeanour as the sullen lot that had brought me up from the boat. Even their clothes were of the identical rough fabric. But I was wrong. What they carried made them fascinating. Both had rifles on their shoulders and wore bullet-belts outside their coats. I had never come across serviceable firearms but these looked well-oiled and in good repair. The question was, were they for show or, impossibly, could they work?

The young man spoke. 'Me Robert. Me men tell me yen have a ship at the quay. Yen trader?'

'Yes, my Lord.' The arcane title had always flattered these chiefs in the past so I stuck to the well-tried formula, remembering to move my accent into scavenger mode as I spoke.

'What trade-yen?'

'Meat, grain, tins, cloth. Anything me find or hunt.'

'Yen hunt the meat you cook on the quay?'

'Plenty more where it come from.'

'Why not me just kill yen and rob yen ship?'

'Then me never come back with more. Me happy to make bargain if you give me yat me want.'

I saw Robert hesitate. *He knows they can't last much longer*, I thought.

'Yen eye state me people. What yen think we have that me possibly have to trade?'

'Perhaps more than you think. Me don't just trade food and cloth. Me interested in City builder stuff.'

'How be that?' On the surface the voice was mocking but behind it there was a keen interest.

'Yen heard a books?' As I said this I noticed that the woman, who had not paid much attention until now, raised her head slightly and started to concentrate on what was being said. 'Yat a book?' Immediately she touched his arm, leaned over and spoke in his ear. 'Me woman say she know.'

I tested her. 'Yen what yey, me Lady?'

'They are the stories of the City builders, collections of writings, like this.' From inside her jacket she took out a small green volume. It was battered but the leather of its cover and the spine were embossed with a complex pattern to which gold leaf still clung. There was also gold on the edges of the pages. She handed it to me.

I looked at the spine, *Bloomfield's Poetical Works*. Then opening the book I thumbed through the early pages, stopped at the first poem and read aloud the first stanza.

> *Though Winter's frowns had damped the beaming eye,*
> *Though twelve successive Summers heav'd the sigh,*
> *The unaccomplished wish was still the same;*
> *Till May in new and sudden glories came!*

I closed the book and handed it back to her. As I did so I touched her fingers and from the deep, irrational side of my brain came the thought that I was touching fingers I had once loved. 'A fine volume, my Lady.'

'Yat you seek as trade?' said an incredulous Robert.

'Yes and other rare City builder stuff. In this once great city, me sure you have much to trade wi me.'

★ ★ ★ ★

The Lady had a small collection of books, two more volumes of poetry, though none as finely bound as the *Bloomfield*, and three novels of which only one was complete. She said she had found them when scavenging as a girl, and took me to the spot. It was the ruin of a big stone and brick building near to the city centre. All that was left of the building was one external wall, but from this and some clues in the rest of the rubble, I was able to work out what I thought was its general ground plan. Vitally, there was no evidence that the building had been burned, rather it seemed to have collapsed from neglect and natural damage.

'If there's anything left it will be underground,' I told her.

'What are you hoping to find?'

'I think the building was where there was a store of books, what the Builders called a library. All the books above ground were destroyed years before you found your poetry book but I think libraries had storerooms below ground. If there's one here then there may be dozens of books preserved in it.' I saw her green eyes flash and her pale cheeks flush at the thought of the books.

'Have you ever found a library before?'

'Two or three times.'

'What was it like? How many books did you find?'

'About a hundred in total.' I was getting used to the confusion between the real woman and the woman of my memory but it could still catch me out. Objectively she was the most beautiful woman I had seen in years, full of life and vitality. Better still she could read. But that was not the real fascination of her. I imagined tracing the tip of my finger down her breast to a perfectly formed nipple, all the time reading Shakespeare to her. Would the body beneath the clothes resemble the memory as accurately as the face and the gestures? If I was to fall in love, would it be with the present or the past? Then I pulled my mind away, experience had shown that desire was dangerous where I was concerned. In the past I had got into trouble too easily. Too often forays had developed into frantic pursuits by cuckolded husbands or outraged mobs. Scavenger Gangs, though sexually promiscuous between themselves, could be very puritan when it came to seduction by Ostlander.

'How did you learn to read?' I asked.

'My mother taught me. She was the old chief's mistress, as I am Robert's.'

'What happened to your father and mother?'

'Robert killed them when he took over,' she said calmly. 'He was the chief of a small gang on the outskirts of the city. They

17

were not doing well, then Robert made his discovery. In desperation, they'd started scavenging out into the countryside and they came across a house with a securely locked cellar. It raised Robert's curiosity. After a bit they managed to open the door. Inside they found a case full of working hunting rifles and ammunition to match.'

'So those weapons his bodyguard have aren't just for show?'

She shook her head. 'They work well enough. He used the rifles to attack us, killed my father's entire guard in an afternoon, captured my father and mother, made him watch as he raped her. Then he beheaded them both. He took me as his prize.'

I knew such things happened. Changes of authority in the Gangs were usually violent but this was a particularly brutal story. 'And he made you watch?'

She nodded her head. 'Don't fret for me Tobias. As a trader you know how it works among Scavengers. At least this way I don't starve. How do we find the books?'

'Well, I think we start over there by finding the wall that would have been the outside of the building.'

Chapter 3

Francesca lay still. She could feel every contact point between her body and the cool sheets: heels, buttocks, shoulder blades, elbows. Anya's body curled around hers, her lover's head in the hollow between her shoulder and her neck, a bent leg hooked over her stomach. It was that point of perfect relaxation, of oneness after passion as breathing and heart rate slowed and companionship replaced placated lust. She stretched, arching her back like a cat waking in the grass of a summer's day. Anya moved a little in response and in return Francesca pulled her closer.

'There, that's a lot better than worrying isn't it?' said Anya.

'Of course it is.'

'I'm not going anywhere. After all where would I find as good a singer to serenade me in the winter's cold?'

'And where would I find as good a...' Francesca tried to find the right word to sum to what she really felt but failed. All she managed was a wholly inadequate '...friend as you?'

Anya sat up in feigned anger. 'Or as good a lover?' They kissed again and Francesca relaxed back into a peaceful mood. She began to hum gently to herself.

'Is that the beginning of a new song?'

'Perhaps. I've been working on the words for a while.'

'Can I hear them?'

'I don't see why not, it's about us,' and Francesca began to recite:

> My love, let not my love be called idolatry,
> Nor you as friend be known for idol show,
> Since all as one my songs and passions be
> To one, of one they shall be ever so.
> Kind is my love today, tomorrow kind?
> She will be constant in her loving way.
> Therefore, my song lends constancy of mind

Though modest, my response all others say.
Fair, kind, and true, is all my argument,
Fair, kind, and true is all her counter-spell,
And in that bargain, love is truly met,
And in our bed are all thoughts made up well.
Three themes in one, which wondrous scope affords,
Fair, kind, and true may often live alone,
But in my house the three keep seat in one.

'That's marvellous and so flattering.'

'It's not quite right yet. I'll have to work on it, especially when I get a tune, but it's coming on.'

'I don't know where your ideas come from.'

'It may not seem it but mostly it's everyday things that set me off, a bird, a flower, something one of the Crèche children says. Though not in this case. This time the words wrote themselves.'

'Well wherever they came from I shall be very proud when you first sing them in the Gathering Hall. I'll go round, nudge everyone and say "That's my Francesca that is".'

'What, even the Council?'

'Yes, even the Council, especially that misery Peter. Just because he has the Red-book to read it doesn't mean he can be snooty about people like you, who have to learn their songs by heart.'

Francesca frowned. 'You know that's always puzzled me. Why is it only a few of the Senior Gatherers who ever learn to read? If I could read and even better write, I could write down my poems and songs. Then when I die they'd still be there to be sung, even if no one remembers them by heart.'

'They never said we couldn't learn to read or write in the Crèche.'

'No but if you asked, though the nurses always said you could learn, somehow it never happened. There was always something more important to do.'

'Did you ask?'

'Yes, lots of times.'

'Why don't you learn now?'

'Who would have the time to teach me? As far as I know there are only ten Gatherers in the whole community who can read. Besides, I'm too old to learn now.'

'Can't be. Not all the leaders of the Council could read before election. They say Peter was the first one in years. The leader has to know how to read from the Red-book, so others must have had to learn when they were much older than you. Go on, ask again.'

'Maybe. But not until after they've made me a Gardener. I wouldn't want to look like a troublemaker until that happens.'

'How can asking make trouble? Promise me you'll ask when you're a Gardener?'

'Well, alright. I suppose it can't do any harm. I promise.' They kissed again.

'Now I don't know about you but I'm still feeling energetic.' Anya moved round to straddle her.

'Well then I'll have to make sure you get the exercise you need,' said Francesca.

★ ★ ★ ★

The bell rang as the signal for the Council to enter. In front of High Table, exactly opposite where Peter would sit, stood Jeremy and Caleb, traditional coronets of wild flowers in their hair. A pace behind them stood their supporters Francesca and Anya, Susan and Christine. Peter smiled at the two young men as he stopped in front of them. The Community fell quiet, disturbed only by one insistent voice from the Crèche tables that carried right across the hall. 'I'm hungry,' followed by a sharp 'Shsh' from a Crèche Nurse. This was the first Declaration for some time.

'I see that we have two who wish to declare their partnership,' said Peter. 'Who stands for them?'

'I do,' replied Francesca. 'As oldest in our house I stand for them and recommend them. Here are their sisters of the house who also stand for them.' This was the third Declaration she had stood for but she still felt as nervous as a child when she had to speak in front of the Community.

Peter spoke again. 'That is good. Jeremy and Caleb, do you petition the Council to recognise your partnership?'

'We do.'

Francesca felt a pang of envy at the confidence in Jeremy and Caleb's voices.

'Have you considered carefully the purposes of such partnerships?'

'We have.'

How much she wished she could have such assurance.

'And what are those purposes?'

'Comforting each other, in loving harmony. Working together to gather and grow. Providing an example of stability to all.'

'Well said.' Peter raised his hands. 'Does anyone oppose this partnership?'

There was a nervous silence. As far as anyone could remember no one had ever objected but there was always a first time for everything. Peter ended the suspense. 'In that case do we consent?'

A great shout of 'Yes, we do' came back from everyone in the hall followed by clapping and stamping. Peter shook hands with Jeremy and Caleb and handed them the evening hardbread. 'Be the first this night to divide the bread.'

Caleb took it, broke it and handed a piece to Jeremy. 'Power to the bread,' he said solemnly.

'Power to the gathered food,' replied Jeremy delivering the sign of blessing. Then he took the hardbread and did the same for Caleb.

'May your partnership be long and happy,' concluded Peter to more clapping and cheering. Then as custom demanded the couple were clapped round all the tables, starting with the Council, shaking hands with as many people as they could manage.

Finally, order was restored, Jeremy and Caleb were back at their normal table and food was arriving from the kitchens.

'Congratulations you two,' said an enthusiastic Anya, hugging both of them. 'A long and happy partnership.'

'And so say all of us,' added Susan.

'Jeremy and Caleb,' they all saluted.

'So,' said Anya to Jeremy, 'how do you feel?'

'Well, a bit stunned to tell the truth. After all I'm the youngest of you all, well, you know, I'm only…'

'Seventeen,' they all chorused at him and then laughed.

'Yes, we know,' said Christine, 'and less than two years out of the Crèche.

'And catching Caleb, who barring our patriarch Francesca…' choruses of *may she live forever* '… is the oldest. Carry on like this young man you'll be the heart throb of the Community.' Choruses of *Ooooooo!*

'That's enough of that,' chipped in Caleb. 'This is no three-year romance. We intend it to last as long as we live,' and he bent over and kissed Jeremy.

'And that's how it should be,' said Susan. 'Let's hear it one more time, Jeremy and Caleb.' Choruses of *Hurrah!*

'So I wonder what the next big event will be for us?' Susan continued. All eyes looked at Francesca.

'You know I heard the Council are going to send the next new Gatherer to herd the sheep,' said Christine.

'Or fish from the boats,' added Jeremy

'Poor Anya, all those pooey fish scales.' Caleb held his nose and pulled a nasty-smell-face like a small child.

'Whatever it's going to be for Francesca the Gatherer, it's not going to be anything to do with plants,' said Susan and they all laughed as Francesca blushed.

They were right. She had tried out herding the sheep, which she liked, and fishing, which she loathed. But they all knew that she wanted to be a Gardener and hoped with her that the Council would see it the same way.

Whilst the Council tried to put people into the jobs they wanted, any jobs that Gatherers did were essential for the survival and wellbeing of the Community. Everyone had to work for the good of all. It was the bargain of being a Gatherer and having a full voting say in how the Community was run, that you did the task given to you without complaining and as well as you could. As the promises Jeremy and Caleb had just taken made clear, everyone needed to find their role. That was how the Community had survived in the past and that was how it would survive in the future. It gave its members identity and stability, it was mother and father to them all. She knew she would serve it as well as she could even if it was not as a Gardener. The alternative was to starve.

★ ★ ★ ★

A few days later Francesca got a message from Joseph, the Gatherer who organised the field-work details. Please would Francesca report to Sylvia in the Glasshouses. Dutifully she walked over there, wondering what to expect.

The Glasshouses were really a single chainlike structure. The core of this chain was the domes. Varying in height from ten to twenty metres, linked by simple tent-shaped tunnels, they were the most complicated buildings in Heron Fleet. Through the whole chain ran an open stone trough which channelled water from a reservoir near the entrance. Each glasshouse took what it needed for its plants from this stream. Plants grown at the top of the chain required the most water, the most drought-tolerant were in the lower houses.

The Glasshouses had two essential purposes: to provide seedlings for planting in the fields during the growing season and to supplement the winter stores of potatoes, corn, millet and wheat, with fresh vegetables, zucchini, marrows, celeriac, onions, and herbs. In short to add variety to what would otherwise be a boring winter diet.

At this time of year, near to the midpoint of the growing season, the houses were at their emptiest. Most of the seedlings had gone to the fields and the beds were being prepared for next year, with mulches made from different materials. As she followed the flow of the water, Francesca could identify the smell of each of these materials: the fruity smell of sheep and goat manure, the warm mottled smell of the leaf-mould and finally the salt and metallic taste of sea-weed. As she passed through the domes, groups of Gardeners stopped work to wave at her. Perhaps, she thought, they watched her a bit longer and smiled more intensely at her than normal, but she might be wrong. Though, whatever was the reason for her being summoned, it was out of the ordinary and they knew it.

In the centre of the chain where the two most important domes, the heart of the whole system. The first was the largest. In it were most of the main controls, including those for the gravity-fed sprinklers in the lower houses and the levers for the ventilators in the central section of domes. The second dome was much smaller but just as vital. It was the propagation chamber, the most exactly controlled area in the whole complex. In all the other houses, the borders where the plants grew were at ground level. In the propagation chamber, there were rows of benches with trays of soil and boxes. Strung above these on cords were cloth baffles that could be used to control temperature or light intensity. Seeds or tubers, kept from the previous season in the cool store outside the houses, were planted either directly into soil in the trays or into the boxes. After they germinated they were grown on a little, until they could be pricked out and transplanted.

Anyone coming into the houses needed to report to Sylvia, the Head Gardener. She was usually to be found in the main dome but when Francesca got there she could see no one. In search of help she drifted into the propagation chamber. Sylvia was in the middle of the benches talking to Simon, one of the Deputy Gardeners. Francesca walked towards them.

Sylvia was tall and sinewy, with black hair, olive skin and bony features. She held herself rather stiffly and carried a staff of knotted alder wood. Years of working as a Gardener had taken their toll on her joints. Her fingers, once long, thin and dexterous, were beginning to swell and stiffen. The staff helped her walk, as arthritis weakened her legs and knees.

The Rule was clear, mating between male and female was destructive and reprehensible. All births were the result of intervention by the Crèche Nurses, who specialised in pregnancy and birthing. They selected the right male for the right female. They collected the male seed and transferred it to the chosen female. They helped at the birth and remembered the pedigree of the child born. It was rumoured that not even the Head of the

Council was allowed to know what the Crèche Nurses knew. Francesca thought of them, when she thought of them at all, as Gardeners of people.

As a result it was a taboo for anyone to so much as whisper about who their birth mother or father might be. The young children accepted this as they accepted that they could not remember their birth-mothers. The only life they could remember was in the Crèche with the Crèche Mothers. It was only as time went by and they got to be teenagers before becoming Apprentices that they started to play the game of *Guess which Gatherers were my Mum and Dad*. Sometimes it was very difficult since there was no resemblance between a given child and any Gatherer. But when young, many of her friends had remarked on the resemblance between Francesca and Sylvia. And as Francesca grew the similarity remained, for though it was true that Francesca was a little bigger in the breast and slightly shorter in the leg than the austere Head Gardener, in general bearing and in reserve of character, they were very similar. Francesca knew if she got her wish and became a Gardener that would prove the point to many who had speculated a link before.

'So when do you think the mulching will have be finished?' It was Sylvia speaking.

'In about a week.'

'In good time then. Is the quality good this year?'

'Yes. Last autumn was as placid as I can remember and we got loads of good quality leaf mould as a result. Since the mould always improves the soil texture I'm expecting this year's seedlings and small plants to make the best start in years.' Simon paused as he saw Francesca, hopping from foot to foot. Sylvia turned, aware that Simon's attention was now on something behind her. She took a steady and appraising look at Francesca.

'Are we certain Simon? As it was said last night, does anyone oppose this partnership?'

'Well she looks a bit too much like a slip of a girl I remember coming to see your predecessor when she was an Apprentice, but she did all right and I don't see why this one shouldn't be nearly as good.'

'Do you hear that, girl?'

'Yes, ma'am.' Francesca's head was spinning.

'Well, do you agree?

'Yes ma'am.'

'Well in that case I want you here every day from now on until the growing season is over. If you do well over that period, from Harvest Festival onwards you'll join as a Junior Gardener, working for Simon. I've asked the Council for you early because I want you to see a whole year from beginning to end as soon as you can. For us that year starts now, as I think you already know. The bags of seeds on these trays are the beginning of next year's harvest.' Sylvia turned to go.

Francesca thought she must say something before Sylvia left. She wanted to run over to Sylvia and throw her arms round her in shear joy, to dance and sing on the spot but in the presence of a senior community elder like Sylvia, such a demonstration of joy would have been unthinkable. All she said was, 'Thank you ma'am... Thank you so much.'

Sylvia looked hard at her again. 'If by some miracle I'm still alive in thirty years when you're as old as me and in pain because of all the work you've done in these houses and in the outbuildings over those years, you can thank me then, not before. I'll believe you then. Simon, show her what you want her to do tomorrow.' Then leaning on her staff she moved off towards the central dome.

Simon smiled at Francesca as they watched Sylvia go. Then he shook her hand. 'Welcome to the Honourable Company of Gardeners. Now as you've seen as you came in it's muck-spreading. So guess what you'll be doing tomorrow.'

'Raking and digging?'

'That's about the size of it. But the first thing I want you to do tomorrow, before you come here, is to report to the Smithy and collect a full set of Gardener's tools. They will know your coming. Mind now, don't accept any faulty stuff from them. Your tools will be your friends for many years, pick them as carefully as you'd pick a partner.'

Chapter 4

The sledgehammers of the two guards Robert had sent to help us smashed into the stonework. The Lady and I ducked out of the way to avoid being cut by flying splinters.

It had taken us two days to get this far. The first task had been to establish the line of the outer wall. Then we had cleared the rubble that had filled the space below ground next to that wall. The breakthrough came when we unearthed a window protected on the outside by a metal grille but with intact wired glass beyond.

The stonework round the grille crumpled under the sledgehammers. The guards prised off the grille and set to work on the glass. When it finally gave way it released a dusty but dry smell. A bit more clearing of the sides and there was a gap big enough for me to climb through.

Out of my pocket I took a silver and black cylinder with a wrist strap. In a slot at the bottom was a crank-handle which I pulled out and started to turn. The others looked on in amazement, briefly giving me a childish satisfaction of superiority. After about twenty turns, I put the handle back into its place and pointed it into the dark beyond the window-space. I pushed the switch on the top. There was a click and a pool of bright blue light appeared on an object a metre or so inside. The Lady and the guards gasped and stepped back, even more cause for childish pleasure.

Being careful not to cut myself on any glass left around the window frame, I pulled myself through and stood upright on a rough wooden floor, under a low ceiling which one scan with the torch showed was intact.

'It's safe enough,' I called back through the window. Then I turned and offered my hand to The Lady. 'Would you care to join me?' I said.

'Do you want one of us to come with you?' said one of the guards.

She immediately replied, 'No. Wait at the entrance and keep your ears open. If you hear us call or think we are in trouble then one of you come in, the other should go immediately for help.' It crossed my mind that this was a planned move. Something Robert had suggested to her. Something along the lines of, don't let the guards see too much until we know what this stranger is really after or what he's worth to us. If this was the case my trick with the electric torch would be well worth reporting back.

After she had climbed through we could start investigating properly what we had found. In front of us was a row of fifteen to twenty metal racks with shelves, facing each other so that you could walk between them. On each shelf there was a row of books, some neatly upright, others stacked in disordered piles. Some books had fallen on the floor and one of the racks had fallen against the wall near the end of the row but the place was generally orderly and undisturbed. Most importantly there was no indication that either fire or water had penetrated the room. It was dry and did not look as if it had ever been disturbed from the day the City builders had left. It was quiet as well. Even sounds were muted here in this sacred place of the books.

We walked slowly down the aisle between the nearest racks. The Lady was mesmerised. With a slight smile on her face she ran her fingers down the spines of the volumes, disturbing the dust, occasionally stopping to brush off and read a title. 'I've never believed that this number of books could possibly exist.' She was trying to suppress her excitement but it still inflected her voice. She pulled down the book her finger had just stopped on. She smoothed her hand over its cover and opened it. She read aloud while I held the light.

A squat grey building of only thirty-four stories. Over the main entrance the words, Central London Hatchery and Conditioning Centre and in a shield, the World state's motto, Community, Identity, Stability.

She closed the book and put it back in its place, finishing by running her index finger down the spine as she pressed it home between its companions. We moved deeper into the store.

Beyond the first row of racks was another, divided from the first by a corridor. On some of these shelves there were half-boxes, out of the tops of which showed smaller documents, just like the one I had found as a boy. The coloured pictures of long-dead heroes and heroines were still bright and clear. I passed one to her. On the next rack, I found one of the things I most wanted, it was full of boxes of newspapers.

I could not remember exactly when I had first realised that there had been such things as newspapers. After the old man taught me the letter sounds, I started to try to read the magazine I had found. Slowly I got the hang of translating the letters and then saying them aloud so that he could recognise the words. Soon all I had to do was sound the words inside my head to decode them. When I had read the magazine out to the old man several times, so he could confirm I really could read, I became dissatisfied with only having a meagre few sheets. After that scavenging became as much a search for reading material as for food. Gradually my resources grew, a book here and magazine there but only once had I found a newspaper.

The fragile sheets were buried deep in a pile of trash. They were stained and battered but readable. I hid them away and went on scavenging. That night when most people had gone to sleep I took the newspaper out and by the light of the small fire we had at night in our camp read it. I was fascinated. There were several different stories but they were not about people in the way the stories in the magazines had been. These stories seemed to be about what had been happening in the city and even beyond. There had not just been one city but many, and the City builders had run not just their own cities but had come together to run whole areas of land. I was engrossed which was why I did not hear him coming.

'What got you there?' said a voice from above my head. I tried to stuff the paper into my shirt but he grabbed my hair and wrenched me backwards so that I lay on the ground. He immobilised me by putting his knee in my chest and snatched the paper from me. 'You know rules, Toby. I gets first pick of what all my team find.'

'No interest you. Nofin to eat,' I shouted back, trying to sound like a man but knowing I simply sounded what I was, a boy trying to impress. He slapped me across the face for my cheek. Then he looked at the paper, turning it over and over in his hand.

'What int'rest this? He said in puzzlement.

'Nufin,' I said again.

'You spend good time on nufin. Me watch you from shadows.' He increased the pressure of his knee on my chest. 'What you doin'. Cast a spell on me do you? Don't think we don't know you got funny ways.' He looked at the paper one more time then threw it on the fire. It kindled and flared. He watched to see how I'd react but the hate I felt made it easier for me to look impassive. As the paper turned to black ash he gave in, punched me in the face then let me go.

That was the turning point. What I had read confirmed an idea I had had from the start, that the City builders used reading to pass on information, in this case what had been happening only a few days before the newspaper was written. That meant that from reading I might discover how the City builders had fed themselves and built the cities. It also showed me that if things were to be improved, if we were ever to climb back to where the City builders had been, then the Scavenger Gangs were no basis as a start. They would consume everything until nothing was left and then they would die. I had to go on reading and that meant I had to get away as well. See if I could find more cities and more books and the knowledge they contained.

The Lady had been looking at my face as I looked at the newspapers. 'This is what you've really been looking for isn't it?' she said.

'Yes.'

'Why especially these and not the wonderful books or poems?'

'I have friends out there. They need information to help them grow more food and survive better.'

'Do all your friends read and have books?'

'Most do.'

'And do they scavenge and kill and starve?'

31

'No, they farm and are at peace, which is why they have time to read, and to write as well.'

Suddenly she was very close to me I could smell the leather of her coat and the sweat of her body. Smell and taste evoke memory more sharply than anything. In the confined space of the book store that memory was too strong to be resisted.

She reached up and stroked my cheek. 'Take me with you when you leave. Take me to such a place.' There were tears in her eyes and a note of pleading in her voice. She was speaking for herself this time, not using some formula Robert had devised.

I was torn apart. One side of my mind desperately reminded me how dangerous it would be to say yes but I could not blaspheme against the memory. I rested my hands on her waist beneath her jacket, and pulled her to me. 'I'll try,' I whispered as I kissed her.

★ ★ ★ ★

That evening, we brought back some samples from the store, books of poetry, a novel or two that the Lady fancied and a couple of boxes of magazines. She told me Robert couldn't read, so bringing back the newspapers shouldn't have been a risk but I was worried I might give away my own excitement in finding them. I persuaded her they needed special care and she agreed to leave them behind.

When we got back, Robert was holding court in the meeting room. His two bodyguards with their rifles were there as well as his spear-bearer. There were six other men in the niches behind him. I thought they were the captains of his guards. For good measure there were two extras guards armed with rifles, one each side at the top of the main steps. As soon as we entered, the Lady took up her place in Robert's entourage. I sat in one of the niches near the steps and tried to look as inconspicuous as possible.

In front of Robert was the woman and the child that had been the first to come to my fireside at the quay. Robert was questioning her.

'Guards tell me you be on boat, yes?'

'No, Lord, no me.' The voice was weak, husky and full of fear.

'You tell me Leonard lying-you?' Robert's voice was low but had an edge of threat.

'Me took scraps only. Never go boat, never Lord.' She was pleading and her legs were shaking.

'He swear you on boat.' Robert's voice was louder and he pointed to one of the guards at the head of the steps as he spoke.

'No, no me Lord, no me.' Robert got up and circled her. The baby whimpered, wrapped its thin arms round its mother and buried its head in her neck.

'So you him liar-callin'?'

'No, Lord. He make...' she hesitated '...mistake. No boat. No me.'

Robert stopped in front of her and sneered. 'We no make mistake,' he said, leaning towards her.

She saw it coming and tried to turn and run but she had not got fully round by the time he had raised his pistol and fired. The bullet smacked into the side of her head from no more than a metre. A small entrance hole spouted a fountain of blood. The bullet's exit took half her skull, and showered blood and brains onto the stone floor in a fan-shaped pattern. The report of the shot echoed round the room like a wave trapped in a sea-cave. As her body hit the floor the baby was knocked from her arms. Covered in blood it started to crawl back towards the corpse. Robert nodded and his spear-bearer stepped forward and stabbed it. A moment's twitching, then it was still.

Robert thrust his hands in the air in joy, his head back. 'Remember all you,' he roared at the beautiful ceiling, 'we no make mistake!' Then he relaxed, returned his pistol to its holster and swept out through the private door, followed by his entourage leaving only the two guards at the top of the stairs and me alone.

When he had gone the guards leant their rifles against the wall and relaxed. The one Robert had pointed to came over to look at the corpses. Emotionless, he looked down, then he hawked and spat into the congealing pool of blood. I recognised him as the guard who'd been left as sentry on my boat.

'Leonard, why you not clean up yen mess,' said the other guard.

Leonard shrugged his shoulders. 'No fault me. She'd had it commin. She were too fess to part er legs,' and he spat again. 'Ramshacklum she is now, ant serve er right,'

'You no heart. Kiddy no urt yen.'

'Why you worry? Two less to feed.'

Out of the darkness of the stairs came three older women and a man. All were thin and badly fed, though not quite as emaciated as the dead woman. They washed the floor of its blood with mops and buckets they had brought, and put the bodies on a blanket. Then they carried them out. As they passed Leonard, the oldest woman held out her hand to him. Leonard spat into his own hand and shook hers.

'Make sure you stick to yen bargain,' said the other guard. 'Bad luck if they get leery. Yen pay or them come for yen in the night,' then the guards left, leaving me alone.

I'd seen brutality of all kinds in Scavenger Gangs but this was one of the coldest killings I'd witnessed. Most chiefs made pretence of helping their subjects, of trying to be seen to be fair. They realised that it was one of the things that kept the gangs together. Of course, it didn't make any difference in the long run. As the resources of a city dwindled to exhaustion more labour was needed to accumulate even survival rations. Well-run gangs slowed the process of starvation but they didn't prevent it.

Very few gangs I had met grew anything or developed new relationships. One or two were near enough to farming communities to trade raw materials like metal and brick from city ruins for food. It was possible they might survive in the future by a sort of symbiotic relationship but most went round and round the same vicious circle out of habit. The end came quickly when cannibalism took hold.

The four who had taken the corpses away might well be cannibals. That might account for why they were reasonably well-fed. Perhaps the remark about them being leery, which I had taken to mean upset but it could also mean hungry, carried more of a real threat to Leonard. Perhaps it meant that if Leonard did not pay for their services, they would cut his throat one night and eat him. It was not so long a step from making use of the bodies provided by Robert's violence, to killing to feed yourself.

I got up and walked to the other side of the room to relieve the stiffness induced by the cold of the stone and the cold of foreboding in my heart. I could not think of Robert as much more than a mindless murderer but maybe that was a misjudgement on my part. Perhaps he saw the end coming. Perhaps he was choosing to drive towards it as hard as he could, rather than sit and wait timidly for the end. There might be a sick nobility in such a course of action. Either way how was I to find a way to negotiate with him?

Then there was the Lady. Perhaps she could see disaster coming as well by comparing the situation now with her father's day. Maybe she was just sick of Robert's abuse of her and everyone else. I was convinced she had been looking for a way out before I'd arrived. Then I remembered the kiss and desire was like a clenched fist in my stomach and a tingling in my genitals. Flashes of what The Lady would feel like naked intruded into my thoughts. I could feel the promise of the future blending with vivid memories from the past. I knew I should cut-and-run while I could but, as they say, when your brains are in your balls, prudence stands no chance. I would take her with me when I left no matter what.

So the whole problem would revolve around how much I could convince Robert that what was on offer was really valuable to him. Bad news, for judging from the display I had just witnessed value in Robert's eyes meant what gave him the most power and satisfaction minute to minute. If I failed it would be a bullet in the head at short range, for me and the Lady.

★ ★ ★ ★

There was a kiss on my forehead, a sense of someone soft close to me. I woke up. It was early morning but still dark. I could just make the Lady out as a dark shape kneeling next to me. I reached for her but she stopped me.

'I can't, he'll miss me if I'm not back soon. I came to warn you,' she whispered. 'I showed him the books and the magazines. He's interested in two things, where the goods you have come from and what power the books give you to make it worth you risking your life to get them. He'll send for you in the morning. Then will be the time for a deal,' then she was gone.

I lay awake for most of the rest of the night, thinking about how my meeting with Robert next morning might go. I worked out a few strategies but didn't have much faith in any of them. Breakfast came too soon for me. There was no obvious way out and I knew it.

I ate with the guards, so I ate as well as anyone except Robert and the Lady. By definition what scavengers ate was what they could find. This morning there were tins of pressed mixed meat and some of tomatoes, luxuries to add to grey, watery porridge to give it some taste. I longed to get down to the boat for some of the salt bacon and fresh eggs stored in the hold but there was no chance.

Across the table from me was the second guard from the night before. He was pleasant-looking with thinning red hair and a decent colour to his cheeks, a man doing well despite privations. He caught my eye but showed no sign of recognising me. I smiled and nodded. Maybe he hadn't seen me the night before.

'Where frumenty come from?' I said.

'Frumenty? More rafty-mixen, think me,' he laughed. 'Big store found when we come. Too ramshacklum for yen, Trader?' there was sarcasm in his voice.

'Had worse.' I laughed and added some of the tomatoes to the porridge. 'Me name Tobias.' I held out my hand to him. He looked suspiciously at it but in the end shook it.

'Angus,' he replied.

'Bin Robert long-time?' I said

'Yeh. With im in burbs before we gwain. Good day's work that,' he grinned.

'Find it big store scran like this.' I splashed my spoon into the porridge. 'Big boost yat Robert?'

'Sure. Avroze first winter without.' He stirred in a couple of tomatoes to his bowl and slurped the resulting mess. 'Chief afore ad good stores. Yen Robert give food to all. No much left be now.'

'Tot afore duty?' I took a small bottle of apple brandy from an inside pocket, uncorked it and offered it to him.

'Friendly,' he said taking the bottle. He saluted me. 'To yen,' he said and swigged from the bottle, coughed and licked his lips. 'Me no taste nufin that-like years. Mehbe your really are wot captains jaw yen.'

'Wot that.'

'Yen last 'ope get loosed way.'

'Wot that?'

'Last 'ope to move where pickin's better.'

He went to give me the bottle back but I indicated he should have another drink. ' No ave nother tot Angus.' He happily took up the offer and took another swig. 'If yen's said why none tried be chief instead Robert.'

Immediately he looked at me with hostility. 'Yen understand nufin Ostlander. All bin Robert long-time. He lucky. He no ramshaklum us. We die for him if yat future.' He corked the bottle and set it on the table between us, a visible symbol of the distance between us. 'Thank for spirit,' then he left. I put the bottle back in my pocket.

★ ★ ★ ★

As the Lady had predicted I was summoned to see Robert soon after breakfast. He was alone in the meeting room except for Angus who had been posted at the top of the stairs.

'Ostlander say me again wot yen trade.'

'Me say yen me gwain, food, cloth, books. Now me found book-store yen got plenty for trade.'

'For tinder yen save us go leery?'

'Yeh.'

'Yen mefool-take. Nune trade chockvul food yen ave for nufin. Wot more?'

'Nufin my Lord, me swear.' He didn't looked convinced. It was going badly.

'Me try nuther path. Wot special yis paper?' Robert picked up a newspaper from one of the niches.

'Wot make yen think it special?'

'She tell me. Yen think it special,' he said slowly. 'Yis ave learnin yen friends need. Friends yo make the cloth and grow the food you trade. Must ave chockvul, chockvul and peacevul.'

He was too close to me for comfort. 'But not defenceless,' I replied.

'Me hazard yen have-no these,' he drew his pistol. 'Me find these great me point-o-view persuaders. She told yen wot these do her parents.'

'She told yen more me meet eye.'

'Yen mean torch no burn. Yeh she told me but it make me more interested. The path me think it yat proves there be somethin' chockvul on yis paper. Haps it can tell you how to make things like torch we no make now. Haps things match power me guns but how we find out?' He tapped the barrel of the gun on his jaw.

'Yat case wouldn't it be better trade-me? In time me might trade knowledge yen.'

'No me style.' Robert cocked the pistol and pointed it at me. 'Me more shoot first, think after guy. Me put yen knowledge to test against me guns direct. Yen gwain me guards, eye yen friends, yen we know surely.'

I had kept calm up to this point, feeling that I could still buy Robert off with a trading agreement I had no intention of keeping. Once I was gone from here, I was not coming back, this man was just too dangerous. But the remark the guard had made at breakfast now made sense. It wasn't just the captains who were wanting to move on, so did Robert and because I had said too much to the Lady, Robert now had a target, one of the farming communities across the channel, and they were in no position to resist firearms.

'Me boat no take all yen guards.'

'No all yem. Only me originals. Ten most. Rest stay. Go leery with rest scum.'

The crisis had been reached. I swallowed hard. 'Sorry, me won't take you. Yen better kill me now and ransack boat. Yat all yen get.' There was thirty seconds of silence as Robert seemed to weigh up my resolve and I tried to hold my nerve sufficiently to die well.

Then Robert uncocked the gun and shouted, 'Bring she in Leonard.' The private door opened and Leonard forced the Lady in to the room. 'Yen may be prepared yen die but she and yen attached.' The image of Robert's joy when he had shot the starving woman came to me. I knew I would be entirely unable to stand here while Robert shot the Lady. It would deny something so deep and so precious to me that I would not be able to do it. Robert and I both knew I was beaten.

RSPB Birds, March 2016

Grey Days Ahead

A new RSBP study based in East Anglia has shown that migration patterns of Grey Herons, normally considered a resident bird in the UK, have changed and there is now a net outflow of the birds to southern Europe in the autumn.

It has been suspected for some time grey herons (*Ardia cenera*) might be changing their migration habits in northern Europe but this has been hard to prove. Grey herons have rather erratic migratory patterns with birds from Scandinavia migrating to over-winter in the UK in bad years, with some UK birds moving to southern and central Europe.

Results from ringing studies are further complicated by low rates of retrieval of rings from both migrant and non-migrant casualties.

Last year a large group of birds were specially ringed in specific nesting areas in Norway, Sweden and Finland, as well as in East Anglia. This was combined with intensive satellite tagging of groups of herons from the same areas.

Paul Engliss from the Snape reserve said: 'The results were unambiguous. Herons are leaving both Britain and Scandinavia in the winter in much bigger numbers than we had thought. Some of the Scandinavian herons do winter here but more only stop off and are joined by British birds when they continue to move south in late autumn.

There is clear evidence that many that winter in southern Europe do not return but nest in the south the following summer, increasing the resident populations. If this trend continues the grey heron will become a rarity on our rivers and wetlands in future.'

New Scientist, 20th January 2029

IS A NEW ICE AGE FOR BRITAIN JUST AROUND THE CORNER?

Could Britain's central-heating system be about to break down? Last week an Anglo-French group of oceanographers took the unprecedented step of calling an urgent international press-conference.

The researchers Augustus Benion of Aberdeen's National Oceanographic Centre and Françoise Ramaux of the Institut Europeén de Recherche de la Mer in Brest were drawing attention to the results from their latest research using a new computer model of sea currents in the North Atlantic. Their findings suggest that global warming will lead to a sudden, catastrophic drop in temperature on the European seaboard sometime in the next twenty years. This would fling Britain into a new ice age.

A network of currents links the oceans of the world together. These currents are driven by winds and by a more complicated process called thermohaline circulation – THC for short – which depends on heat and salt.

In the North Atlantic, water flows towards the Arctic from the Caribbean in the warm current known as the North Atlantic Drift. As it heads north, evaporation makes this water saltier. It is cooled by cold winds from the Arctic ice-sheet. Both these effects make it denser and as a result it sinks somewhere off north Norway. It then spills back to the south over undersea ledges and through undersea trenches displacing deep ocean water that emerges off the coast of Africa as a cold current that flows back towards the Caribbean. This flow completes the circle in what is called the South Atlantic Gyre

This process has been broadly stable for millions of years but as global warming gets worse, the rate that the Arctic sea-ice melts increases, and more and more fresh water is released into the Atlantic between Greenland and the North of Scotland. This fresh water dilutes water in the North Atlantic Drift, reducing its density and making it more buoyant, which reduces the sinkage and the overall flow rate in the South Atlantic Gyre.

For many years it has been proposed that at some point the fresh water input could reach a critical rate and the sinking will stop entirely. Then the North Atlantic Drift will no longer bring the warm tropical waters to the western shores of Britain to keep us warm in winter and summer.

Until now it has always been assumed that the deep ocean water displaced by the sinkage water moving south diffuses back into the system over very large areas of the ocean. The twist that the work of Benion and Ramaux has given to this theory is that much of this water may come back to the surface in two local areas, off Spain near the Bay of Biscay and off the coast of Labrador. For the first time, by measuring the rate of this upwelling, oceanographers would have a direct measure of the health of the North Atlantic Drift.

Previous computer modelling of what would happen if the THC collapsed and the North Atlantic Drift stopped predicted that Britain's average temperatures could fall by -1 to -2°C. whereas the rest of the world would see average rises in temperature of 2 to 3°C.

Is all this theory? Well geophysicists believe the Northern Atlantic Drift stopped temporarily once before about 20,000 years ago. Before restarting, the effect of the cold reduced the far north of Scandinavia and Russia to the tundra and icy moorlands we see today.

Chapter 5

Everywhere Francesca looked was a smoke filled-hysteria. At large stone anvils male and female Gatherers slammed hammers into glowing metal, producing small fountains of white-hot sparks. Sweating Apprentices pumped wildly at bellows, feeding air to dull-red beds of charcoal that shimmered in their own heat. Pieces being worked on, plunged into baths of quenching river water, produced flamboyant clouds of steam, which exploded as the water hissed and boiled. Occasionally, a completed hoe blade, rake head or spade was placed on a rack to wait for its handle to be fitted by one of the wood turners who worked on foot-lathes nearby. Then the smith would saunter out to the pile of rusty metal at the rear of the building, carefully select the best piece available for his purpose and return to start again making one of these vital tools. Although where Francesca stood in the yard the day was bright, clean and fresh, under the canopy of the Smithy it was misty, smeared and sulphurous.

Francesca couldn't see the Head Smith but eventually she caught the eye of one of the Apprentices on the bellows. He nodded to her to show she'd seen her and then had a word with another Apprentice who was refilling the baths of water. He disappeared into the fog at the back, emerging in a few moments later with the Head Smith.

'You must be Francesca.' He was cleaning his hands on an old piece of cloth, which he pushed back into the pouch on the front of his leather apron. He held out an enormous hand that swallowed hers as he shook it. 'Enoch. Simon said to expect you. He also said I wasn't to give you anything but the best. He seems to think you're going to need your tools for many years.'

'Yes, he told me much the same.' Francesca felt nervous and in awe of this giant.

'Well come this way and we'll see what we can find.' He led her to a small thatched storeroom across the yard and opened the door. 'Take your pick. These are all Gardener's tools, none of these is lent out to workers in the fields.' Seeing she was reluctant, he looked her up and down and pulled out a long-shafted hoe with a large flat blade. 'Try this one. It's bigger in the head and longer in the stave than you've been used to, but you're tall and lithe, and a well-balanced hoe will probably suite you.'

He handed it to her. The point of balance fell under Francesca's hand immediately. A few practice prods, as if she was weeding, and she realised that it would give her extra reach across rows without reducing accuracy or control. She smiled, not knowing what to say.

'Well that's the hoe then. Spade's another thing though. Try this for length.' He passed her a spade, the open handle of which came up to her waist. 'Put your foot on the blade as if you were going to push it home.' He eyed her position carefully. 'Umm... too long...try this one.' It took a few more goes until both of them were satisfied the height was comfortable. Then they turned their attention to the blade size, settling on a small one. 'You're too thin of frame for a big blade. What you win in speed with that hoe you'll lose in having to dig more often with the spade.'

They added a rake to her equipment and then there was only one tool left. For this they went to another store room. When the door opened Francesca saw on the bench, catching the sunlight, five new trowels. Whereas the blades of the other tools were clean and in their new state shiny enough, the trowels were totally different. She picked up one. Its surface was so polished she could see her own reflection in it.

'Beautiful,' was all she could say.

'Made from the best metal we have. The silver-steel we call it. It's hard to work but it shines when it's polished and as you use it the edge sharpens itself. It's the mark of the Gardener. Which will you have?'

She looked at them. Each seemed as graceful and beautiful as its neighbour. She did not know how to choose. Then she saw one whose handle had a strong, dark grain, like the grain in Sylvia's staff. 'That one, please,' she said.

'Good choice. Fine blade, though I says it who made it. And the ash handle sets it off beautifully.'

★ ★ ★ ★

It didn't take long for Francesca to realise that the life of a Gardener was perhaps a bit more physical than she'd originally thought. True, she was saved the effort of carrying her tools to the Glasshouses each day; they were safely stored in a place of her own in one of the upper domes. But there had been an awful lot of digging and racking to be done as they prepared the beds for replanting. She thought her back was prepared for it by the work in the fields but after the first week she was as stiff as she'd ever been. One other snag was that since she had to be in the Glasshouses to close them up at the end of the day, she was always late back to the roundhouse and missed walking home with Anya. When she got home this evening Anya wasn't even in. This vexed her until she remembered that Anya must be down at the river giving Jonathan his first swimming lesson. But the more she thought of swimming the more she thought it might be a good way of getting the creases out of her back. So she picked up a drying cloth and walked down to the river.

There were not that many places for a novice to swim and the best was where the Crèche Mothers taught the children, a bit upriver from the bridge, so she made for that. Sure enough as she approached she could hear Anya's impatient voice.

'Oh come on Jonathan. It's not that bad.' Her partner was standing up to her waist in the river. Her wet hair, flattened down into black tresses, glistened in the evening light. She looked totally in command of the element. Jonathan, on the other hand, had only made it in up to his knees. He was flapping his arms up and down and hopping from one leg to the other; the perfect picture of someone very afraid of water, who found the shale of the riverbed sharp on his feet.

Even with flapping arms and looking more than ridiculous he was a tall, well-made young man, if you liked that sort of thing. Good shoulders and firm chest muscles came down to a flat stomach.

Anya spotted her. 'Look, *you* tell him Francesca.'

'Oh no,' wailed Jonathan, 'it's bad enough with you, let alone her as well.'

'That's not very polite,' retorted Anya. 'If I get you in here I might just drown you to make up for being so rude to my partner!'

'Sorry,' said Jonathan. Francesca stripped off her clothes and paddled over to him.

'You have to bear in mind that she's never been frightened of anything in her life,' she said to him. 'Now I can remember how frightened I was when I went for a swim the first time. So you just come with me and we'll do whatever Anya wants us to do together. Then she can take over and teach you how to swim properly.' As Francesca had spoken she had drawn him deeper into the water by the arm. It was now above his waist. She let go and put a hand on his shoulder instead. Anya saw that Francesca was doing the trick and came up on Jonathan's other side, adding her comforting hand to his other shoulder.

'Take a big deep breath, Jonathan,' Anya said quietly. 'Then all three of us are just going to bob down below the water and come straight back up. If you're frightened just remember that there isn't anything in this river Francesca and I can't save you from. Ready.'

'Yes. Alright. I'll try.'

'One, two, three,' said Anya and down they went. The cool water flowed over Francesca's head, she opened her eyes and saw the pale green world of the river: weed, sandy bottom, shoals of small fish. A second later they were up again in the air. Jonathan spluttered and breathed hard but after recovering and a bit more reassurance, he was ready to do it again. After three goes they persuaded him to open his eyes underwater and then to count to five before coming up. After a few more goes, he could float with his feet off the bottom and allowed them to tow him gently out into deeper water. After that Francesca left Anya to it and swam up stream, feeling the stiffness in her shoulders melting away.

★ ★ ★ ★

46

'Look, it's not me,' the male voice was angry and upset. 'I don't care what you think but it's not me. You've changed, not me.'

Whoever it was could not see Francesca and with a bit of luck she could keep it that way. If she was careful she could back off round the side of the roundhouse and not embarrass them by letting them know they had been overheard. She started to retrace her steps.

'You may not think you've changed but you have. You used to like spending time with me but now...'

'Now what? Now I can't bear to look at you, can't bear to touch you? You know that's not true.'

There was something in the way the voices intersected that made her shudder. It reminded her of conversations she'd had with Ruth just after she'd begun to notice Anya. She had denied vehemently that she had changed but she had known that she had, even as the words had come out of her mouth in her own defence. She had denied it because she denied it to herself. Denied she was falling for someone else, that Ruth's care of her, which had once been charming, had begun to pull and restrict her. That Ruth's steadfastness had become dullness. What she wanted was a lover more likely to take risks; one who would let her grow.

She backed off slowly and then made it to the shelter of the next roundhouse so she could go well to the left of the voices. As she glimpsed the place were they must have been talking between the roundhouses, she saw Jonathan hurry off in the direction of the river. So it was Jonathan who had been arguing with Hamied. She remembered the exasperation in Hamied's voice on the bridge the day Anya had pitched Jonathan into the river. She hadn't thought twice about his tone then, thinking he had been cross with Anya for her prank on Jonathan but now maybe he had been exasperated with Jonathan as well. And the real source of that exasperation was now clear. She thought it a great shame since they had looked so happy when declaring their partnership two years ago. She hoped that whatever happened as they broke up it would be quick and easy to heal.

★ ★ ★ ★

The hot days of summer were beginning to come to an end. Increasingly, the clarity of the sunsets was marred by the presence of cloud, low on the horizon, that gathered during the day. The Fishers were reporting seeing squalls forming out to sea. The Shepherds had taken the seasonal hint and had started to bring the flocks in toward their winter quarters nearer the Gathering Hall. The Gardeners who had been on field duties had returned to the Glasshouses, where the racking and digging was over. And planting had begun.

Francesca had been coming and going all over the place. One day it had been taking bulbs out of cold stores, the next it had been sowing seeds into pots. No sooner had she got the hang of one job than Simon sent her off on another. It was interesting and exciting but she felt she was being filled up with gardening knowledge as fast as the Gardeners could pour it into her and wondered if she might overflow at any moment. Even now, though it was the end of the day, she had one last errand to run.

The Glasshouses not only supplied culinary herbs for the Kitchen but also medicinal herbs to the Infirmary. They grew poppies and harvested the sap for the relief of pain, feverfew for lowering the temperature, valerian as a sedative and foxglove for pain of the heart, as well as several other plants for specific medical purposes she didn't yet understand. One of the children had been taken to the infirmary last night suffering from a fever. Normally, the sick children stayed in the Crèche. Since this one had been taken to the Infirmary it must mean the case required medical experience beyond that of the Crèche Mothers. Late in the afternoon a message had come from the Infirmary that they need fresh feverfew and valerian. So Francesca had been despatched to gather the required herbs and to take them over urgently.

She had come out from the top end of the Glasshouses and had picked up the track that led back towards the suspension bridge. From this path she could see all the north side of the community. The Gatherer longhouses were on the north side of the Gathering Hall. There were a dozen in all, set around courtyards; each with room for five couples. All the Gatherers lived on the north side; the seven Apprentice roundhouses were on the south side. The Crèche was to the southwest next to the Infirmary. The working areas, Smithy, Pottery, Solar-ovens and Kitchens were to the northwest. Between Hall and river there were no buildings, except the small guardhouse where the path to the suspension bridge cut the protective bank-and-ditch.

Since she was going as fast as she could, she was soon at the top of the stone steps down to the suspension bridge. Near the top was Sylvia, who was having difficulty managing to get down the first few steps due to the stiffness of her joints. Francesca hesitated. Sylvia was very independent and the pain she experienced often made her sharp-tongued. She might not thank Francesca for help down but passing her on the steps without helping was impossible. But the herbs were urgent and if she waited for Sylvia to make it down under her own power it might take some time. Francesca hesitated.

'Stop farting about, whoever you are; you'll just have to wait.' Sylvia had her head down and was prodding at the next step with her staff.

'But, err, ma'am it's the herbs.'

Sylvia turned slightly. 'Oh… Ah… Francesca. Well I suppose you're right. I shouldn't get in the way of one of my own on an urgent errand. But the fact is I can't get back up to clear your path so I'm afraid you're going to have to help me down if you're going to get on.'

Francesca gingerly climbed down on to the steps. The herbs were packed in her bag so her hands were free but she didn't fancy having the responsibility of getting Sylvia down safely. Dropping the Chief Gardener on the steps would be a bad black mark and Francesca was conscious she was still on probation as a Gardener.

After a bit of negotiation Sylvia gave Francesca her staff and put her arm over her shoulders. With Francesca supporting her weight, they went slowly down step at a time. When on the bridge Sylvia was able to pick up her pace and took back her staff.

'Thank you young woman. If you breathe a word of this to anyone you'll end up as manure in the borders of the main dome.'

Francesca smiled, 'Your secret's safe with me ma'am.'

'Well you better get along now. Just one thing before you go. I was going to tell you tomorrow but now is as good a time as any. The Council will confirm you as Gatherer at the Harvest Festival as planned. You've worked as hard as anyone I can remember to learn everything we've been able to show you. You'll more than do.'

FE modelling of deep ocean currents by ALMA, Journal of Physical Oceanography *30, 7, 750-753, 2030*

High Density Finite Element Analysis of Thermohaline Currents in the North Atlantic

L P Troubadour★, T J Smith★, F Ramaux★★ and A J Benion★[1]

★National Oceanography Centre, Aberdeen, UK
★★Institut Europeén de Recherche de la Mer, Brest, France

Abstract

This paper presents a pilot study into the opportunities that the use of Advanced Large Multicore Array (ALMA) computers may offer to higher density modelling of ocean bed currents. The experiments reported used finite element analysis of the thermohaline currents in the North Atlantic with special reference to interaction with North Atlantic Drift. The simulations improved convergence of model by between 100 to 500 times at resolutions 100 times higher than conventional simulations of the same problems. Simulations connected surface current predictions to deep ocean bed currents and suggests that significant localised areas of upwelling and sinkage of water between the surface plane and the ocean bed may be present at the borders of four ocean floor basins east and west of the mid Atlantic Ridge. These findings were consistent for a wide range of boundary conditions used in successive simulations.

Keywords: ALMA, finite element analysis, ocean current modelling, thermohaline currents

Introduction

Recent advances in multithreading approaches to finite element analysis on Advanced Large Multicore Array (ALMA) computers have raised the possibility that high density finite element analysis of ocean current fields could be applied at improved resolution. When combined with details of ocean floor maps from the GOCE Gravity Survey this has made it possible to consider modelling of not only the surface currents and temperatures but also the difficult-to-observe ocean floor currents, offering the possibility of new insights into the details of thermohaline circulations.

This paper reports the results of an initial study using the ALMA at Aberdeen to model the ocean floor current structure of the thermohaline circulation of the North Atlantic.

Method

A triangular finite element grid of 10^6 points was set up to cover a quadrilateral section of the North Atlantic from 25.6° north, 47.9° west to 94.9° south, 5.5° east.

Initial conditions were obtained from a combination of publicly available data sources [1] and our own research data [2, 3]. Mean gravitational vectors and initial mean water pressure data for each element were calculated using ocean floor height and water column data from the GOCE Gravity survey [4]. Initial salinity and surface sea temperatures were derived from the World Ocean Database [1].

Hagen-Poiseules Equation was then used to calculate the mean flow vector in each of the elements at the surface and at the ocean bed. The Beatty-Smith relaxation algorithm [5] bounded by global limits on

---

[1]   Corresponding Author: Prof. A J Benion, Room G986, The National Oceanography Centre, 1 The Parade, Foreshore, Aberdeen AB7 9NN, UK. E-mail: Augustus.Benion@Aberdn.ac.uk

groups of functionally related elements were used to resolve any boundary condition conflicts by semi-local smoothing. Convergence of the model was determined by the Whittaker-Green criteria [6].

There were three phases to each stage of full model iteration. After the boundary conditions had been set surface current patterns were partially establish by multiple iteration across the surface field without modification of the ocean floor layer. When interactions of the surface model were broadly stable according to the criteria employed by Ramaux and Smith [7], the surface layer was allowed to interact with a still unmodified ocean floor layer to identify significant points of sinkage of water from the surface to the ocean floor and of upwelling of water from the ocean floor to the surface layer.

In the last phase points of significant upwelling and sinkage were fixed and the ocean floor layer fully connected to the surface layer using them and Gaussian assumptions of diffuse sinkage and upwelling between the fixed points of significant sinkage and upwelling. The fully connected model was run to local convergence before smoothing criteria between cells was applied and a new stage of iteration initiated.

The iteration process was deemed concluded when the mean RMS error from model findings and 100 known data check points across the whole region modeled were below 0.1%.

Results

Full iterations took from 10,000 to 100,000 stages depending on exact boundary conditions. We estimated an improvement in time to convergence of the model using the ALMA of between 100 to 500 times for comparable models run on other machines at resolutions 100 times lower.

While there were differences between details in the different interactions the results they produced were very consistent. These are well represented in Figure 1 which shows the typical results of modelling at the surface (1a) and ocean floor levels (1b).

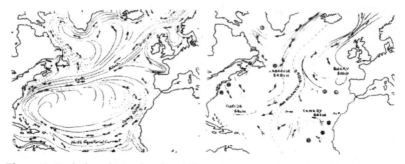

Figures 1: Typical results results of modelling of currents at the surface (la) and ocean floor levels (1b)

Key: ⟶ Warm currents in the surface layer, ‑ ‑ ‑ ‑ ‑▶ Cold currents in the surface layer, ⊗ Local area of significant sinkage of water from surface layer to ocean floor, ⊙ Local area of significant upwelling of water from ocean floor to surface, ⟶ Drift per hour each thick stroke above the shaft indicates 1.0 nautical mile per hour, each thin stroke below the shaft indicates 0.25 nautical miles per hour.

Figures 1: Typical results results of modelling of currents at the surface (la) and ocean floor levels (1b)

Discussion

Clearly the expectation that the use of ALMA architecture machines in this computer-intensive type of modeling task is justified by the results of this short study. The challenge will now be to improve the design of the mathematical algorithms driving the finite element analysis to exploit this advantage in speed and resolution.

However, it would be remiss of us not to consider the implications of the model results in terms of what they may indicate about the structure of thermohaline circulation in the North Atlantic. The consistency of the models in their predictions, particularly of the ocean floor currents, was unexpected and they challenge several established assumptions.

The first is that even in areas such as the South Atlantic Maelstrom upwelling and sinkage is a broadly diffuse process. Whilst in many ways the model is consistent with this assumption it identifies a set of well focused regions of upwelling and sinkage across the area which if present cannot be accounted for by standard assumptions.

Second, the modelling suggests that there are four defined ocean bed basins which form on the western and eastern upslopes of the mid-Atlantic ridge.

It has been known for some time that the undersea trenches between the Outer Hebrides and the Iceland, and Iceland and Greenland are the main bottlenecks in the return of water from the North Atlantic Drift when it sinks in the area between Norway and the Polar Ice Cap.

Our modeling suggests that the effect of these two trenches combines with the barrier of the mid-Atlantic ridge to partition the feedback of the water from the North Atlantic Drift unevenly between west of the ridge and east of the ridge, approximately in the ratio of 1:2. As the water from the trenches flows down each side of the ridge it settles into the low lying areas off the continental shelf of the Bay of Biscay and the Canary Islands in the east and off Labrador and Florida in the west. The influx of this water displaces the cold water from the ocean floor in these area areas mainly diffusely but on the borders of what we would describe as these functional ocean sea basins, areas of significant upwelling and sinkage arise.

We would hypothesise that these local areas of upwelling and sinkage contribute significantly to the cold surface Canary Current and the cold currents off Labrador and the east coast of the USA.

Conclusion

If the structure of deep ocean basins suggested by our modelling can be confirmed by direct observation then it will radically affect our understanding of the dynamics of North Atlantic Drift. In turn this would have a marked effect on our understanding and predictions about what may happen to weather patterns in the North Atlantic if global warming affects thermohaline circulation by weakening the North Atlantic Drift.

References

World Ocean Database, National Oceanographic Data Centre, www.nodc.noaa.org

Benion, AJ Sinkage and Upwelling in the North Atlantic. Journal of Physical Oceanography 2025; 20(3): 230-245.

Troubadour, LP and Rameaux, F Annual variation in surface temperature at the junction between the Canary Current and the South Atlantic Maelstrom, Limnology and Oceanography 2024; 30(4): 371-387.

GOCE Gravitational Variability Data www.esa.com

Beatty, SF and Smith, PG Relaxation algorithms for current field extrapolation: Smoothing and Relaxation Criteria Ocean and Climate Modeling 2028; 12(3): 120-125.

Whittaker, KL and Green, JW Convergence in large finite element fields, Finite Element Analysis in Hydraulic Engineering 2029; 14(12): 450-461.

Ramaux, F and Smith, T J Mathematical stability in surface reaction fields Mathematical Methods in Physical Oceanography 2029; 13(8); 560-565.

Chapter 6

I had transferred as much of the book store as I could to the boat given that I was going to have to house eleven or so 'guests' for the trip. Robert had allowed me to include all the newspapers and magazines but I didn't take this as a gesture of generosity; on the contrary. The books were merely part of the agreed cover story which was that Robert had done a deal with me of which the city builder stuff from the store was part. After the deal had been announced a rumour had been started that said when I came back I'd bring three other ships with me, all full of food. That kept everyone happy. Ordinary scavengers had started shaking my hand as I passed and suddenly the guards were respectful.

Robert had been careful to keep me away from the Lady, which suited me. I couldn't make up my mind whether she had been part of an elaborate plot to trap me from the start or whether Robert had simply seen the emotional impact she made on me and played accordingly. On balance I thought it was probably a bit of both. She would have to have played along once Robert had told her to pull me in. I had observed that when up against it human beings had great deal of difficulty in being honourable no matter how good their intentions. That took real determination and strength of character. People in the past had called it moral fibre and I clearly lacked it. I could not let Robert succeed but I had no plan to stop him. I probably didn't have the courage either. I comforted myself in the fact that that was the journey and the sea was always an unpredictable place.

'We fit for voyage yen?' Robert was standing too close to me for comfort, deliberately impressing on me his physical presence. Over his shoulder I could see the Lady at the prow of the boat with a guard. Robert had come on board to check my progress and brought her to remind me of what was at stake.

'Getting there. How much food you want take up to city to fool people?' I asked.

'None.'

'Surely they fight if see you running?'

'So what yem do; plenty bullets.' Not only was Robert prepared to condemn his people to starvation but he was quite prepared to rub their noses in it at the same time. 'Anyway yem not see us go; me go at night.'

'Then your men going have to row. Channel too narrow use the sail at night, Need all my time, steer a safe course. Only rowing do.'

'They learn under your wise instruction.'

'And me need all light as I can get. When moonfull?'

'Me think of that; night after next. We'll go then. Me not as stupid as yen think Ostlander.' He left my side and wandered forward to the Lady and in full view of me, cupped his hand under her chin, forced her head back and kissed her on the lips.

The anger started in my guts and rose up through my chest. My pulse increased and I knew I was going white. It wasn't jealousy driving it; it was the realisation of my own foolishness. How, with all my knowledge, all my experience, had I been so easily read and trapped? How? The desire to take the spike I had been using to splice a new rope for the sail, walk over there and thrust it up under Robert's chin, through his tongue, pallet and the bottom of his brain case, into the soft tissue beyond was almost overwhelming. I was disgusted with myself and what I was going to help him do.

★ ★ ★ ★

Eventually I persuaded Robert that they should keep up the sham of me coming back by holding a feast. I had told him that the journey to the nearest community, one that was rich and that would be easy to conquer, was no more than three days, so they could afford to cover their departure with a celebration. At midnight, they would accompany me to the boat and hail my departure.

So, I had brought enough food from the boat to make a decent meal, built a fire in the main hall and put the rest of my venison to roast over it on a spit. When the guards and the rest of the gang members arrived, two kegs of brandy were opened and tots of the spirit handed round to everyone except those who were to sail with me. The remnant of the hardbread from the boat's hold was distributed to the ordinary gang members; the venison was kept for the guards.

It was the first time I had seen all the gang together in one place. The whole group did not amount to more than sixty. Robert was right to be keen to go. They were closer to the end than I had anticipated. The social fabric of the gang, such as it was, was about to implode.

I sat between Robert and the Lady. Her touch was painful, made worse by the fact I could not speak to her or exchange glances, since we were under Robert's eye. At what I estimated to be midnight Robert got up to speak. The hall became quite.

'Friends. Tonight marks new beginning. The Ostlander has brought us new hope. Tonight he leave. In few week he be back with more food. Friends, I give you Tobias the Ostlander.' Robert held out his cup and drank; cheering followed from the guards and the rest of the gang. Robert fired his pistol at the ceiling. Like Robert the forty-nine who were to be left behind were drunk; the nine who were coming were sober.

'Friends let us give yem good send off.' Leonard and Angus seized hold of me and put me on their shoulders. They carried me out of the hall and into the night followed by all the guards and the cheering people.

The boat had been prepared; even its four oars had been placed ready in the rowports. On the pretext of moving the boat so that it pointed downstream, I had even managed to train a few of the guards to row. We arrived at the gangplank and they put me down. I waved and grinned at the crowd. 'Thank you friends. When return yen no more hunger.' Strictly not a lie, I thought, for even if I never came back death would soon come to end their starvation.

Robert patted me on the back and ushered me onto the boat. The chosen guards followed. The four who would row sat on the benches by the oars. The rest came aboard. To the crowd on the quay it must have looked like Robert was giving me a great send-off. The last two guards to come aboard were Leonard and Angus. They turned and tried to pull the gangplank quickly onto the ship before anyone else could board. But one of the captains who was not in on the secret was standing on its end. Robert drew his pistol and pointed it at the man. The crowd went silent.

The man looked at the gun. 'Robert, what yen do?' He understood as Robert pulled the trigger. The man fell from the plank into the dock and Leonard and Angus pulled the gangplank on board as fast as they could.

'Push us off,' I shouted to the oarsmen. 'Push us off before they come at us.' The boat began to move away from the quay. A groan went through the crowd as the truth dawned. One or two of the guards dived in after the boat but Robert's pistol settled them. As the boat slipped away the last thing I could see in the moonlight was the silent, terrified faces of the gang members and the shadows of three or four bodies floating in the dock.

★ ★ ★ ★

We picked our way down the channel. I set Angus at the prow to watch for anything in the water while I took the rudder. At first, the men at the oars were rather erratic but they gradually got a rhythm going. By shouting instructions to them I was able to use them, to turn the boat instead of the rudder. Gradually, the channel became wider and the navigation easier. Though it was still dark there was a breeze in the air. The atmosphere was more open and I knew we had left the city. There would be willow growing near the banks and grass in the fields. If I had been on my own I would have beached the boat near some group of trees taken my bow and waited for a hart to appear for its morning feed. It would have been a fine way to see the sun come up and fresh venison was always welcome.

As the channel got wider I had more time to think. At the mouth of the main river we would join later, was a large island. On my inward route I had steered to the west of this island a route that offered the most shelter from the east winds getting up this time of year. But if I took the easterly course then I would come out into the channel at a point where I knew the sea would be rough; where currents coming around the island from two sides met. I still had no concrete plan of how to stop Robert and prevent him attacking one of the farming communities, but a resolution was forming not to do it. I would have to play for time and the eastern passage offered at least the fun of seeing the quality of my new crew's sea legs.

The first sign of light was appearing, the skyline turning a pale pink. Details of the trees on the banks and the meadows began to appear washed and diffused by a thin mist. Pink turned to blue not just at the rim of the skyline but reaching further up into the arch of the sky. Now I could see the banks. A heron eyed us suspiciously as the boat moved down the centre of the channel. Then it turned, its wings outstretched in downward-facing arcs and it wheeled gracefully across the meadows upstream, not wishing to have us disturb its chance of an early fish. As the sun broke over the hills the wind I had been waiting for arrived.

'Stop rowing,' I shouted to the men at the oars. 'Hold oars still in the water to steady the boat. Leonard, Angus give me hand.' We hoisted the main sail and trimmed it to the wind and when it was set just right I called to the men to ship the oars. The boat hesitated as the sail filled but then she was away. The sound of the crackling of the sail and rushing of a bow-wave replaced the monotonous creaking of the oars. The guards cheered, partly in relief of not having to row anymore but also, I felt, for the freedom of the boat's passage and I cheered with them.

★ ★ ★ ★

Breakfast was hours ago and Robert had not been on deck for some time when the river started to broaden out. We were coming to where it joined the estuary of the larger river of which it was a tributary. He had disappeared into my cabin with the Lady just after eating. I tried not to think what he was about down there on my bed, though sleeping off the brandy he had drunk last night was probably playing some part in it. As the flat shape of the great estuary came into view I realised that the men were becoming restive. After breakfast they had taken to lounging around on the deck or the hold covers. Some were asleep, some playing games, but now they were beginning to crowd at the front of the boat, looking worried and talking in the quick whispers of those who are anxious.

Eventually Angus came to talk to me. 'Do we have to go… there? he said pointing to the estuary.

'Yes. That worry you?'

'No not me, understand yen, but some don't like open spaces much, big wet open spaces specially.'

'Only big river, that all. There be a bank other side, long way off so difficult see it. Tell yem safe; me no sail off edge.'

'That be a relief to yem, some of yem think we will.'

'Any else trouble?' I said

'Yes. How you know which way you go?'

In answer I pulled out a small wooden box from my jacket and hinged back the top. Inside was a rotating disk with letters round its rim.

'This compass. Now it tell me we go southeast but when we join big river we south. That how I know which way we go. As well, me sailed so much round here, up and down coast and across channel, I good idea where I am most of the time simply by looking.'

Angus seemed satisfied and went off to reassure the other men. So they had lived for so long in the city that they were frightened of wide open spaces. If the estuary frightened them, what would they make of the sea?

As he passed, the cabin door opened and Robert emerged. The turn into the estuary was no more than 200 metres away. Robert blinked at the light and rubbed his eyes He was clearly just waking up and had a headache. As he started to take in where he was as the boat reached the turn. I threw the rudder over and the boat heeled as it came out into the main stream and was taken by the stronger current of the larger river. Robert staggered and grasped the top of the cabin roof to steady himself, then he saw the expanse of the estuary. As if to welcome us to saltwater a pair of gulls flew low over the boat squawking and clamouring. Robert ducked away from them and then I saw that he was clinging with both hands on the cabin roof in panic.

The boat steadied itself and I adjusted the sail to the new angle of the wind to the boat. Robert was still hanging on but as the boat came round on an even keel, he took control of his fear. Unsteadily, he turned and walked back to the rudder. His face was still a little white.

'Where we Ostlander?'

'Bout thirty kilometres from the city. Twenty more from sea.'

'How far from target?'

'Bout hundred.'

'Nuther day an half.'

'No nuther two day an' half. We can't sail at night at sea. We find somewhere along the coast rest tonight.'

'Can't sail or won't sail?'

'Can't sail, not near coast. Currents and rocks that would tear boat apart if we didn't miss them. Need daylight that. So no sailing night. Unless you want to be out on cold, windswept rock, soaked in salt spray, with nothing between you and the flat open sea.' I saw Robert swallow hard.

'S'pose yen know best,' he replied. Then he went to talk to his men.

★ ★ ★ ★

The moon was up in a clear sky. It was so bright that it trailed a wake of silver as far out as I was able to see. The boat rode at anchor in the bay as peaceful as I could have wanted. These were the nights I prized in my life. I would have been sitting happily out under these stars if it was not for the black shapes of the two guards fore and aft.

We had emerged from the estuary late in the afternoon and I had taken the eastern route as I had planned. The increase in the breadth of the sky had an immediate effect on most of Robert's men. Some could hardly bear to look over the side and even those less affected seemed on edge, only Leonard and Angus seemed at home, positively elated by the wind and the waves. We reached the cross-currents with the sun low in the sky. There was a brisk tide flowing up the channel and the waves within the maelstrom were as violent bad as I had ever seen. I put the men back on the oars and ploughed ahead.

The boat pitched and yawed fiercely as the prow broke into white water. Two of the weaker-stomached individuals were immediately sick over the side. Robert was at the prow when the first wave broke over the rail, the water, flecked cream and aquamarine, leaped up and rattled against the sail giving the chief a mild wetting in the process. Until that point Robert had done a good job of holding his fear of the open space in check but the spray was just enough to break his resolve. With a bit too much haste he retreated to behind the hold-cover, hanging onto the rail there. He had tried to cover up his discomfort but several of his men noticed his hasty retreat. Not a good thing for a despot such as Robert to show weakness in front of his men, I thought; tends to undermine authority.

The pitching of the boat would be reverberating through the hull and would be quite frightening below. After a few more heavy waves, the cabin door opened and the Lady came on deck. She looked more curious than perturbed and was surprised not to be stopped by a guard or Robert, but everyone was far too engaged with their own problems to worry about her. To my delight I saw she was not at all afraid of the view of the sea or the motion of the boat. As soon as she came on deck the wind took her hair and her checks reddened with the exhilaration. She even glanced back at me and smiled.

Then she saw Robert clutching the hold rail: his discomfort obvious in his body language and in the colour of his face when he glanced round. As soon as she saw him she started to laugh. 'At last,' she shouted at him. 'At last something you can't threaten or kill. The great chief defeated by a few waves.'

She was delighted but her triumph would not last long. Despite feeling sick Robert wasn't going to take what she had said. He turned and threw himself across to the rail at the cabin entrance cover as the boat pitched and yawed again in a large wave. Then hand over hand he worked his way round to her using the rail. She stood her ground. When he got to her he slapped her backhanded across the face. I saw a thin line of blood on her cheek. Robert raised his hand for a second blow but I pulled the rudder round so the boat took the next wave on its windward quarter. The boat rolled and Robert lost his grip, being thrown across the boat and hitting the leeward rail with the small of his back. He collapsed on to all fours, winded by the blow to his kidneys, and immediately spewed up on the deck.

'Get back in the cabin,' I shouted. 'Get out of his way. This won't last much longer.' She nodded and went down again through the door.

In half an hour we were through the maelstrom and into the calm waters in the lee of the island. We sailed on until the sun was setting in earnest and then found a sheltered bay for the night. The guards and Robert were shattered and tired. Seasickness and fear had taken their toll and without much discussion, they all went ashore, preferring dry land beneath trees on the shoreline to even the gentlest of rolling on the boat at anchor.

Point-blank I refused to go ashore and Robert did not put up much of a contest, except that he had posted the two guards to keep me company. Robert probably wanted to go ashore more than most of his men after he had vomited in full view of them. It crossed my mind that the odds of stealing the boat away were probably as good as he was going to get with only two guards on board but the Lady was on shore and I felt a responsibility for her. The weakness and fear Robert and his men had shown must be to my advantage, if I could think of a way of exploiting it.

Times, *Saturday May 25th, 2032*

Anglo-french expedition sets sail amid storm of controversy

Later today the oceanographic research ship *Loch Fyne* sets sail from Aberdeen on an expedition that will prove if the North Atlantic Drift, that keeps Britain warm in the winter, is failing.

Two years ago researchers Augustus Benion of Aberdeen's National Ocenographic Centre and Françoise Ramaux of the Institut Europeén de Recherche de la Mer in Brest published controversial computer modelling results that suggested that it was possible to test the theory that the North Atlantic Drift was weakening by making direct measurements of ocean currents at the surface in two key areas in the North Atlantic.

Over the next six months, backed by the EU, the *Loch Fyne* Expedition will sail to an area off the coast of Spain on the edge of the Bay of Biscay and then to the area around Labrador to make these measurements.

At a hundred sites in both places pods of scientific measuring equipment will be lowered slowly from the ship to a depth of five kilometres. The pods will measure salinity, temperature and local current both across the ocean floor and vertically. The expedition will be looking for upwelling of water from the ocean floor, part of the return water from the North Atlantic Drift. If the upwelling is weaker than expected from the computer models of a healthy North Atlantic Drift, then the researchers believe this will give indicate that the European seaboard is on the verge of a sudden catastrophic collapse in temperatures.

As joint expedition leader Augustus Benion said at yesterday's press conference, 'What we thought would only happen over many years might be about to happen in a matter of twenty years. The centres of upwelling our computer models suggest would have the effect of intensifying and accelerating the effects on climate of a collapse or even weakening of the North Atlantic Drift. These measurements will be vital in changing the way we think about the effects of climate change and how we should respond.'

But many oceanographers disagree violently with Professor Benion. Professor Olga Christiansen of the Icelandic Oceanographic Istitute has labelled the *Loch Fyne* expedition as a monstrous waste of money. She is quoted as saying 'The *Loch Fyne* measurements will be meaningless. The process of return of North Atlantic Drift water into the main South Atlantic Gyre is predominantly diffuse. Any upwelling they find will be purely a local effect.'

Chapter 7

It was harvest, when the whole community turned all its collective attention to the bringing in of what was in the fields before the first storms of the autumn. It was a time that was a mixture of joy, relief and panic. Everyone who was physically able was out in the fields. Lines of Gatherers scythed their way across the wheat fields, followed by teams of children who tied the sheaves together. The smiths then stacked them on wains and they were hauled back to the barns, sheltered under the eaves of the wood, by the community's only two horses.

Francesca, Anya and the rest of their roundhouse harvested the sweetcorn and millet they had sown. Francesca was astonished how the millet had grown and she worked particularly energetically to harvest what she thought of as her own plants.

The community olive grove on the most southerly slope above the sea was stripped of its fruit, which was inspected, segregated and sent to be packed into barrels filled with salted water for winter storage. Any damaged fruit was sent directly to the Gathering Hall for the evening meals which were cold and basic since there was no one in the Kitchens to cook and the solar ovens were taken up with heating preserves and blanching vegetables for storing in earthenware pots.

Every night partners fell into bed exhausted. But despite the hard work and the stiff limbs, it was the happiest time of the year, when all ages mixed and the youngest Apprentice could find themselves working alongside the most senior Councillor on equal terms. It was the embodiment of community identity and ideals.

On the last but one night of harvest week, tired and dirty, Francesca and Anya were just coming away from the Gathering Hall, having eaten, when they met Jonathan. By now Francesca was not the only one who had realised that Jonathan and Hamied's partnership was breaking up. Many had noted that they had been working apart during harvest and had come to eat at separate times. As he came towards them, his head was down and it was clear that his personal problems were getting to him. But when he realised they were there he looked up, smiled and his face brightened.

'How are you getting on?' said Francesca. There seemed no reason to pretend his and Hamied's partnership was not in trouble and she sympathised with him.

He laughed and quickly changed the subject to the swimming lessons. 'You better ask my teacher that. Have I passed the test Anya?'

'I think you need to curb your enthusiasm a bit,' Anya replied. An odd remark, thought Francesca, maybe they had had an argument about the lessons.

'Well have a good supper. There's only one more day to go in the fields and then it's the Harvest Festival and a few day's rest,' and they moved on.

'He's not yet ready to admit that it's all over between him and Hamied,' Francesca remarked to Anya.

'Would it be better if he did?' replied a thoughtful Anya.

★ ★ ★ ★

The Gathering Hall was a riot of action and activity. Francesca and Anya had hardly stepped over the threshold when a gaggle of children besieged them offering plaited corn dollies.

'Francesca! Francesca! Look at mine.' A little girl was holding out a dolly in the shape of a sheaf of corn.

'Very nice Phyllis. Did you make this all yourself?' Phyllis, suddenly overcome with embarrassment, went dumb. 'Well it's very nice but I have to keep my hands free so I need a coronet this evening.'

'Over here Francesca, over here…' It was a little boy this time: 'I've made a coronet.'

'Let's see Alan.' She took the pale yellow circlet from his hand. The boy had done a beautiful job. The twists and turns of the basic shape were even and he had woven through these sprigs which reminded Francesca of corn standing in the fields ready for the scythe. She tried it on. Alan looked on hopefully but the coronet was too small and his face fell.

'Oh dear what a shame,' she said. 'Have you any more?'

'No… sorry… Francesca, that was the last one. I only had time to make three.'

'Well if it won't fit me perhaps it will fit someone else I know, who's smaller than me.' She walked over to Anya who was looking at the produce of three other children.

She put her hand on her lover's arm. 'I was wondering if this might fit you?' and she handed Alan's coronet to Anya who took it in two hands and placed it on her head. It fitted perfectly.

Francesca turned to Alan, 'It seems your coronet has found a home,' she said. Alan, who had been near to tears, laughed, smiled and hugged Francesca.

'And one good turn deserves a mate.' Francesca turned back to Anya and found she was holding out a second coronet, this one twisted in the form of the sea with fish woven into its waves. Francesca put it on. It too fitted and the partners kissed at the exchange of their gifts as the delighted children danced round them.

'You'd better go to join the singing group,' said Anya, as the children broke off, seeing fresh potential customers. Francesca looked over to the centre of the hall where the singing group would be situated for the evening's ceremonial, just beyond the fireplace. The lute players were already there and Anya was right, it was time for her to get over there as the rest of the choir where arriving.

'Yes,' she replied. 'As sad as I am to leave you, I better go and help.' She kissed Anya again.

The previous day, the hearth had been uncovered and the new winter fireplace built. There was a head-high pile of pale-grey driftwood from the beach, fallen branches from the trees, corn-stokes and olivewood prunings. She looked up and saw the open flue hole in the thatch above the fire. Earlier in the day the lightest and most agile of the Apprentices had shinned up the outer side of the roof and had opened this chimney-trap. Who had done this job was always kept as secret as it could be, revealed only when the person so honoured, brought fire back to the Hall that evening and lit the wood in the hearth; a symbol of the turn of the season.

'Francesca…' She turned at the voice. It was Peter intercepting her and carrying two earthenware beakers. He gave one to her.

'I couldn't help notice that you didn't have a drink of elderflower champagne and I believe it's a favourite of yours.'

Even though it was the tradition, that Gatherers, Apprentices, in fact everyone mingled together at Harvest Festival, she still felt awkward at being offered a drink by the head of the Council. He held up his cup to her.

'Francesca, nearly our newest citizen!' then he drank. Several people within earshot noticed his gesture and joined in, making her blush.

'I just wanted to be sure you knew what to expect this evening,' he said quietly. 'I want to put your induction last this evening, just before the lighting of the fire but after I declare the number of children for the next year. It's the first induction of a Gatherer at Harvest Festival for many years and it's doubly significant since you're going to be a Gardener.' Francesca nodded and sipped her delicious drink, trying hard to appreciate its taste as well as take in what Peter was saying.

'You don't need to worry too much, I'll call you up,' he indicated the platform built on the other side of the hearth, 'as soon as it's time. Have you any questions?'

'No, I don't think so.'

'Good. I'm looking forward to you becoming a Gatherer. I can't remember anyone whose calling and duties have matched better.' Then he left her.

Ruth was in the singing group, helping increase the number of voices and helping the children who would sing.

'Am I glad to see you,' she said as Francesca took her place in the group.

Ruth had a good voice but she lacked confidence in it, as well as the natural musicianship of her former partner. As a result she was too nervous to make the most of it and only made up the numbers on feast days.

Francesca looked back beyond the hearth, expecting to see Anya, but she had gone. Look as she might Francesca could not see her. Anya had apparently vanished in the time Francesca had taken to walk the few metres to the singing group. Francesca immediately felt nervous and her old uncertainty about Anya's affections came back to her for the first time in months.

'Ruth, did you see where Anya went?'

'Don't worry, I'm sure she's only disappeared with her special friend.' The remark was cold and carried an edge of spite.

'Has Anya offended you?' said Francesca, surprised.

'You mean any more than having taken you away from me? And all for nothing!'

Francesca was shocked. She wanted to let the remark go but Ruth's tone had changed so abruptly she didn't feel she could.

'Ruth, you're not still angry are you? I know I hurt you but surely you're happier with Carole than you could have been with me?'

'It's not you I'm cross at but it hurts to see how she treats you.'

'I don't understand,' said Francesca.

'I saw her and that Jonathan on the river bank the other evening.'

'Yes, she's been teaching him to swim.'

'Well I've heard some names for it but swim is a new one. It's a good job it was me and not a member of the Council who saw them swimming!' She moved off over to the other side of the choir leaving Francesca upset and confused.

There was no Council procession; the Council being already there in groups across the hall. At Harvest Festival people settled in informal groups and children adopted any group they fancied. At one table Francesca noticed Sylvia sitting with Simon and his partner. Next to Sylvia was a small boy who had adopted her for the evening. The forbidding Head Gardener was happily telling him about all that he could see and the absorbed attention on the child's face showed she was doing a good job. Francesca wondered if Sylvia had ever had a partner.

Quiet fell and the choir started to sing.

The autumn time has come,
our festival is made,
the corn and grain are gathered in,
safe in our storerooms laid.
The weather will now break,
the wind and frost will come,
but we are here and all is well,
our Gathering is made.

A line of children came in from the Council doors at the ends of the Hall. Each carried something from the harvest. Francesca could see an older girl, thirteen or fourteen, carrying an olive branch with the olives still on it, a small boy was carrying a freshly-caught, silver, black and blue fish in his arms. Others of various ages were bringing sheaves of wheat, another a fleece of wool. At the head of the line a small boy and girl, the youngest in the procession, carried a loaf of hardbread made in the shape of a sheaf. It had been fresh baked and was still warm from the ovens. The smell wafted out into the Hall.

Immediately in Francesca's mind the smell fused with the words of the song. She could remember being in the procession herself. It was as if the she of now was watching and being watched by the she of the past, as if they could nod to each other across the years and the space of the Hall.

The sun falls to the hills,
the evenings draw in dark,
but round the fire we all will meet,
to spin the thread or card.
The strength of each is here,
held in our common bond,
The strength of all, the strength of one
community's strong song.

The children wound their way through the hall between the tables which were set in rings round the fire and the central platform on which was a table. They showed to everyone in the Hall, the whole community, that the harvest was real; proved that they could rely on there being enough food in the stores to feed them despite whatever the winter might bring, until another growing season came.

The silver moon grows red,
hard down upon the shore.
The tattered clouds will hide its shine,
the tides will rise and fall.
But though she wax and wane,
pointless her scowling face,
for all is now secure within,
against the winter race.

They reached the platform and went up the steps to join Peter who was waiting for them. He took what each of them had and having thanked them, put each of their contributions on the table. By the time all the procession had passed over the platform, the table overflowed with samples of all the food and goods that the harvest had yielded.

And so we will survive
and prosper in our time,
our hall will stand though storm may blow,
its hearth will warm our kind.
For we have never failed,
to loyally keep our Rule
to work and gather from our land,
and bring our harvest home.

None of the children remained, except the small boy and girl who had headed the procession. Their wheat-sheaf loaf had pride of place at the centre of the table. As the song ended they came forward. In the dead silence in the Hall they begin to recite.

Many years ago, the Founders came here to Heron Fleet. There were twenty of them and they had travelled far across Albion. We do not know where they came from but we know that they were hungry and tired and could go no further. There were few places where plants still grew and animals could be found in those cold times, but here they found plants growing, and flowers under the trees and a few goats and sheep hiding near the sea. They found a cave in the river-cliff and they gathered what they could from the plants and made camp for the winter thinking it would be their last but they were wrong and they survived. They had seeds of corn and barley with them and they planted these the following year. They fished at the river mouth and they rounded up enough goats and sheep for a small herd. At the end of the first growing season, they celebrated their first harvest and named themselves 'The People who Gather'. This is our story and we the youngest remember it, so none of us will forget.

As the children finished their recitation the whole community stood up and said together the words said at every meal time:

Reaping and sowing,
sowing and reaping,
this is the world we have.
All we know is the cycle of life.
Power to the greenwood.
Power to the field.
Power to our gathered food.

Then they began to clap the children, who were overcome with shyness until their Crèche Mother came up on to the platform for them and they were lead happily away to sit with her. Peter held up his hands.

'Friends, as the youngest with power to tell the story have reminded us, we come to celebrate another harvest, a harvest as plentiful and successful as anyone of us can remember.

'But we have had our losses since the last Harvest Festival. Five Gatherers have died this year: Thomas lost at sea while fishing, our oldest Gatekeeper Jake who will be badly missed by all, Miriam and her partner Alice who died within a few days of each other last winter, and Jacob who was our oldest Gardener. Let us remember them and pass on their memories in the stories we tell of them.

'But we should look to the future. Five youngsters will become Apprentices in the spring this year and a new roundhouse will have to be built for them. The Council has decided that we should not only bring the number of children up to replace them but in the light of such a good harvest three extra babies should be birthed, making a total of eight.'

'Why, that's the most birthing in a single year ever,' whispered a Crèche Mother who was standing next to Francesca in the choir.

Peter went on. 'But at this Festival, we look to the future in other ways too. Welcoming a new Gatherer is always a great occasion both for the individual and for us all. If this is done at Harvest Festival it is twice as meaningful if that Gatherer is to become a Gardener. Francesca will you join me here along with Sylvia and Enoch.'

Francesca felt her heart race and her legs felt unsure; she could hardly get up. She looked around for Anya but she still could not see her and she remembered what Ruth had said. But hands were pushing her to her feet and she could see Sylvia, coming determinedly forward with Enoch behind her. She had to go up the steps in front of Sylvia so her nerves and doubts would just have to take care of themselves for now. She walked to the bottom of the steps and having paused to allow Sylvia and Enoch catch up, ascended as steadily as she could.

Peter placed her on his right and Sylvia and Enoch took up their places on his left. Francesca saw that on the table was the Red-book. Peter picked it up and gave it to her.

'Repeat after me Francesca,' he said. 'I solemnly promise...'

'I solemnly promise,' she repeated.

'Remembering all those who have gone before me...'

'Remembering all those who have gone before me...'

'That I Francesca will play my role in the community as a Gatherer until my life's end.' She heard herself saying 'until my life's end' in a sort of dream.

'That I will uphold the Gatherer principles of community, identity and stability and take a full part in how the community is governed.' Again she repeated her reply in a dream.

Peter turned to Sylvia. 'Do you sponsor Francesca as a Gatherer?'

'I do,' replied the Head Gardener, 'and I confirm that she will be invited to join the company of Gardeners.'

'In which case, Francesca, I declare you a Gatherer. I believe Enoch has something for you.' Enoch stepped forward. In his hand was the trowel she had selected in her visit to the Smithy. It still looked beautiful with its deeply grained handle. He showed it to Peter.

'Is that correct?' he asked.

'It is,' Peter confirmed.

Enoch turned to Francesca. 'You know the trowel of a Gardener is buried with them?'

'Yes.'

Francesca knew about the tradition but in the moment she realised that this trowel would define her even beyond death. This astounded and trilled her. She thought of Jacob buried out in the fields, his trowel placed with him in his grave and how that would be her fate. She was now committed. A Gatherer she had been declared but to be a Gardener was in her blood. It was her calling and she embraced it with joy. Only one thing marred the moment; even from the platform she could still not see Anya.

Then she spotted her. She was standing at the far door with Jonathan. He was holding out a flaming torch for her. No wonder she had disappeared so mysteriously, she was to light the fire. Ruth was simply jealous of Anya, that was all there was to it. Francesca felt she had been very foolish.

The cheering and clapping for Francesca's induction extended to greet the fire. Anya, torch in hand, walked quickly down the hall towards the hearth. The clapping and cheering rose to a crescendo as she arrived and plunged the torch into the pile of kindling.

It was only a small thing. Even the people near them would not have noticed it, but to Francesca it was like a knife through the heart. As Jonathan had passed the torch to Anya there was a moment as she grasped it when his and her hands had touched. At that point, instead of releasing his hands as soon as Anya had the torch in hers, Francesca saw Jonathan slide his hands down the torch to cover Anya's. It was no more than a slight pause but Francesca saw them look into each other's eyes just as Anya and she looked into each other's eyes at every evening meal when they passed and blessed the hardbread. Anya and Jonathan were emotionally involved. Ruth must have seen them embrace or similar on the river bank. That was what she was referring to.

Though it was impossible, it was true. Anya was the reason Jonathan and Hamied were breaking up. Anya was challenging one of the basic tenets of The Rule itself, by which Francesca had just sworn to live.

You Never Can Tell! *May, 2032*

Mammoths back in London?

We're all used to scientists coming up with loony ideas, well here's the latest – *Mammoths are coming back to London.*

Using a computer that's been in *You Never Can Tell* before[2] for being used to predict the lottery numbers, Aberdeen University scientists have predicted that Britain is on the verge of a new ice age and that pretty soon we'll all be chasing woolly elephants round our local parks.

This stupid idea has been worked out by nutty professor Augustus Benion. By number juggling on his pet computer nicknamed Big Alma *(ooh Mrs!),* Augustus has says he has shown that in a few years a cold snap to end all cold snaps will plunge us all into the deep freeze.

Augustus says that it will be due to changes in the ocean currents in the Atlantic. Winters will get longer and colder, summer will practically disappear and we won't be able to grow food in Britain anymore. And all this will happen in over less than 15 years!

So girls get your winter drawers on. For if idiots like Augustus are right then pretty soon you won't be popping down to the supermarket for frozen beefburgers, you'll be hunting polar bears in Tesco's car park – as if.

But don't despair entirely that holidays on the Costa Dubai are over. Augustus also says that the effect will stabilise after about a hundred years and summers will get warmer again, probably hotter than now

---

[2]   Students use computer to fix lottery numbers. *You Never Can Tell* March 2031

though winters will still be colder. Your pals at *You Never Can Tell* can hardly wait!

But seriously, *You Never Can Tell* is outraged that when all us hard-working taxpayers are being asked to pay more and more for services like health and schools by wasteful central government, loonies like Augustus can be spending millions on this sort of rubbish. If you think it's time we put a stop to Augustus and his like then fill in the lastest *You Never Can Tell* campaigning rant at on our website and put a stop to Augustus.

The Founder's Diary I

Day 1

I write as an act of magic. I write because the journey will be dangerous, so I can say to myself, I will not die because I am writing. And I choose to start today – the day we leave.

We came here from the south, from a city where a weak sun shone through haze. We came out of our arguments. He had said that we all once lived in harmony with nature but I did not accept this. I said it was his fairy-story. What I saw was that we had always lived by feeding from nature. But in the past, he said, nature could repair itself but now it was dying.

He quoted facts and figures at me but my mind shut them out. Then he would get angry, frustrated, grieving about what he saw. He would shout that we had fallen from grace, from paradise to empty lives in hell. We had to return to Eden or die.

Sometimes I would stand with my man. At the gates of a power station I stood with a placard. I cheered him when he told us that it was our selfishness and greed that was killing nature. I cheered when he accused me of squeezing and exploiting the earth like a filthy harlot. I cheered when he pleaded with us to see that our lungs were filled with pollution, our blood poisoned by toxins and our minds cluttered with useless information.

Even when we were alone, it was the same. He pleaded with me. How could I be happy when nature suffered from our actions: the cutting down of the forests, the fouling of the seas with oil, the balance of climate wrecked by carbon dioxide belched from our industries. Then he would weep and I would hold him and stroke his hair; tell him all I wanted was his peace of mind.

Then one morning I went into my garden, into a corner where white snowdrops grew; a patch that returned each year. I was proud of their beauty and glad that they were with me. I went that morning to see them again. But instead of the delicate curve of the heads towards the good earth, their stems were bent and twisted. I bent down and lifted some of the blooms gently upwards; they shed their petals and disintegrated. With my fingers I loosened the soil around them. Their bulbs were rotten, their flowering not a sign of health and promise but a last desperate act of defiance. Then I believed and I too wept.

That changed me but unlike him, who was all fire in his fear, I did not rally and chafe against my impotence. I did not go his way, throwing myself towards the doom I perceived, as if my body and anger could prevent it. I was cold but looked for escape. I reasoned that even in the past when disaster had come a remnant had survived. And if a remnant survived then I would be part of it. So I searched and I found Winter's Hill.

I had become aware of it through stories in our group. They argued about it. They called it escapist and labelled its members traitors to the cause but it sounded practical to me. I saw an article in a magazine with an address. I wrote and asked to visit.

I found a farm below the moorland, with pollution-free air with people growing crops together. At the end of two days I asked to stay and even he was peaceful enough not to fight. So we stayed, built our own house from thatch and cob. Dug our fair share and settled.

Those years on the farm were fulfilling. Thirty grown-ups living together had their disagreements but we settled them in the Council.

As he became more contented he gave in to me and we had the children I had always wanted. Charlie was born in the spring of the second year, Alison two years later.

The Winter's Hill community was led by James. He had gathered the other first members together: Naomi and Jacob, Dina and Andrew, Chloe and Christopher. Winter's Hill was James's dream and every tree stump and field expressed his ideas. His vision of Winter's Hill was not as a way of escape, nor a base for protest but a place to preserve the best of the past and to rediscover how to live without technology. It was a place where we ate the food we grew, but we would invent as well and not just be locked into the past.

At first, as the temperatures dropped, we adapted and changed our patterns of farming a bit here, a bit there. When troubles hit the cities we watched and waited. Even when we heard that food there was scarce we were not afraid. Then suddenly it was time to go.

Today we put all we had on the wagon. James set light to the farmhouse and we left. He destroyed it as a symbol to all of us that there was now no going back.

Day 4

It was not that we were out of touch. We did not live cut off. We were always in touch with the outside world through the radio and the people we met occasionally from the surrounding farms. But we were self-sufficient and we expected that there would be a crisis of some sort; that was why we were at Winter's Hill. So, though we heard the news about the calculations, the predictions of the models, the confirmation of the expeditions, we did not panic. We took it in our stride and waited.

The cold came quickly. At first it was nothing more than a poor April; a snap, nothing more. A blip in the weather, the people on the radio and in the cities all said. But it lasted long enough that so many birds died their bodies had to be cleared with shovels from the city streets.

Then winter came back more quickly. After a short summer there was heavy snow out east. And so it went over the next few years. Each year winter was earlier. Each year it was deeper. Each year there were signs not even the city people could ignore.

When the scientists had first made their predictions people thought they were mad. So they denied that there was a possibility of disaster and continued. Now here were things they could see and they were fearful. Panic set in.

The rich were the first to move. There were reports of groups of boats, some privately owned, others hired, gathering in out-of-the-way places in the summer months. They set off south to Africa or the Mediterranean, anywhere warm where the cold would not come. We waited.

83

Next, food was rationed in the cities. This helped for a few seasons but eventually there was not enough food coming out of the farms to feed the cities under any circumstances. The ration was cut to hunger levels. There were street riots which undermined the economy so that the government could no longer buy food on the world markets. They prevented money leaving the country and banned migration. More riots followed and this time the army opened fire on the rioters, killing hundreds. Airports were taken under military control. Ports were closed with blockades of armed ships but the coast was long and there was always somewhere to get away. Finally, the army took over.

Then the cities' councils made independent arrangements with local army commanders. Together they mobilised the people and were successful in pulling in more food from the countryside near themselves, but this divided the army and without a united army, any vestige of national government collapsed.

Chapter 8

'If you don't want a fucking hole in your head get over here now!'

Robert had clearly decided to deal with the problem of having lost face with his men the day before by all-out bullying and bluster. The subject of his wrath was one of the men he had set last night as a guard on the boat to take care of me. The unfortunate man was trying to row the skiff to the shore to bring Robert and the rest of the group back on board. Try as he might the guard, who was not one of the ones I had trained to row, could only navigate round and round in circles.

Robert was beside himself but the rest of his men were beginning to see the funny side. Every crossed oar or crab caught had started to be accompanied by a cheer or laughter. The more the men laughed, the worse the man rowed and the angrier Robert became. Finally, he took out his pistol.

'I warned you,' he shouted and fired in the skiff's general direction.

'Angus. Have you got a line you could throw him?' I shouted. Though Robert might not be trying too hard to cause the rower any bodily harm, I didn't want my skiff full of holes by accident. Angus looked round. Then I saw him run back to where what baggage they had was waiting, rummage round a bit and emerge with a rope. He got back to the shore just in time to stop Robert firing again. After a well-aimed throw of the rope, that the man in the skiff caught, he was able to pull the boat to the shore. One of my trainees took over and Robert, with The Lady and his spear-carrier got back to the boat first. As soon as he was on board he bustled up to me all bullying and nervous anger.

'How far we from yem friends?'

'Bout hundred and sixty kilometres that way,' I pointed out to sea.

'How long it take us?'

'Tomorrow midday.'

'That include night sailing do it?'

'Yes.'

'You told me you no sail at night?'

'I can't sail at night near the coast but once we're out there,' I waved my arm at the open sea, insisting he look at the empty grey sky and flat space. 'Nuthin hit us out there; water deep. But me will need someone to steer me, I need sleep. Angus would be good choice.'

'We get there tomorrow in time to attack?'

'Yes, My Lord.' A bit of obsequiousness never came amiss.

After ferrying everyone on board, we got going about an hour later. Not that it worried me, the longer the better. I put my compass in its place on the rail next to the tiller and once away from the shoreline, with the sail up and trimmed, I steered southwest. Twenty hours on that heading would bring us in sight of the far coast. The sky was overcast but looked fair enough, and the wind was steady from the northwest. There was only a light, even swell and the boat was already making good speed.

I hoisted the small slave sail and coupled it to the tiller mechanism. With this steering sail engaged the tiller would automatically respond to small changes in wind direction and the helmsman was left only to take account of slow variations that might take us off course due to current or tide. After dark I expected the wind to veer to the east, at which time the slave sail and the tiller mechanism would have to be realigned, but that done, with a bit of luck, any change in wind direction would make very little difference to our progress.

Angus came to join me. 'Robert say you want see me.' So Robert had paid attention.

'Yes, member this,' I showed him the compass again. Angus nodded with interest. 'Me teach you how use to take boat as far as you like.' Angus smiled, he was fascinated by the boat and I intended to use that to my advantage. 'You see markings on disk?' I indicated the letters and the pointed triangles that marked the compass direction, 'And this line.' I pointed to the compass graticule. 'Me want you to keep that line between this mark and this mark, by using the tiller.' I indicated the S, then the W. 'D'y think you can do that?'

'Well, me try,' said Angus.

'Good. Start now while me piss. Just take the tiller and gently move it to keep the line where I showed you. I'll be back quick.'

I went off the back of the boat and got down on to the small lavatory platform below the transom. By ducking down no one on deck could see me unless they looked directly over the rail. Quickly I took my watch from my pocket, wound it and noted the time. Then having relieved myself I went back to join Angus.

'Any trouble?' I said to the guard.

'No...' He paused. '...But me thinking, don't me have to watch the wind do to the sail like.'

'Yes. But the small sail do most that at present. Me show you how to read the wind without it in a bit. Me get you controlling the rudder properly then me can get sleep before dark. Me take over from you when the sun sets.'

Angus was as natural a sailor as I had thought him. After half an hour I took down the slave sail so he had to cope with wind and current variations together. He rapidly learned to watch what the boat was doing and to be slow with the tiller and not panic if a wave took the boat off course. A couple of times he heaved a bit hard and the sail lost wind but I felt sure enough of him to get about the boat and look to some of the ropes and pulleys that I hadn't been able to check before we had left the city. Halfway through the afternoon, I hoisted the slave sail again and gave the boat entirely over to him. Then I told Robert I was going to sleep in the hold and left the deck, but sleep was not the main thing on my mind.

From a locker in the hold I took a hammock and slung it between two beams amidships. Then I dug out a pillow and a couple of blankets. When I was sure no one was likely to check up on me I pulled out some of the barrels at the far end of the hold, uncovering a small hatch in the floor which I opened. After a bit of fishing round in the bilge water I pulled out a sealed trunk, dried it off with rag from the locker, opened its catches and dialled a code number into a keypad on its lid. There was whirring sound and a click.

Inside there were various emergency materials sealed in oilskin bags. In one there was a thirty-five centimetre hunting-knife with a flat double blade, one side serrated, the other plain-edged. I checked it was sharp, put it back in its scabbard and hid it in the bottom of the hammock under the blankets. Then I put the rest of the bags back in the trunk and hid it again under the false floor panel, finishing off by carefully and quietly moving the barrels back. I took off my boots and swung myself into the hammock. Some sleep was essential; it was going to be a long night, with an even longer day to follow.

The sun was nearly on the horizon when I came back on deck to relieve Angus. My watch told me that we had been running for nearly ten hours and even if Angus had drifted off course, I estimated we were halfway across the channel. Certainly, there was no sign of land on either horizon. I checked round. Only one or two of the guards were still seasick but the unease of yesterday had returned, no doubt accentuated by being out of sight of land. Robert was not on deck nor was The Lady. The cabin door was shut.

I wandered over to Angus. 'Any trouble?'

'Nufin me couldn't sort out.' The guard was pleased with himself. 'I could go on for hours doing this if yen want?' He seemed hopeful that he get to continue to use his newly discovered skill.

'I'd let you with pleasure if it was day, but it's a different problem at night: especially if there's no moonlight. Well done anyway. If you like, I'll show you a bit more when we get near the coast again after sunrise,' and I took over from him at the tiller.

Gradually the sun went down and half an hour after it had gone, the stars were out in the blackest of blackest skies before moonrise. The wind backed to the east as I had thought it would, and the boat settled down for the night, guards sleeping where they could. I wound the electric torch and strapped it to the rail so I could see the compass. Gradually over the next hour, before the moon rose, I brought the boat onto a northwest course. Then

I took a small piece of iron from my pocket, slid it round the edge of the compass box until it appeared that the boat was in fact on the original southwest heading. Then I wedged the iron home between the box and its place in the rail so it didn't show. The moon rose. Now it was only a matter of time and seeing where we came out on the northern shore.

★ ★ ★ ★

Leonard was the first to wake. After stretching he wandered back to the tiller.

'Fine morning Trader?'

'Not bad.' I was non-committal though it was in reality it was a very fine morning. I did not feel as easy with Leonard as I did with Angus, I sensed the violent streak that had made this man stand by and watch a woman and baby killed because she resisted his desire to rape her. Leonard looked out to sea across the prow.

'Is that what me think it Trader?'

'Depends what you think it.'

'Land?'

'Yes, from there all round to there...' I traced the curve of the huge bay. On the right was what appeared to be a small island but I knew it was attached to the mainland by a causeway. From there was a low grey line, with pale green hills beyond. Further round, white cliffs rose up until the arc was completed in the distance by one cliff, higher than the rest, which seemed to wear a gold cap.

'Not long now. Me go and check my rifle.'

'Me do that, if I was you. As you go past the cabin door, tell Robert we land in about two hours.'

I checked the course of the boat. The prow was dead in line with the point where the great stone beach, the grey line I had shown Leonard, met the cliffs. From here, it looked like a solid line but in fact there was a gap at that end. Through that gap a river flowed out from a set of lagoons behind the beach, lagoons which offered a safe anchorage in any storm. Once through, by sailing a little east, we would reach the point where the same river came down from the hills. We would anchor there and then follow the river on foot as it climbed up and round on to an exposed moor, wide to the open sky.

★ ★ ★ ★

Robert was addressing his men on the bank of the river. 'In hour we see our target. It rich, it peaceful, it poorly defended. Tonight we eat much food. Take many women.' The men cheered and whooped, glad for the promise of better times, glad to be on firm ground and done with sailing.

'Leonard will check rifles. Angus give you bullets you need. Make every shot count. But remember we need the people afterwards; they grow food, make cloth. No unnecessary killing.'

The crowd broke up as the guards started to check their rifles and bandoliers were handed out. Robert came over to me.

'I want you out in front Ostlander, where me see you. If anything go wrong you get me bullet in your back. Understand?'

'Yes My Lord,' I said lowering my eyes to ensure he thought me afraid. 'What you do with The Lady?'

'No business you but since you ask, she stay me.' Angus came up to us.

'Everythin' ready, sir.'

'Good we start.'

I led off with Roberts's spear-bearer. It was warm and if there was any breeze it did not get down under the trees to the level of the river. After about a kilometre, the path steepened and the track became single-file only. I began to sweat but I plugged on as best I could.

It took us a little less than an hour to climb up onto the open moorland, where the river was reduced to a collection of small streams. As soon as the terrain became more open, four of the guards spilt off into two teams scouting wide of us and a little in front. We continued to climb on to the rounded flank of the moor then quite suddenly there it was on the skyline.

It towered over us, three tiers of banks, the last bigger than the first. I had no idea how old it was but the way large, dead trees grew out of its sides in places made me think it must be very old indeed. Maybe older than the cities. On the third bank there was a series of watch towers. The guards threw themselves flat on the grass when they saw them.

Robert pulled me down next to him, 'If this trap, Trader, you dead.'

'No one in the towers My Lord. No man yem long time. You see no one on this side 'til you get to gate. Follow me.' Before Robert could react, I got up and in a crouching trot started to traverse the line of the lower bank. Robert and the rest followed.

Another quarter of an hour and the ground opened out, and a more definite path appeared. I stopped to let Robert catch me up.

'Gate just round where bank turn left. You rush it from here,' I whispered.

'A frontal charge?' Caution was not something I had expected from Robert. On the way up I had been disappointed not to see more unease in the him and the guards, as the moor became more open and the sky more impressive, but maybe this new-found restraint was the product of the corrosive effect of their fear of the open. Maybe they were getting used to it and wouldn't panic; a grim thought.

'Me no soldier,' I replied.

Robert hesitated again and looked hard at me. 'I think you may be playing games. Perhaps man and a woman on own provide distraction.' He pulled on a rope I had not noticed before. It was attached to The Lady's hands, which were bound. With it he hauled her up to where we were. 'Take her with you but leave her hands bound.' He drew his pistol and pushed the barrel under my chin. 'I see you all way. I better shot with rifle.'

The Lady was freed from the rope but her hands were left bound. We moved off towards the path. When we were out of earshot I spoke to her.

'Don't look at me but listen to what I'm going to tell you. If you want to get away from him, do exactly what I say. About a hundred metres from here we come to the gate. It's really a set of interlocking short banks. Just before we get there this path turns to the right and Robert will not be able to see both of us. At that point I'll cut your ropes. Then run for it. There's a clear path that goes straight downhill from the gate. Run as fast as you can until you reach the trees and then keep on downhill until you get back to the lagoon. You should be able to see the boat. Work your way back to it and wait for me.'

'Why are you doing this? I betrayed you.'

'You remind me of someone I once knew.'

I bent down, drew the hunting knife from its sheath on my leg and cut the ropes. Then as she started to run I turned and yelled to Robert. 'Now! Now! The gate's clear! Charge! Now's your chance.'

Whether Robert believed me did not matter, the guards, rattled by their agoraphobia, just wanted some action. They charged up the path and through the deserted gates. Robert, far from leading his men like a hero, straggled at their rear.

I watched them race past me and then I sprinted back the way we had come. I was back on the single-track path before I heard the first shooting. I knew what they would see when they got to the top. The inner area of the fort was a ruin. The last time I had been here, only a few buildings were left; there would be fewer now. I had been surprised the watchtowers were still there.

There had been a community once but the moor had proved to be a windswept and difficult place to farm. The group had given up and moved on. Robert had no one to fight and nothing to conquer. The only satisfaction he would get was if he caught me. There was an idea to get the legs pumping.

The wood was in front of me; the trees offered some cover but not much. I was gambling that since they had come up by this path they would stick to what they knew and not take the quicker, direct path The Lady was on. As desperate as I was to be the first back to the boat I knew they would catch up with me before I could get underway.

I was within 300 metres of the lagoon when I heard shouting behind me. I crashed on as the first bullet hit a tree about thirty metres behind me; not far now, not far now! I could see the water beyond the trees and the reflection of the boat.

Where Angus came from I didn't really understand but suddenly there he was blocking the path. He started to raise his rifle but he was too late – I crashed into him, knocking him unconscious.

The skiff was on the bank, I grabbed its prow and pulled it behind me into the water. Then I threw myself into it and rowed like a madman. I had just reached the boat when Robert arrived on the bank. Bullets peppered the water but I was able to shelter behind the hull and get aboard. By crawling across the deck I was able to tie the skiff to the transom rail and heave the main sail up. Bullets made small holes in the fabric and some hit the mast but the sail filled. The hunting knife made quick work of the forward anchor rope and the boat began to move further down the lagoon to the east, out of range of Robert and his men and towards where The Lady would have come down on her path, but away from the exit to the sea.

Where was she? I scanned the bank. Any minute now the red mist would leave Robert and he would realise that if two of his guards swam out and attacked, one on each side of the boat, then I was finished. Where was she?

Then he saw her break from the trees about twenty metres away. She threw off her coat as she ran and dived into the lagoon. The guards followed the line of the boat's course and saw her. If I could get the bulk of the boat between them and her I could save her; I just needed to make five more metres. 'Swim towards the boat!' I yelled. 'Swim to me!'

She was making good progress until her arms went up and I saw the water around her go red. She stopped moving and her body rolled onto its back. I got a last sight of her beautiful face before the weight of water in her clothes dragged her under. Helpless I put the tiller over and the boat came round. It hesitated for a moment when the rig went slack but I had enough momentum and the sail refilled on the new tack, heading for the sea channel.

The amount of firing diminished as the guards realised I was out of effective range. They also began to realise that they were stuck in the open on a strange shore, under the open sky, with limited ammunition; in his arrogance Robert had left the reserves of ammunition on the boat.

Only Robert and one or two others kept up firing, moving down the bank with the boat as it sailed down the lagoon. I made it to the point where the river turned round the last spit of the beach and looked back. Robert was standing with Angus and Leonard up to their knees in the water to get as good a shot as they could at the narrowest point of the turn. I had to hold on to the tiller and so as I made the turn they would have their best chance as the transom came round and they got the last clear view of me.

Which one shot me I couldn't tell but before I heard the reports of the rifles a bullet took me and threw me across the deck. The pain was fierce and immediate, and I knew my right arm was broken just bellow the shoulder. I pulled myself up with my left arm and took the tiller again. As I did so I felt the boat rise to the swell of the open sea.

The Founder's Diary II

Day 6

We had been walking for a few days. At first the children, Alison, Charlie and the rest, played together as we walked though never too far from our old horse that pulls the wagon with our food and gear. It was no more than a holiday for them. No more than playing round the same wagon when we had used it to take in the grain at harvest time. Now they were quiet and closer.

Away from the shelter of the moor land it was colder than we had expected. Frost rimed the trees in valleys and in some sheltered pockets there was still deep snow. The next surprise was how quiet it was. The few people we saw ran away, even if we greeted them.

We saw the village on the horizon, a small hamlet by a beck. The water flowed quickly over the stones and we could hear it gurgling as we got closer. The road curved down the hill towards a stone bridge. On the left was a public house; its brightly painted sign swung in the wind; a white swan and two cygnets.

We pulled up outside the pub. James, with a few others, went in. I waited with the cart, starting to take the horse out of its traces for a rest. The children were playing tag round me. Suddenly we heard the raised voices and then the shots.

The men tumbled out of the door. 'Scatter,' shouted James. 'Take cover.' I pulled Alison to me and hid behind a wall. Through the door came a man: withered, grey, gaunt. He had a shotgun he was trying to reload. James had swung behind the wagon. As the man fumbled with the cartridges James rushed him. The horse shied and reared, knocking the man over. He and James struggled for the gun. Then it went off and only James stood up.

We buried the man and searched the buildings. He had been alone. In one house we found the body of a woman and two children in a bedroom. It seemed she had smothered them and then killed herself with a knife. I helped Naomi carry the children's bodies to the graves we dug. They were a boy and a girl, not much younger than Alison and Charlie. I carried the girl. She was holding a teddy bear so tightly I could not break her grip so it went with her as I placed her in earth. We laid their mother next to them. Naomi and I wept over all three of them as our men pushed back the earth.

We stayed the night in the pub for the sake of some shelter and to give the horse a rest in a barn we found. There was no food in the village and the only way we could make a fire was by breaking up furniture from the pub for kindling. We had a Council before we left and decided to take the shotgun just in case of more trouble.

Day 11

Before we set off from Winter's Hill we formulated a plan. We reasoned that if were to survive we must find a place where the climate is sheltered, protected from the worst of the cold. Somewhere wooded where there might be game to hunt, near the sea so that we could fish. 'The last thing to die will be the sea,' James said and I believe him. 'Fish will survive the longest and if there is a recovery it may well start at the coasts.' Since the coasts seem our best bet we have been heading towards a part of the coast remote from people.

The whole philosophy of Winter's Hill was not just about surviving for a short time but to plant something permanent and lasting. So we carry seeds to plant in any new home and we have all our know-how of planting, husbandry and building. All we have learned about how to sustain ourselves. If we can find sheep where we are going we can produce a new herd. We will not give in until the last.

Day 13

Today has been difficult. We are coming near to a city we cannot entirely avoid no matter which way we go. The nearer we get the lower our spirits fall and the more anxious we get. All day, so we will attract as little attention as possible, we have tried to use green-lanes. Of course we do not have any direct evidence that this city or any city will be hostile. Except for the man in the pub, no one has threatened us. When I think it through most of our fear comes from our assumptions. Most of us fled the cities to Winter's Hill to try to live outside the destruction of nature by humans. Now the consequences of the damage our kind has done are here we assume that it will be in the cities that the blow has fallen worst.

After the military took over the cities news became spasmodic. TV went first, requiring more technical knowledge and power to transmit, but radio lasted longer. City-based radio stations appeared, some of which were independent and under the control of local people. They did not paint an encouraging picture. Eventually, they closed down, we presumed due to difficulties of different sorts but there was always the thought that they were they were silenced by the authorities. There were only official radio stations after that and they were upbeat, with messages of things getting better. We listened but they seemed a bit too good to believe.

Day 19

We had a Council last evening to decide our route through the city. After some arguing we have decided to cut across the western side, between the main part of the city centre and a large, satellite town further out. This town shares some suburbs with the city. We hope this will reduce our time in the outskirts and that in the no-man's-land of the suburbs it will be safe.

Day 20

Today we got our first good look at the city. The high buildings in the centre were clear. In fact the sky is clearer, less hazy with pollution than I remember. But in places thick smoke was rising in columns and it looked from where we stood that fires must be blazing in the denser parts of the houses. I wondered how long has this been going on?

Day 21

We have found a small building about a mile from the motorway that circled the city. It seems once to have been a garage or a haulier's. In any case it was a place where lorries ran from; there were three wrecks in the yard. Whilst the women and the children hide, James and a few others have gone on reconnaissance. They will be back in a few days. The children are restless. We must not let them out to play for fear they will be seen, so to pass the time we repair clothes and tend to the horse. We had the good luck to turn up some oats and hay for him in one of the out buildings.

Day 23

The scouting party came back in the afternoon and a Council was called. James said that the suburbs were very quiet. In places fires are burning but they seem to have started accidentally, at least there is no evidence of them having being started deliberately. But despite the quiet there is evidence that people are active. The scouts had come across a large number of tyre tracks and it was clear that lorries and other vehicles were still running about.

They had traced some of these tracks back to a large mill which had a guarded compound with army vehicles going in and out, driven by soldiers. In some of the lorries they had seen groups of what looked like civilians. The party suspected that this was not the only 'fort' in the area since they'd seen other sets of tracks that led in different directions. 'But this may not be bad for us,' said James. 'I think there will be spaces between the forts with few people. We will be able to travel through those spaces without problem.'

Day 24

We began at break of day. Three men scouted well out in front of us and another group scouted behind. They took turns to circle the rest of us, who stayed close to the wagon on which the children ride. Two of the oldest were put high up on the load to use the advantage of being high up to act as extra eyes and ears.

We crossed under the motorway and went towards where the first fort had been found. We avoided the main roads where possible, though we still had to cross them from time to time. On some of them the tyre tracks, coming and going, were clear. Once or twice we heard the faint sounds of engines in the distance. Once the sounds were loud and three lorries passed close enough for us to have to pull into a garden behind a big three-storey house to hide.

Day 25

This was our second day in the city and, partly due to the rain, our progress was slower than we had hoped. The weather was bad and it drizzled as we trudged on getting wetter and wetter. We are so nervous that we hide at the slightest sound.

To our relief we have found an empty dry building to sleep in tonight. At Council we discussed moving at night but decided that it would be difficult for us to find our way. Besides we do not know what sorts of groups might come out at night. It seemed to me as the discussion went on, that there might be far worse than the fort people lurking in the dark.

Just as we stopped for the night we heard shooting in the distance. We passed the furthest point the scouting team got today, so tomorrow we will be in unknown territory.

Day 29

I have to write this very quickly. It is the first chance I have in three days. What we feared happened. They took us on a road that had high buildings on both sides. We were going along as we had done for the previous two days, then suddenly there were men in battle fatigues armed with rifles dropping from the buildings. They blocked our way front and back using a pickup with a machine-gun mounted on its tailgate and a lorry. We were surrounded. Shots were fired mostly into the air but my man, the father of my children, had the shotgun and he pointed it at one of the soldiers. The soldier shot him and I screamed as I saw his body fall from the wagon. He is dead, Alison and Charlie have no father and I am alone. They did not let me bury him. They did not even let me go to him. The last I saw of his body, it was being kicked into the gutter with blood smeared across his beautiful face.

Chapter 9

You are terrified. The wind roars in the thatch and a fine dust is falling onto your face. The roof seems far away but its beams groan and chafe against the fixings as the gale tears at the outside. Something bangs into the wall behind you: is it a branch or a stone? Again and again there are impacts with the walls. There's another one. It's coming for you. You wince and shiver, and scream for help. Part of the roof gives way, revealing a lightning bolt. How far the sky is away; how small you are.

'Come on, come on...' A kind face looms over you. 'Get up quickly. Take my hand.' You swing your legs over the side of the bed. The door slams open and rain, spiced with salt, curtains in as the door flaps about in an icy wind: bang, bang, bang.

You throw your weight at it, pumping with your legs, hands spread out on the leading edge, arms stiff, forcing it shut with all you have. As you get it back into place you feel a great hand pushing you backwards. A strong man is forcing the door, trying to get in. You feel him through the wood. You compete with him. Now there are two people behind the door, forcing you aside, then three as the typhoon monster rises to contain you, to trap you, to kill you.

Anya's face shimmers within swirling gobbets of water that howl and dance through the door-crack, while wind and lightning tear at the hole in the roof. She is screaming at you, 'Come back, come back,' but you are not taken in. Jonathan is running after you, down the slippery length of the bridge that swings and skitters in the gale. 'Come back, come back.' But you run harder. You have escaped them.

There's a hand in yours. 'This way, this way...' Someone is pulling you along, as the water sucks at your knees and you wade through it, salt-tears of fear mix with the sea-salt in the wind and fill your mouth; you are drowning.

The wind scrabbles at your thin sleeping-dress, pummelling your body, assaulting you as you run. 'Come back,' their voices join with the wind's scream through the bridge cables but you can hear them laughing as well and run harder though you seem to be getting slower and you think it must be the water that is slowing you down. They are coming but you are free, you will act, and you will not go back. Impossible, impossible but you know.

'Hold on,' shouts the hand-voice near to you now, next to your ear. 'Hang on to the ropes.' But it is too late the, wind and the rain fling you over the side, only for the hammering wave to push you back and dump you on the deck. 'Try to stay calm,' says the voice and you hear it quietly despite the wind and the panic, 'Think how trees bend. Accept the storm and survive.' 'Never!' you scream back.

You reach the end of the bridge and turn right. There is only one place to go, one place for action. The path to the beach is sheltered. The wind choruses in the pines above you like the choir that sings the storm into being, but the rain falls even more coldly here. Then you are out into the gale again and the shingle crunches and clutches so that running on is harder and your footing slides away from you as you run towards the sea.

'Now, now. Do it!' shouts the voice now in your head, now in a far place and time and not in this storm as it mocks at you, 'Time to swim!' and you crash into the waves that are white foam in the dim light. Thrown back you turn again and run at them again. A white fountain hammers you over, burying you in a pall of white. Beach-stones lash your feet. The current takes you and down you go, rolling at the bottom of the wave, as the faces laugh and kiss. Then it takes you up and smashes you against something hard and rough. A wall but there are no walls nor rocks on the beach. Despite yourself, you flail out your arms and whatever it is scratches at your skin. It is wood. Then there is a rope and steps. You try to avoid them but the waves throw you back and invite you to climb. It is the side of a boat.

On the deck the mast is down and the beached boat rolls madly. Again you try to throw yourself back like a floundered fish into the sea but it rejects you as an unworthy offering. You stagger towards the stern. You see a figure, a man rolling backwards and forwards in the waves. He is like a doll and his blood stains the deck. You hold him below the arms and pull him up into the shelter of a hatch. Your strength goes. The part of the mast still standing comes down and hits you on the back of the head. The faces swirl away; hers, kissing his. Last before the blackness is the voice. 'There, there, child it's over now.' Hands and arms have you safe and there is a kiss on your forehead and the touch of yellow hair on your face.

★ ★ ★ ★

The first thing Francesca could recall for sure about her recovery in the Infirmary was a passing memory of the smell of herb tea combined with pain from her side and head as she had attempted to roll over. After that there was a gap, which might have been seconds or days.

Next she could remember her head being supported as the rough edge of a beaker was put to her lips and a kindly voice encouraged her to drink.

On one occasion, she was suddenly conscious and screaming with pain. Someone seemed to be gouging at the back of her skull. She tried to raise her hands to protect herself but she did not have the strength. She endured the pain until they stopped whatever they were doing to her and it went black again.

After that memories became more common. She remembered someone bathing her eyes and that she opened them and saw a blurred face before the shock of the brightness of the light made her shut them again. But the pain in her head was not as bad.

★ ★ ★ ★

Wind blusters in the roof, fingers trying to unpick the fabric of the building that is your safe home. The storm is an animal trying to break through the ceiling way up there above your bed. It means to kill you. You cover your ears with your hands and bury your face in the blankets, as the roundhouse is shivered by the thunder and the lightning is so intense that you can see it through the thatch.

Then she is there. Hands reach out and pick you up. Her voice whispers in your ear and you cling on to her neck, burying your face in her yellow hair, as she rocks you back and forward, whispering and comforting you.

The door explodes open and he comes through, trailing wind and water. He forces the door shut again. 'We must go,' he says, 'the river is rising.' You do not understand the words, the fear simply communicates itself. They wrap you up in two blankets. Then he takes you and you are flung out into the storm.

★ ★ ★ ★

But then there were the dreams. They were worse than the awake-pain. They were vivid and disturbing, and she could not impose on them any sense of time or order. She must have called out in these dreams, for once she remembered the night and someone holding her hand and asking gently what was the matter and stroking her hair and saying it was all right and to go back to sleep. Then she slipped back into the dream again, back to the rain and the lightning.

★ ★ ★ ★

The water is still round your feet. The man has had to put you down. He holds your hand as he pulls you through the water while he helps the woman as best he can.

'Get to the bridge,' he is shouting. 'We must get to the bridge before the water brings it down.' He stoops and whispers in your ear, 'Hang on to the ropes,' and you do. Your hand moves from one to the other as the water rises but you make it. You climb the bank on the other side and then there are two others; a woman and a man. The man picks you up. 'You're safe, my girl. The flood won't make it through the ditch.' The woman helps the lady with the yellow hair. You pass through the gate and it is shut behind you. You feel the wind drop, though it rages above in the unsheltered air. The man gives you back to... who is she? You put your arms round her neck and hear a voice: 'There, there, child it's over now.' Hands and arms have you safe and there is a kiss on your forehead and the touch of yellow hair on your cheek.

★ ★ ★ ★

In her memories there was a point when there was a face above her and again that smell of herb tea. Her legs were stiff and uncomfortable and so she tried to roll over but the movement triggered aching from what she could tell immediately were bruises all along her sides, and there was still the sick pain in her head but this time it was different. She tried to open her eyes but they were sticky and thick with matter. Effort was required for the first blink. Once that was accomplished more effort went into making her eyes big, to stretch back the lids until she could hold them open without blinking. Then, miraculously, the world came into focus and the first thing she saw clearly was an ash staff leaning against her bed.

'Welcome back to the land of the living,' said the familiar tart voice, though quiet and gentle in a way Francesca had never heard before. 'Would you like some of this herb tea I've just brewed?'

'Where am I?'

'You're safe and in the Infirmary but you've had a very bad blow to the head, so try to lie still.' Then Sylvia's voice snapped back into its normal commanding tone: 'Keeper, one of your charges is awake.' Immediately, two Infirmary attendants were at her bedside.

'If you can help her up into a sitting position she can have some of my herbal tea,' continued the Head Gardener as if it were a simple question of planting out seedlings in her own Glasshouses.

'All in good time Sylvia,' said an equally authoritative voice in response, 'I give way to your knowledge on medicinal herbs and their effects, but this is my Infirmary and I want to see how my patient is and if she's ready for any of your so-called tea.'

Two attendants helped Francesca into a sitting position, propped up on a pile of lambswool- stuffed pillows. 'Look at me,' said the Keeper. Francesca looked into her blue eyes, whose focus flicked from one of her eyes to the other and then back. 'So far so good. Your pupils are even.' She held up a single finger in front of Francesca's face. 'Focus on this, please and follow it with your eyes but don't try to move your head.' The finger went slowly from left to right, then up and down. 'Good,' said the Keeper, then she put both her hands on Francesca's shoulders and probed with her long, persistent fingers into the muscles all the way up the neck. Occasionally Francesca winced but the only thing that this elicited was a low grunt from her torturer.

'How's your head?'

'Very sore.'

'Can you see clearly?'

'Yes, I think so.' The Keeper of the Infirmary and the Head Gardener both let out a sigh of relief. 'Have I been very ill?' said Francesca.

Sylvia put her hand on her arm. 'Yes, very ill. You've had the worst head injury anyone can remember in the community; certainly of anyone who has survived.'

'Can you lean forward so I can see how your head is?' said the Keeper.

'I'll try,' though she knew her strength was beginning to fade and she was beginning to feel faint. But with the help of the attendants, she was able to lean her head forward. There was a bandage and the Keeper lifted its corner. Then she sucked her teeth.

'It looks alright but I don't want to disturb it much yet, though it will have to be sewn up as soon as possible and the bone put back if it's to heal and keep out infection. But there's no fresh blood oozing from it so it looks as though the pressure has been relieved and the scalp and skull are healing. The fact that she's properly conscious suggests that as well,' she spoke half to herself.

'Do you want to resume giving her the poppy juice?' said Sylvia.

'I think so,' said the Keeper, 'but at a reduced dose. I want to see if she can start to sleep again naturally. You can give her a dose of some of that terrible concoction of yours if you want to. Wonderful thing. the recovery power of the young,' she remarked as she left them.

A fresh herb tea was brewed and Sylvia sat on a stool close to the bed as she helped Francesca sip it.

'What is wrong with my head?'

'You got a very bad blow to your head in the storm.' Francesca looked blank. 'What's the last thing you remember?' Francesca thought hard.

'Anya lighting the fire at the Harvest Festival.'

'Well let's just say you got up to quite a bit more than that later in the night. Now rest. I've got to see about the other patient in here.' Stretched out a few beds down was a tall grey man, with a dishevelled beard, whom Francesca had never seen before. He had a heavily splinted and bandaged right arm, as well as some other facial bruises and cuts.

'Who is he?'

'Don't worry about that now but without you he wouldn't be here. Now rest and try not to move your head too violently. We had to drill a hole in your skull to relieve the pressure. That's what's under the bandage.'

As the effort of sitting up and the effect of the poppy juice took hold and she drifted off again to sleep, she watched Sylvia stop at the end of the grey man's bed and look thoughtfully at him. The expression on Sylvia's face was strange; half the care of the herbalist for her patient; half suspicion and doubt.

★ ★ ★ ★

In the next few days, Francesca gained in strength and could stay awake for longer and longer periods. On the following day she had a light meal and on the day after that they decided to redress the bandage on her head. When the Keeper inspected what was underneath properly she decided to seal it up. Francesca was given a draught of something that made her confused but pain-free, while they cleaned up the wound, replaced the plug of bone they had removed and sewed back her scalp over it. Afterwards her head felt sore but better than it had.

Sylvia came each day to tend to the grey man and more and more in passing to talk to Francesca.

'How long was I unconscious?' Francesca asked her on one of these visits.

'Four days,' said Sylvia.

'Four days?' Francesca was astonished.

'As I said when you first came to, you've survived the worst head injury anyone in the community can remember.'

'And you've been here all that time?'

'Well, in and out, for both you and him.'

'Has he got a head injury?'

'No, he had a broken arm, which has been set. But that combined with the effort of navigating his boat to Heron Fleet running before a storm had exhausted him. We've given him some sedatives to let him recover while the arm sets properly. He should be up and about in few days, as will you be. In fact the Keeper has allowed Anya to visit you. So you won't have to put up with only my company anymore. She'll be here later on to bring you your evening meal; you're to go onto normal food from the Hall.'

'Oh ma'am I sorry to have been such a trouble.' Francesca was alarmed the Head Gardener had taken offence.

'Nonsense,' said Sylvia sharply. 'I can deal with your sort of trouble easily enough. Now concentrate on getting well. There's quite a lot of preparation and cleaning up to do in the Glasshouses and I don't want to be short-handed for long.'

★ ★ ★ ★

In the evening Anya arrived carrying a hot tagine from the hall complete with some hardbread and a flask of elderflower champagne sent by the Head of the Council. Anya hugged and kissed her, then sat on the stool so that they could eat together.

108

'You gave us all the most terrible scare,' Anya said. 'When we found you, we thought you were dead; you and the man on the boat.'

'I'm afraid I don't remember anything after you lit the fire in the Gathering Hall.'

'Nothing at all?'

'Nothing at all really but I have had some very vivid dreams though most seem to be about when I was little. All I've managed to piece together so far is that in some way I saved the grey man over there.' Anya shifted on her seat as Francesca said this.

'Don't worry, even if you never remember it won't matter. Do you want me to fill in any of the gaps?'

'Yes but just the bits about him. I think it will be better if I let the rest come naturally.'

'Well he was on a boat that went aground on the beach in the storm. We don't know how or why but you swam out to it and had pulled him out of the surf which was engulfing the back of the boat. If you hadn't got to him he would have drowned. You'd dragged him back behind a hatch cover but then you got hit on the head and collapsed. You were both unconscious when we found you.'

'What sort of boat was it?'

'That's one of the mysteries about him. His boat is much the same design as the ones the fishers use but far bigger. You'll be able to see for yourself in a few days. After the storm had gone they managed to bring it round into the channel and it's now in the river anchored near to the bridge.

But there's a mystery about that too. No one but the Council is allowed on board. One Apprentice from Robin's roundhouse got his ears boxed by a Gatekeeper for having the audacity to swim round it to get a better look. The only things that seem to have been brought ashore from it have been taken to Peter's longhouse.'

Through telling Francesca this gossip Anya's mood had been light and happy but as she finished it suddenly changed. She leant forward and put her hand on Francesca's arm. 'You know I love you don't you?'

Francesca responded, covering Anya's hand with hers but slightly surprised at the sudden turn in the conversation, 'Of course I do,'.

'You know I'll always love you, no matter what?'

'Yes,' said Francesca puzzled.

★ ★ ★ ★

The following day, two of the attendants helped her out of bed. She was a bit shaky and getting on to her feet revealed all sorts of other cuts and bruises, but with help she was able to walk the length of the Infirmary.

As she passed the bed of the grey man she took the opportunity to have a closer look at him. He seemed not to have moved since the previous day, though she imagined he must have had to move when the attendants checked his broken arm. And he must have been woken to drink and have some food. She had noticed that she had been very thirsty when he was first awake and that the attendants had insisted she drink as much as possible now that she was conscious.

She concentrated on his face. The features were sharp and bony, the skin a deep weathered brown. In the community only the fishers and the herders went that colour, being out in all weathers all year round. And there was a yellow, metal ring in his ear, something she had never seen before. He was clearly an Outlander, and interesting and rare enough for that alone, but beyond that she could make no connection with him.

The Founder's Diary III

Day 31

The fort to which we were taken is in some sort of converted industrial building. We are prisoners, though the soldiers who guard maintain they are doing this for our own good. The women and the children have been segregated from the men and we don't know where they are or even if they are alive. All our belongings have gone. They shot the horse for meat and stole all our salt mutton; requisitioned is the way they put it.

I cannot free my mind of the image of his body. I want to weep but I must remain strong for the children. It seems impossible that someone so full of life and fire should be so easily extinguished.

Day 32

He is dead and our dream is at an end. If it was not for the children I would kill myself! But the others want me to go on writing and so I will for their sake, if it makes them feel better.

The soldiers feed us but the food is rationed and basic. At the evening meal Naomi reported that she had glimpsed the wagon tucked away in an empty part of a store room. Our job when out is to forage in the no-man's-land between the forts. The gangs we work in are about ten-strong plus an armed guard. The women have been divided into two gangs led by a couple of more experienced women. Miriam leads our gang. She is kindly enough but has her job to do. We have spoken. She lost her man last year which gives me a rudimentary bond with her.

Day 33

The men are alive! Those of us who believed they were still alive had assumed they where being kept somewhere else, perhaps in another compound, but tonight Isabel saw Jacob near where the lorries are off-loaded. She got close enough to get a word with him before the soldiers saw it and broke them up. Jacob said he'd make sure that there's someone near the same place each day.

Day 35

The men are held at the other end of this building and they have found a spot round the back of our latrines, where there is a crevice where a pipe comes into our part of the building. They think they can put messages there. They will try to send us something tomorrow. It's up to us to find where it comes in on our side.

Day 36

It worked. We found the pipe and this evening we got our first note from the men and sent them a first note from us. It gave us a great hope.

The men always knew we were OK. They had seen us on our way out on the lorries a couple of times and had heard us in the latrines. They are in much the same position as we are. They are put on guarded lorries for forage work.

There's one difference. They are being worked on by the soldiers to join them. They have been told if they become 'volunteers' they will get better rations. There are several forts in this area which are at war for the food that is left. Sometimes they launch attacks on each other. The fort needs all the soldiers it can get to survive, so they need the men to help them fight.

Day 40

Tonight's note from the men sounded ominous. Instead of being put into foraging gangs this morning they were put into a separate room under guard, away from the other civilian men who are housed near to them. They had wondered what was going to happen and some feared they would be killed because they would not join the soldiers. In fact they were visited by the Commander of the fort.

He told them that he was expecting an attack in the next few days. He said that he greatly respected us. We had been watched from the time we came into the sphere of influence of the fort. He had been told how well-organised we were and how careful. He had seen our preparations on the wagon and said he could not have been better prepared himself. He had also been impressed how hard we worked and since our men were strong and well-fed, compared to the other civilians, he pleaded with them to help repulse an attack if it came. The men said they would consider it. The Commander has asked that they give him a reply the day after tomorrow. Our men want to know our view.

Day 41

We met in Council this evening and we have sent our reply to the men. We were divided. Some said we should not fight. They said that the soldiers were the people who had destroyed our world and as such we should not collaborate with them. Others were fearful for their children if an attack came and said we should fight. We could not agree and so we voted and sent the men a message with that vote on.

Day 42

The men replied this evening. They too were divided but adding their votes to ours gave a majority for fighting. So it has been decided the men will fight and we will do what we can to support the fort.

Day 44

It has been quiet except for shooting as the soldiers train the men to use the rifles. The foraging has been curtailed and we have been drafted to prepare a makeshift place for wounded to be brought when the fighting begins. Miriam has been helping us set this up. I asked her whether there have been attacks before. Once, she said. She didn't seem to want to discuss it but I needed to know more so I pressed her. She said that then about ten people had been wounded and four had died. It had been a night attack.

Day 45

It started in the darkest part of the night. It wasn't clear at the time but this is how it all happened as far as I've been able to work out since.

The attack started with an explosion which blew a hole in the outer fence, somewhere near our part of the building. This was not expected; all the main defences of the fort are focused on the main gate. Pretty quickly soldiers arrived but not quick enough to prevent a second explosion which opened the inner fence. Shooting started and there was shouting above the noise of the rifles. The occasional flash showed that someone had thrown small bombs at the intruders. At the height of the fighting there was another explosion at the front gate. The attack on our side had been a blind, a feint. But the Commander had not been taken in and the majority of our men were still on the front gate.

The first wounded came in soon after. It was one of the soldiers. I was glad it wasn't one of our men; otherwise I think I would have gone to pieces. The soldier had been wounded in the leg and was bleeding badly. Miriam showed me how to give him an injection of morphine while she inspected the wound. 'The bullet's gone straight through,' she said to me, pointing at the jagged hole in his thigh. 'Apply a tourniquet above the hole to reduce the bleeding and then clean the wound up so I can see what I'm doing.' Another man had been brought in and she went to attend to him.

I turned to the soldier and tourniqueted his leg. A spurt of blood from an artery stopped. I cut the fabric of his trousers back and started to wipe the lips of the wound. 'Jesus and Mary!' he shouted, 'be a bit fucking careful!' I pulled back. He looked up and smiled. 'Sorry. Bit sharp that. Not your fault. Give it a bit longer then the morphine will kick in and I'll be able to grit me teeth. Not the first time I've been shot.' I started to cry. 'Don't worry, you're doing fine. Say, your lads can fight when they 'ave to. That leader o' yours, James, 'e took control as soon as 'e saw the fence was down. Born bloody officer if ever I saw one. OK, luv, you can 'ave another go now.'

By the time Miriam came back the soldier had passed out but the wound was clean and she tied off the artery and sewed it up. Then the first of our men came in. It was Jacob. He was still alive but he'd been shot in the jaw. Miriam looked at him and shook her head. He died a few minutes later. Naomi found him in time to keen.

After that it was a blur of blood and bodies. By dawn I could move from case to case and assess what had to be done even before Miriam had told me what to do. Strange place to find a talent you never knew you had. By the time the fighting started to die away we had six wounded and four dead around our dressing station. Three of the dead were Winter's Hill men.

Day 46

This time we buried all the dead, soldiers and men together. The Commander read the burial service over the graves and said how proud he was of how everyone had fought. I thought I'd rather have the men back, or have died with them. I didn't think there was much difference between us and our enemy. In the end there will be no future for any of us, especially not in foraging and fighting; only growing food will give us any long-term chance of surviving. It seems to me it is create or die.

Chapter 10

'Just walk up to the end of the room and back,' said the Keeper. Francesca did as she was told, trying to hide the limp.

The Keeper looked thoughtful. 'Sit on the bed,' she asked. Then she picked up a foot stool and sat down in front of Francesca. 'Slip off your sandals and put both your feet in my lap.'

She moved both her hands over Francesca's ankles in synchrony, one on each. 'All the bruising is gone but you've got a swelling just here,' she prodded it and Francesca winced. 'Just as I thought, it's still sore. You can put your feet down. That swelling's causing you to limp. I think there's a small bone on that side that's either displaced by an injury below the skin we can't see or the bone itself is broken. We'll have to strap it up again, you'll have to rest it and we'll see how it gets on. Less walking I'm afraid and no return even to light duties yet.'

In one way, Francesca did not mind the delay. Though she was keen to get back to work, her mind was not at ease. Dreams persisted and her memory was unclear. At first she had thought that she could remember everything up to Anya lighting the fire but gradually she found that she couldn't remember key details of the procession or what she had been doing before her induction.

Even so after a couple of days of enforced rest, when she felt better in every way but her ridiculous ankle, she was bored and frustrated. Except for Anya's visits with the evening meal, the only relief was that she had time to observe the Outlander.

As the Infirmary staff became happier that the bone of his arm had knitted properly they gave him less poppy-juice and he started to be conscious for longer periods. Francesca had tried to speak to him, hoping for some boredom-breaking conversation. But he was remote and difficult to talk to, so she stopped trying until one afternoon.

She had dozed off but was woken by raised voices. Standing at the bottom of the Outlander's bed was Peter.

'I don't care how well you're feeling, you're not going back to your boat yet!' Peter was as cross as Francesca had ever seen him.

'What right do you think you have to keep me here?' replied the Outlander.

'The right of ensuring that your stubbornness does not undo all the effort of care that the Infirmary staff have put into keeping your ungrateful frame alive, or the initial bravery of that young woman over there.' Peter's finger jabbed in Francesca's direction.

The Outlander snorted. 'Alright, alright,' he replied, 'I suppose that would be ungrateful of me. But won't you at least let me go and make sure my boat is alright?'

'Look Tobias, take my word for it, your boat is safe, sound and harboured in the river. We have even pulled her up to the jetty now the fishing boats have come ashore for the winter. We had to remove some of the stuff in the hold so we could patch up some damage below the waterline but what we took ashore is safe in my longhouse. There's nothing for you to worry about except getting well.'

The Outlander snorted again. 'I'd like to see for myself if you don't mind.'

'Oh really! I haven't got anyone who I can spare to take you on board. The storm did quite a bit of damage to the community buildings and I don't want to be caught without repairs having been done.'

'I could go on my own.'

'What if you fell and broke that arm again?' Peter's tone became a more gentle. 'If that break is undone you might never have the strength in that arm to sail her again. I know how much of a blow that would be to you.'

'If you're worried about me falling, it would only take a youngster to prevent it. Don't you have a lad who can do me this service?'

Francesca empathised with him. She realised how frustrated he must be with not being able to see his boat. 'I'll go with him if the Keeper will let me,' she interjected.

The Outlander immediately seized on her offer. 'There Peter, you've got a volunteer who cannot work.' He turned to Francesca. 'Young lady I accept your offer with thanks.'

'Hold on a minute,' said Peter, trying to regain the initiative. 'Francesca has a broken ankle. She's not fit to wet-nurse you!'

'I'm still willing to go with him if the Keeper says it's alright. I'm as frustrated as he is and I'd love to go outside for a little while and see this boat I've heard so much about.'

Peter hesitated and in the instant knew he had no real argument if the Keeper said yes.

★ ★ ★ ★

To Francesca's surprise the Keeper had been in favour. 'Neither of them will rest until they've got outside for a bit. I don't think it will do either of them any harm unless they overdo it and I trust Francesca not to allow that.'

So Peter gave his permission. Anya brought some outdoor clothes for Francesca, and Peter sent some of the Outlander's clothes over from the boat. The following day, after breakfast they got dressed and when the strapping on Francesca's ankle and the Outlander's sling had been checked, the Infirmary attendants let them out.

At first it seemed very strange. It was a fine day and though the wind, coming in from the sea, was sharp it was not unpleasant. They walked down through the roundhouses towards the jetty. As they passed the Gathering House the Outlander stopped and looked at it for a long time.

'Do you think we could take a detour so I could have a look inside?' he said to her.

'I don't see why not, sir,' she replied.

'Sir! Well that's a promotion,' he laughed. He turned and held out his good hand. 'My name is Tobias and that's what I'd like you to call me.' Francesca shook his left hand awkwardly with her right. 'May I call you Francesca?' he said.

'Of course,' she replied and blushed. There was something about him that made her smile and feel embarrassed at the same time.

118

They went round to the east door of the Gathering House. The sky was cloudy and the light diffuse but even so the west window, with its great optimistic sun over the Council Table, still looked magnificent. Tobias stopped at the threshold. She saw he was impressed and was pleased. Wherever this Outlander had been, it was clearly not as fine as the Gathering Hall.

The central hearth contained only a small fire. Once lit at Harvest Festival this was never left to go out until the new growing season was declared next year at Mayday but today's weather only required a small fire. The place where the stage had been at the Harvest Festival now contained looms and spinning wheels. About thirty people were working around the fire. They were either hand-carding wool from a pile of washed fleeces, spinning the newly carded wool or weaving cloth from wool gathered and spun earlier in the year.

'One of the main duties of every member of the community is to spin and weave wool in the winter when there aren't other duties to do,' she explained. 'Some cold days, when there's no work that can be done outside, the whole of the Hall will be filled with people carding, spinning and weaving round a big fire in the hearth.'

'And they sing at their task,' he said.

'Yes they do or tell stories or recite.'

'Do you do that?'

'Oh yes,' added another voice. 'She's the finest of all our singers.' It was Anya. She came up and threaded her arm into Francesca's, drawing her close.

'This is my partner, Anya.' said Francesca. 'This is Tobias.'

'Ah, the mysterious Outlander,' said Anya, 'Everyone here is dying to know more about you. Will you join us at the fire and tell us your tale?'

'Thanks for the invitation but Francesca is taking me to my boat and we have to go back to the Infirmary when we've got that done. I promise to tell my tale if I get the chance.'

'What, not even a small tale?'

By now, there was small group round them. 'Well to be truthful, in the little time we have, I'd rather hear Francesca sing.'

'Yes, Francesca,' said Caleb, who had just joined them. 'It would make us all happy to know you're really getting better.'

Normally, shy at showing off, Francesca would have refused but she realised that she needed to know if she could sing anymore. If she could sing properly then it would prove to herself that she was really getting better. It would be a promise that her memory would return and she needed that feeling. She nodded. 'Alright, how about this,' and she started to sing one of the Harvest Festival songs. At first her voice faltered but as she got the feel of the words and the tune, it got stronger until she was in full voice and revelling in the feeling of vitality it gave her. As she sang, details of how the Hall had looked at the Festival came back to her. She could remember the boy sitting with Sylvia, the procession and the smell of the bread. She remembered the community cheering her induction and seeing Jonathan by the doorway as Anya ran in with the torch. She finished the song and the group clapped.

Anya kissed her. 'Now get on about your task. I'll see you later when I bring some food.'

Francesca and Tobias retraced their steps. At the east door, Francesca looked back and waved to Anya. Just over Anya's shoulder she could see a frowning, angry Ruth. Francesca's stomach tightened with an anxiety she could not explain.

'You sing well,' Tobias said as they walked on towards the river. 'Do you compose any of your own songs?'

'Yes I do. I commit them to memory.'

'I should like to hear some of them at sometime.'

They had come through the gate in the ditch and for the first time she had a clear view of Tobias's boat. It was a bigger version of the community fishing boats. It was designed for one large central mast and another smaller mast towards the rear. But though the small mast was intact, the main mast was sheered off about a metre or so above the deck.

'Peter never told me the mast was down?' said Tobias. 'I hope there's not too much damage done to the mounting in the keel.'

'It made a terrible cracking noise when it went,' said Francesca. She stopped, realising what she had said. She could remember

120

the mast coming down and the dreadful sound it had made, so loud she had heard it even above the chaos and violence of the storm. She could remember seeing Tobias's body rolling back and forward in the surf. She could feel the pain in her back and arms as she dragged him across the deck. She was in the cold water being tumbled in the waves and flung onto the boat. The power of her memory made her dizzy. She tried to reach to steady herself on Tobias but his whole focus was on his boat and he had started to walk quickly towards the jetty and away from her. Why had she been on the beach? Why had she been charging around in a storm in the middle of the night? Had she had some intuition that the boat was there?

Tobias was now well in front and she started to try to catch him up but her ankle meant that she could not move as fast as she wanted. By the time she got to the jetty, Tobias had disappeared onto his boat. Carefully she climbed onto the deck. The community fishing boats were open and only had enough room to stow some nets and the catch when they had any. Beneath the stout deck she stood on, there must be a hold with a capacity for large amounts of goods. That was where Tobias had gone to inspect the repairs.

The second wave of memory hit her harder than the first. Now she could remember running over the bridge as it swung in the wind. She could feel the wooden boards under her bare feet. She remembered the wind singing in the pines in the shelter of the hill and the stumbling run across the pebbles before plunging into the sea. She slumped down on the hatch cover and began to sob. She could remember why she had been there and what she had been trying to do.

Tobias stuck his head out of a forward hatch cover. He started to say something but his voice tailed off. In seconds he was next to her, his good arm round her shoulders.

'What's a wrong lass?' he whispered. 'What's wrong?'

'I can remember what I was doing when I rescued you.'

'I doubt that's anything to cry about.'

'You don't understand. I didn't come to rescue you. I was trying to drown myself.'

'What?' She heard the shock in his voice. 'What troubles could one as young as you have that would drive you to that?' He was incredulous and concerned.

'I had realised something I had been told was true. I thought the person was lying but she wasn't.'

'How sure are you? Are you really convinced you remember it properly?'

'Quite sure. It was Ruth. She told that Jonathan and Anya were … involved. But I saw them at the Harvest Festival. I saw how they looked at each other, how they touched each other's hands. That's how I knew for sure.'

Tobias squeezed her shoulders. 'Try to take some deep breaths. It's all come back in a rush. You need to get over the initial shock.'

'But how could Anya do it? What's wrong with me?'

'Nothing, absolutely nothing I'm sure.'

'But I must have done something wrong to drive her away?'

'Not necessarily.'

In the next few minutes, as she tried to get back her self-control, she was very glad that Tobias was there. Partly, it was that she didn't have to feel ashamed in front of him as she would have done with another Gatherer, partly it was the fact he didn't either approve or disapprove. She could just be herself and he accepted that.

Gradually she realised that though it was a terrible shock, at least it explained the dreams and the feeling of unknown anxiety she had felt from seeing Ruth in the Gathering Hall a few minutes earlier. But as the initial emotional impact subsided, it was replaced by the worry of what she was going to say to Anya that evening.

'Is your boat alright?' she said in a rather irrelevant way, simply to pull her own mind away from the image of Anya coming with her evening meal and she not knowing what to say or feel.

'Yes it's fine. I might not want to admit it but they've done a good job on the repairs and the breaking of the mast has not done too much damage to the mounting in the keel.' He paused. 'You know I was running before that storm not caring whether I lived or died. I'd just seen someone I was very fond of killed by the people who shot me. I know how you must have felt.

'But you saved me and though I didn't care about living then, I'm glad you saved me. I'm glad to be alive now. Is there anywhere you'd like to go to think what to do next; somewhere happy, not full of bad memories? I'd be honoured to take you there.'

She smiled at him. 'Take me to the Glasshouses,' she said.

★ ★ ★ ★

By the time they got to the Glasshouse entrance, the most that anyone might have thought odd was that Francesca looked a bit red-eyed. Tobias was clearly impressed by the domes and the other houses as they walked down the path. He took at every detail and craned his neck in delight so as not to miss anything, asking more questions about how they worked than she could answer. When they got to the Central Dome and she left him to look at the controls while she went off to think on her own in the Propagation Chamber.

Seeing the preparations for the next planting of seedlings made her feel much better. She was able to talk to some of the Gardeners who were glad she was up and kept asking when she would be back. It gave her back some of her confidence but it didn't lead to any answers about what she would say to Anya.

She was leaving the Propagation Chamber when she saw Sylvia coming into the Main Dome. If anyone could see through her front it was Sylvia. Francesca dodged behind a tank of fermenting seaweed fertiliser so she would not be seen. From where she stood she could see Tobias in the centre of the dome looking up at the ventilation flaps. Sylvia saw him and went towards him. Tobias looked down and was aware of the Head Gardener.

'Sylvia,' said the Outlander.

'Tobias,' the Head Gardener replied. Their tone was formal but familiar. 'Yes,' Sylvia went on, 'they have done good service. We've been able to add more over the years from your plans as you'll have seen as you came down the main path.'

'Glad to be of service.' He bowed slightly. There was a long pause. 'What happened to her, Sylvia?'

'She died three years after you left.'

'Left!' Tobias shouted. 'Left! The Council put me on my own boat and towed it out to sea! They even tied me hand and foot. I hardly left! If I hadn't found that knife I'd have drowned!'

'We thought we could rely on you to find the knife where we put it. You were always resourceful.'

'You planted it?'

'Yes, Lucia, Peter and me. We thought they'd do you harm if you didn't go and that it might all get out of hand and would threaten the child. She was nearly three if you remember.' Sylvia's face showed sudden frustration and she knocked her staff down on the floor in anger. 'How long did you and Lucia think you could have gone on having a life half in and half out of the community in your own little roundhouse beyond the ring ditch? How long did you think the Council would let you defy the Rule?'

'We were doing alright. They were happy enough to tolerate us while I was building this!' He made an extravagant gesture that took in the dome, the controls, everything around them.

'Yes they were. But for pity's sake try to remember why you built this.' Tobias was silent and looked to Francesca a little sulkily. 'Well since the cat's got your tongue I'll remind you. It was those dreadful growing seasons before the child was born. You told the Council that we needed a way of supplementing what we could grow in the fields. You told them of seeing the remnant of houses made of glass that people had once used in the cities and you reckoned you could find the materials to build us some of our own.'

'And I was as good as my word!'

'Yes you were. These Glasshouses saved us, and better than that as the weather has got more stable, they've allowed us to thrive. But it was dangerous and unstable then and no time for an unplanned child or trying to live outside the community. It was always all or nothing with you. Always respond today, think tomorrow. It couldn't go on. If we hadn't put a stop to it one way or another you and your family would have died. Peter and I couldn't have stood that. We loved you both and when Lucia realised that your behaviour was endangering the child she helped us. Tobias, she chose her daughter over you!'

There was a faint echo as Sylvia's words rolled round the dome before Tobias spoke. 'What happened after you disposed of me?'

'Lucia came to live with me and…'

'…you took her as your partner!'

'No. She only loved one person, you.'

'But you put the child in the Crèche?'

'Yes.'

'What happened to Lucia?'

'Giving you and the child up killed her. She detached herself as best she could but she never really came to terms with seeing her daughter nearly every day and not being able to hold her or acknowledge her. Three years after you left, in the first big storm of the Autumn, she went out into the wind and never came back. I didn't stop her.'

'And the child?'

'Her name was changed and she was treated like any other child. She's grown up as well as any and better than most.'

'She doesn't know? Isn't that her right?'

'Right? To know something that would make her life difficult? Have some sense. She's safe and happy. Be content with that.'

'Can I see her?'

'You already have. But if you mean will I point her out to you, never. I'll not allow the accident of you being swept up here to make her unhappy and undo the good we did.'

As quickly as the pain in her joints would allow Sylvia swept passed Tobias and out of the Central Dome. His head drooped and he looked crestfallen as she passed.

Even given her own troubles, Francesca was astonished; Tobias had once been a Gatherer. She could not conceive of anyone leaving Heron Fleet. To her the community was the whole world. But worse than that he had deliberately broken the Rule, something she had just sworn to uphold for the rest of her life. Then there was a child in the community that had been born out of his and Lucia's relationship. Someone she knew was that child.

But mixed with her abhorrence of his actions was sympathy for him. To have lost Heron Fleet, to have lost his partner and have been cast out so brutally must have been terrible.

She was caught between the emotions, not knowing which to side with.

★ ★ ★ ★

When they got back to the Infirmary Francesca rested. She had waited a decent time before rejoining Tobias in the Central Dome to hide that she had heard the argument between him and Sylvia. Then they made their way back. As she rested she thought about what she was going to say to Anya when she came with the evening meal, but nothing occurred to her.

Then it was too late. There was no more thinking time. At the end of the ward Anya was saying hello to the attendants. Tobias looked up from his bed. He had been discreetly reading some documents brought back from the boat. He looked over and winked.

'Good luck,' he whispered as he packed up the papers. 'If you need me I'll be in calling distance. I'll keep the attendants out of the way.'

Then Anya was there, smiling, making her way down between the beds, carrying the evening tagine and a basket in which would be hardbread and something to drink. In the moment that she saw her, Francesca knew that no amount of reserve or preparation would have been of any use. She wanted to scream simultaneously in guilt and anger.

Guilt in not having done what was necessary to keep her lover happy. To ask Anya's forgiveness for the failing in her that had driven Anya away, promising wildly that it would not make any difference; imploring for forgiveness.

Anger which would demand why Anya had done it. Why she had broken the Rule, rejected her love and the commitments they had made when she had left Ruth and they had become partners.

In the end she did neither. All she could do, as Anya came to her bed and put the tagine and the basket down, was to get up and throw her arms around her, sobbing and kissing her, binding her arms in love so that there was no chance of rejection, no chance of being fended off.

'What on earth is wrong?' was all that Anya could get out.

'I love you! I love you! You know that don't you?' They subsided onto the bed and Francesca had to let Anya go.

'Yes, I know you love me.' Fear came into Anya's face. 'You've not got worse?' She trembled slightly and her voice was unsteady. 'You're not in danger again?'

Francesca started to weep again but managed to shake her head. Anya sighed and the fear passed. 'Then what is it?'

Francesca collected herself as best she could. 'I know,' she said trying not to let her voice break and the sobbing start again.

'Know what?' said Anya.

'I've remembered. I remembered everything that happened at the Harvest Festival and in the storm. It was seeing the boat this afternoon. It made my memory come back.'

'Well that's good isn't it? You'll know how much of a heroine you were, saving the Outlander and all.'

'I remember everything, including what Ruth told me that night.' Anya went pale. 'I know I was trying to kill myself because of what she told me.'

'What did she tell you?' said Anya.

'She said she'd seen you with Jonathan.' Anya dropped her eyes and rubbed her hand across her forehead. Francesca felt sick. 'It doesn't matter you know. I don't care, if we can just go on the way we were. We can keep it secret.' At that moment she just wanted to push time back, to make things how they had been. She would have said anything in the hope of that.

'Don't you want to know how and why?' said Anya. Her voice was controlled but her hands shook.

'It won't make any difference to me.'

'I think you should know what you're attempting to restore before you make rash promises. I think you should know what sort of person you're offering to forgive, go on loving and cover up for in front of the Council.' Her voice broke and there were tears in her eyes but she pursed her lips together and she looked determined to go on.

'I suppose it began when you started to teach him to swim?'

'That gave us the opportunity but if I'm truthful, and you shouldn't have anything except the truth from me, we'd noticed each other before then.'

'But didn't you love me?'

'Yes, I loved you. I still love you in many ways. I'll never love anyone else like I love you.'

'So you don't love Jonathan?'

'No, I love him too, it's just,' she paused, 'different.' She shook her head from side to side so that her swirling hair hid her face for a second. Then she looked Francesca full in the face. 'Have you never wondered what would happen if men and women started to fall in love? If the Rule was broken and we all simply mated as we chose?'

'No, I never have.'

'I always have. I've always wondered what we were being protected from. Perhaps I was wondering what we were being denied. I've always noticed boys. Thought some of them smooth and silky just like the girls. Jonathan was one of those boys and for him I now know that I was one of those girls.'

'But that's not really very different from me fancying you.'

'No, that's not, but when I had the opportunity I thought I'd find out what would happen. You know me – act first, think later.' Francesca tried to embrace her again but Anya resisted, 'No, let me go on, I don't think I'll ever have the strength to tell you this again. I got an opportunity one day, when I was taking him for a longer swim upstream. We were out of sight, on a secluded part of the river. I kissed him and he responded. We felt guilty for days after but we couldn't help but see each other, I had to teach him to swim so every day after work when your muscles are tired and you're most aware of you body, its senses, its feelings. In the end the inevitable happened.'

Francesca started to cry, 'Was I so much a failure as a lover?'

'No, it's not the same. There is the comfort and pleasure of sex, the bonding of equals and companions. You and I have that. With Jonathan that side is not as intense. Not as good.'

'So you can come back to me?'

'Well if that was all there was then yes I could. In that sense I love you more and I think in the end that may be the most important sense. But there is something more, the bit we're being delivered from. There is the promise of children as well. Don't ask me how it works – I don't understand. But that provides a second bond and now I know that it is very important to me.'

'But I'll make it better. We'll find a way.'

'I wish we could but it is impossible.'

'There's nothing impossible for us!'

'No, there is one problem we can't fix. Even if I could, I wouldn't. I'm pregnant.'

The Founder's Diary IV

Day 60

It's been a little while since I wrote. It's not that there's not been things happening but I needed time to come to terms with the fighting.

One of the effects of our role was that we've all been given much more freedom to come and go. We are still housed separately from the men but we can see them with permission of the guards and they can come and see us. Their place is pretty much the same as ours with bunk beds and communal eating area. The other civilians they share with look pale and nowhere near as healthy as our men. I understand why the Commander had been so keen on our men fighting.

I've seen Bill, the soldier I treated during the fighting, a couple of times. He's hobbling around on crutches. The first time I saw him he came in when I was visiting the men. He's quite friendly with them. He sat down and rested his leg. I sat next to him.

'Nice job,' he said pointing at the bandage. 'How long before you think it will heal?'

'You're probably more of an expert than me,' I said. He grinned.

'Miriam says the bandage will have to stay in place for a few more days and then she'll have a look,' he said. 'But it's already tingling so I knows it will be OK. It's great to know that there are lassies like you two around if we get hurt.' And he pulled me towards him and gave me a kiss on the cheek. I pulled away and blushed.

There are sixteen soldiers in all with two officers the Commander and his second in command which means they are hard pressed to put on a guard all the time even when there are no wounded in the camp. Then there are eighteen men, twelve women and five children. Finally there are us: twelve men, fifiteen women and ten children. So our original estimate of 200 in the fort was way short of the mark. When we arrived we must have caused quite a stir; the workforce doubled at a single stroke. No wonder they did not want us to contact each other.

I went round to see Miriam who showed me more of the fort and introduced me to the civilian women I'd not met foraging. As with the men, the children in their group looked sickly and the women listless in contrast with us. I wondered why we should be so much healthier and why they were weaker than us. I supposed that we have kept the conditioning that we had from our life at Winter's Hill. The poor city food and the way we live in the fort has not yet ground us down so we still have the advantage. As soon as I'd thought that, I began to see signs of their weakness everywhere. Over the next few days I started to catalogue our advantages, our strengths. In the end it was certain and I went to see James. 'We're strong enough to escape from here aren't we?'

'I've been thinking that as well,' he said. 'The question is when and how?'

Day 63

All I have been able to think about for the last few days is escape. It's not as straightforward as it seems. First, there are the weapons, though James thinks this is not as big a problem as I imagine. He argues that from what happened in the attack it is clear that fences away from the gate are easy to breach. We could get through them and be away quickly enough to disappear into the night. But if we go silently we will not be able to take food or transport with us. A bigger problem is the winter. If we go now then we will have to travel in the coldest weather in open country.

He has asked me not to tell the others about our conversations until he has a plan. He thinks I am the only one who has realised that there is a possibility of escape.

Day 64

This morning Miriam got permission from the Commander to train me as a second medical orderly. After he'd agreed she came and saw me. She was a nurse before the cold started and says she needs help since she's the only one on the fort with any medical background. That's why she was in charge of the dressing station and treating the wounded.

I talked to James before accepting but he thinks it would be a good thing. It will allow me more access inside the camp. We will need as much inside knowledge as possible to help in planning our escape. This job will give me an opportunity to gain more of that knowledge. In any case we need more medical experience in our group.

Day 70

I have been working with Miriam for a week. She has shown me basic wound care and I've also got a basic anatomy book to read. As well as wounds there are accidents that members of the fort get when foraging.

Reconnaissance groups from our side have found that the fort that attacked us has been ransacked. We don't know if they were picked off by someone else or if their attack on us was a last resort but their building has been burned and all their stores and transport have gone.

Miriam and I went over to see if there were any medical stores left. We found a couple of dead bodies. One was a child of about twelve. She was more than half-starved.

Though we don't know what happened to them a second attack looks unlikely, which should mean that we are safe to concentrate on collecting stores for the fort before winter. Lorries are going out twice a day as we forage further out than we could before.

Day 73

Miriam shook me awake in the middle of the night. 'Come

quick,' she said. 'We're needed on the main gate.' We ran across the courtyard and round to the military part of the compound. In the merciless brilliance of the emergency arc lights for the gates was a sick boy of about fourteen. He could hardly stand and was slumped against the outer cordon of wire. Between the inner and outer gates, an armed soldier and the Commander were watching him. We were told to join them and the guards let us through the outer gate.

Closer up, we could see black swellings on the boy's face. His eyes were bloodshot. He was softly saying over and over again, 'Water... help,' with a voice that wheezed as it whispered. He coughed occasionally and when he coughed, blood dribbled down his chin. The Commander turned to Miriam.

'What is it?'

'I've never seen it before,' she said, 'but it looks like an infection, probably in the lungs.'

'Can we do anything for him?' The Commander was cool. Miriam looked at the boy and then back to the Commander.

'No, I don't think so Commander.'

'Are you sure?' the Commander asked again in a way that seemed to hope that there might be a way to treat the boy. Miriam looked at me and there were tears in her eyes.

'He may even be an infection risk just standing there,' she said.

'That's what I thought. Sergeant.' The soldier levelled his rifle.

The first bullet didn't kill the boy outright. He staggered and started to fall to his knees, clinging to the wire. All he could manage was one wheezed word, 'Please....' which was silenced by a second shot. When he was still, they opened the outer gate, poured petrol on the body and incinerated it where it lay. Miriam and I turned away and helped one another through the inner gate.

I came back here and tried to go back to sleep, but all I could see behind my eyelids was the picture of that boy, so I got up to write this.

Day 74

I had not appreciated the choices that survival in a dying world would require. I had thought that since we were right, that would be enough. We could survive with our humanity intact because of our morality. Our cause and beliefs were all that we needed. I was wrong. At the first test of those beliefs, beliefs about caring and community, I was willing to see the boy at the gate shot down. We killed him to protect ourselves. It is no comfort to imagine what terror the infection he carried would have produced inside the fort. It is no comfort to know that the choice Miriam and I made was necessary. We did it without knowing anything of his story. Who was his father or mother; where were his brothers or sisters? How many more necessary, inhuman choices will I or others make before anything is reborn out of this chaos?

Day 77

Today has been devoted to my new duties as a nurse. Miriam and I have been practising bandages and slings. We had great fun in tying each other up. She has no children but is interested in how my two have adapted to living in the fort. 'Not bad,' I said and it is true. At first they were unhappy but they have found tasks in the Winter's Hill group and we have returned to the pattern of teaching we had before we left the farm. As our freedom round the fort has grown, so the children have become more useful.

Just as Miriam and I were talking, Charlie came running in, asking to go to the gate because Bill was on guard. I gave him permission but I'm very wary of him getting too wrapped up in the life of a soldier. As he ran off, I caught Miriam looking at me.

'You don't like him near the soldiers do you?'

'No,' I said as flatly as I could.

'Bill's a good man you know, reliable and kind. He likes you. He's quizzed me about what you might think of him.' I was revolted at the thought. 'You don't like him?' she persisted.

'It's not that I don't like him but I couldn't... I couldn't...'

'You couldn't think of another partner just yet?'

'Perhaps it's more than that. I'm not sure I will ever be able to think of another.' I was surprised I had been so frank so easily but she nodded.

'It's like that for me too.' We return to splints for fractures of the femur.

Day 78

A flurry of secret notes has started again between us and the men. More freedom of movement has meant that we haven't had to pass notes for some time but what we have now started to discuss has forced us back into secrecy.

It is not only me who has been able to hunt round and put two and two together. Our ability to escape occurred to Naomi as well. As a result she went to where she had found our wagon to have a better look. Our clothes and some other things like our seeds are still there. She has made what she has found common knowledge and publicly suggested we should think about escape. As a result James decided to make public what he was thinking.

Day 79

Views on what we would need to escape have started to be exchanged. A majority think transport is our biggest problem. They argue that we stood some chance of feeding our old horse as we went along, though what would have happened to him if we had had to travel in the winter they do not discuss. But there are no pack animals in the fort to replace him and none of us have seen any when foraging. Some think we could take a lorry but others have pointed out the difficulties finding fuel. Some have said that it would at least get us far away quickly and carry enough for us to find a place to hole up for the winter away from the city. Others think it would attract too much attention and might get us attacked.

After transport comes food; where to get enough? Could we steal from the fort stores bit by bit until we had enough? Could we lay aside enough in secret from our foraging to build a store? Neither seems possible. Food is closely watched and guarded.

Day 86

This evening, over a rare communal meal of the whole of the group we started to talk over these problems. But we still could not agree. Finally, Naomi slammed down her plate and stormed out. I tried to go after her but James stopped me. 'She needs some space,' he said. I returned to eating and in about thirty minutes she was back dragging a heavy bundle behind her; our winter clothes from the wagon. 'There,' she said. 'There's something done! There's one problem solved.'

Day 91

Naomi's gesture changed the way we thought about leaving. *It's impossible* became *lets do it* and we have worked away at collecting what we can. We started to conceal things when foraging which would be useful and we got away with it. We found a place to hide the clothes and soon added to it tins of meat, dried survival meals, water-sterilising tablets, salt for preserving fresh meat. Our doubts have been suspended in the activity and thrill of collecting what we will need.

My work with Miriam continued. She talked to the Commander and suggested that we set up an infirmary because she has been haunted by the image of the plague in the boy. She told the Commander that an infirmary would need more drugs than we have: antibiotics, anti-virals and phagocitics. Miriam would like to give everyone a tetanus injection as well. We are also short of bandages and morphine. She told him we need a functioning refrigerator for storage and more equipment such as instruments and a small surgical table. She proposed a raid on a hospital and the Commander agreed, provided she and I can come up with a workable plan of how to do it.

Day 93

We are ready. Initially we had two alternative targets. The nearest hospital was the most dangerous, the one in the centre of the main city. The alternative was the hospital in a neighbouring town. As Miriam and I discussed the choice it seemed to us that our chances of finding a useful store of equipment and drugs were best at the central hospital and therefore worth the risk. The thing that finally swung our choice was that Miriam had worked in that hospital and knew her way round it. As to equipment and transport we proposed that we take a pickup with a machine-gun mounted on the roof. We will rely on hiding and speed rather than pure brute force if we run into trouble. I will drive, Miriam will map-read and Bill will come to ride shotgun. He was pleased to be asked.

Day 95

We set off early this morning and drove out of the city in a northeast loop into the countryside. This was so as to approach the city centre from the east and avoid any forts in the suburbs. The morning was clear and once out into the country I felt free and happy. I had not realised how the fort made me feel cooped up. There were the occasional birds and red, yellow and ochre leaves were still on many trees. We circled around through small villages. We met some groups of people but they all ran for it as soon as they saw the gun. When we were about ten kilometres east of the town we came back towards the city and drove up a hill Miriam knew from which we could get the best look at possible routes to the city centre.

Miriam laid our map out on the bonnet of the pickup. 'The hospital is there near to the university. There is a main road that comes in here.' She pointed out across the view of the city, tying the picture of the map to the details of the view we could see. 'That line there, north of those tall flats, is the elevated section of road that used to be part of the inner ring. It should be the quickest way in.'

'Quickest and the one with least cover,' said Bill. 'They'll be no chance it's free of barricades.'

'Can we follow its line without using it?' I asked.

'Maybe,' said Miriam, 'but the roads around it twist and turn and are visible from tall buildings.'

'So we run the risk of turning into an ambush on the side roads and being fired on from above,' said Bill. We went on discussing the problem but every solution had drawbacks. Picking our way through quietly, street by back-street, was possible some of the way but near the centre the office blocks and flats could came back into play as firing platforms. No matter how we thought about it, when we got into the city centre, it was plain there wouldn't be much cover. Finally, Bill settled the matter. 'Well I'm in favour of a quick dash at the end,' he said. So we reached a compromise, we will use back-streets until we reach the ring road then use our speed to get right into the city centre as quick as we can. We'll just have to accept the risk of running into a barricade on the ring road and cope as best we can.

Day 96

We started before dawn today. The morning air was cold on our faces. It reminded me of autumn mornings long ago when I was an innocent girl in a city just like this one. The sun rose in a lurid mixture of purple and brown, its colours affected by the pollution held in by the buildings. The sun only shone brightly when it was about 20° above the horizon.

We reached the ring road without trouble and hid the pickup under one of its concrete supports. Then we went on a careful reconnaissance of the roadway. The surface was good. The road went up an incline from where we were to a flatter section that curved away from us. There was debris and a few burnt-out cars whose metal surfaces, exposed by the flames, were red with crusted rust. There was nothing that looked like an organised barricade. 'Are we up for it then?' said Bill. Miriam and I nodded.

We went back to the pickup. Bill climbed into the seat attached to the machine-gun. I climbed into the driver's seat and Miriam arranged the map on her lap. We strapped ourselves in. 'Ready,' I called to Bill. He hammered on the roof in response. 'Ready?' I said to Miriam. She looked at me; frightened but prepared. I put my hand on hers and squeezed it. 'Ready.' The engine started and I moved the pickup out from our hiding place.

There was a short run to the point where the raised road started. I swung the pickup round the end barriers and on to the road. I accelerated and we got to the flat part of the road doing about sixty. Bill shouted for the sheer joy of the race. It was like that for about two miles, clear and easy to see. Then the road started to fall and I couldn't see what was in front of us. We slowed at the top of a down-slope which disappeared under an overpass. 'There must be some pollution trapped down there,' said Miriam. 'The exit to the hospital should be no more than half a mile beyond this bit.' I put on the lights and accelerated. There was a twist to the right and then another to the left and the road began to rise again. The gloom thinned and I thought I could see sunlight up ahead.

The barricade was neatly built, moulded into the structure of a bridge above the road. I jammed on the brakes, the pickup skidded left. I heard the grind of the machine-gun mounting as Bill swung it round. He fired a sustained burst at the barricade. From my side windows I saw pieces of metal fly up and fistfuls of dust explode from the bridge concrete. For a fraction of a second I thought I saw a person with a rifle leaning across the top of the barricade but immediately the body was flung backwards as a machine-gun round hit it. I rammed the pickup into reverse, let the clutch out too quickly and stalled the engine. 'For Christ's sake, get us out of here,' screamed Bill…

Chapter 11

After Anya had gone, Tobias came back into the ward. Discreetly he cleared up what was left of the meal and persuaded one of the attendants to return it to the kitchens. That done, he came and sat on the end of Francesca's bed. She was curled up with her back to him, head buried in the covers.

'Do you want to talk about it?'

A muffled voice replied. 'I don't know. Will it do any good?'

'It might,' he said. 'Perhaps not now but it will tomorrow or the next day. Take your time.'

Francesca unwound herself from the sheets and sat up. 'Now's as good a time as any I suppose. She's been having an affair with Jonathan.'

Tobias shot a glance up the ward but they were alone. 'I wouldn't say that too loudly if I were you.'

'Why not? I ought to tell the Council right now. Why not get the whole thing out into the open? Someone else will do it even if I don't.'

'That's true but you will feel guilty if you're the one that tells the Council. Believe me, you'll feel worse if you betray her.'

'And what do you know about betraying someone?'

'More than I would care to admit,' he said. 'You heard my conversation with Sylvia.'

She looked surprised.

'You're too tall to hide easily and I've a very sharp instinct about being watched. Sometimes my life depends on it. You ask what I know about betrayal; well, I betrayed Lucia and my child.'

'But they forced you to go, tied you up in your boat, set you adrift.'

'Yes, but once I was free I could have come back for them. We could have gone away together.'

'Why didn't you?'

'As I said, I betrayed them. I put my pride before my love and sailed away. I persuaded myself that they'd be better off without me. I've regretted it ever since. Now I know that it killed the person I loved more than any other in my life and means my daughter is hidden from me. People persuade themselves of all sorts of things when they have to or when they think they've got a very good reason for doing something cruel.'

'You were a Gatherer?'

'Yes. I even had a partner who I loved and who loved me.'

'So how did you go from having a partner to having a baby with Lucia?'

'That's a long story and it's not going to help you.'

'Please tell me. It might explain something of why Anya did it.'

He frowned and sighed. 'Alright, but I'm still not convinced it will really help. You see I came from the outside. I found this place after I ran away from a city.'

She looked puzzled. 'The cities were places built to hold millions of people,' he said. 'But now what's left of the people are dying out. They live off what's left in the ruins and pretty soon they'll all have starved. I was one of them, a scavenger. They don't make any stable relationships and disputes are settled by violence.

'When I got here it was like heaven. Even better, my knowledge was useful. I fell for my partner mostly because he was the first person to show me love but when I noticed Lucia, well, she took my fancy and there was still sufficient of the scavenger in me to make me take her.'

'Are you saying the only place with any future is Heron Fleet?'

'No. You're right that in the end the only significant groups of people will survive in places like Heron Fleet where they grow their own food, but Heron Fleet is not the only place that does that.'

Francesca was amazed. 'You mean there are others communities like us?'

'I know of twenty all around the coast of Albion and more across the sea on the coast of Bretagne. I live by trading between them. But we are supposed to be talking about you and Anya.'

Francesca sighed. 'Yes of course. I don't understand something Anya said: that there was a difference about the relationship she and I had, and the one between her and Jonathan. She said something about the promise of children.'

Tobias scratched his chin. 'That's not something I've heard put that sort of way before. All partnerships bring companionship, a sharing of life, emotions, memories. But I suppose one might say that in the natural way of things, a partnership between a man and a woman always has the extra dimension of children.'

'I don't know what you mean.'

'Let me think. A few years ago a pair of wrens made a nest in a pile of rope near the prow of the boat. I was cruising some of the bigger rivers across in Bretagne at the time. I wasn't ever very far from the shore, so they could come and go when they liked and still find food. One morning on the hold cover there was a line of three bundles of feathers. Their chicks had hatched. Those parents worked their tiny wings off getting grubs for their young. Then one day they took off, followed by the parents and I never saw them again.'

'And the point is?'

'Well, the bond between those parents provided a safe environment to bring up their young. Only in Heron Fleet is there a rule that makes same-sex partnerships the standard way of pairing up. Here you substitute the Crèche Mothers for the support a child would have from its parents, and have broken the natural bond between pregnancy and the bringing up of children in an utterly fundamental way. As a father and I know it's a strong bond, so I wouldn't be surprised if Anya felt something similar about her relationship with Jonathan because deep down she wants a child of her own. Does that help?'

'A bit. I thought it was Anya just making excuses.'

'No this is serious, not just for you, Anya and Jonathan. When the whole thing comes out it will bring a lot of unhappy memories for Peter.'

'Why?'

'Peter was my partner. I betrayed him just as Anya has betrayed you.'

★ ★ ★ ★

Over the next few days Francesca felt she was waiting for a storm to break. She reasoned to herself that it would take at least two months for Anya's pregnancy to become visible to the community but she wasn't certain. Mothers were kept in seclusion as much as possible before their babies were born. Only the women who had given birth knew the answers to the questions she would like to have asked but they never spoke about the matter, at least not outside their partnerships. As a result, along with the majority of the community, she knew practically nothing about pregnancy.

She was allowed a few more outings with Tobias to his boat, which helped since he did his best to keep her mind off things. His arm was mending well, and Peter had given him a gang of Apprentices and told him to get on with repairing the boat so that it would be weatherproof before more winter storms came.

But Tobias was far too impatient and easily frustrated with the Apprentices when they didn't immediately pick up what he wanted them to do. Soon she found herself explaining to them what was needed after Tobias had explained it to her. To her surprise she rather enjoyed this role and how, as the only Gatherer on the project, all the Apprentices did what she told them.

The first big job was to set a new mast. A large pine was felled in the woods to the north of the community, shorn of its branches and smoothed down. One of the group, Timothy, who hoped to be a carpenter, revelled in being in charge of the mast-making. Since the new mast would be too long and heavy to be set in the boat by muscle power alone, Tobias showed them how to make an A-frame to lift it high enough so it could be slotted through the deck and down to its fixing in the keel.

When the mast was ready, the boat was pulled further up the river and beached, prow-on to the shore. Then the A-frame was set so that it could swing the mast inboard. Two long ropes, arranged to raise the A-frame, ran out on to the shore and Timothy organised volunteers into two pulling teams, one on each rope.

But before the new mast could be set, the broken stub of the old mast had to be removed.

'Does everyone know what they're doing?' Tobias shouted irritably from the bottom of the boat where he was releasing the final clamps that held the stub.

Francesca went to the prow and waved to Timothy who waved back. 'Yes, they're ready,' she shouted to Tobias.

'In that case I'll come up. Signal Timothy to start.' Francesca picked up a small yellow flag and waved it. Timothy lifted his arms and the pulling teams picked up the ropes and took up the slack. Then the pull started. She saw Timothy rocking from right to left as he set the rhythm of the pull and the song they were singing drifted to her on the breeze.

Gradually the A-frame started to rise. By the time Tobias came on to the deck its apex was nearly over the broken mast.

'Stop pulling,' said Tobias from behind her. She picked up a red flag and waved. Timothy stopped the pull, with the teams holding the A-frame steady.

While they waited for him to come aboard, she and Tobias tied ropes from a block and tackle on the A-frame to a metal hoop that had been drilled and bolted into the old mast. Timothy arrived.

'OK if we pull the broken mast out of the keel now ma'am?'

Francesca looked at Tobias and he nodded. 'Be careful not to snag the stub as you get it clear,' he said as Timothy and a small team of Apprentices who had come with him took over the free end of the rope through the block and tackle.

'Yes, sir,' said the boy.

'When did he start calling you "ma'am"?' said Tobias to Francesca as they watched the team start its work.

'He's been doing it for days. I can't stop him,' she blushed, looked embarrassed and then grinned. 'Actually I think it's rather sweet.'

'Hum. You'll be getting power mad if you're not careful.'

The bottom of the mast was just about to clear the deck and Tobias steadied it so it wouldn't swing. Though it was now free it needed to be higher if it was to clear the prow. 'Nearly to the right height,' Tobias called. 'Get ready to tie off the lifting rope.' There was a creaking and the A-frame twisted.

The mast stub was yanked out of Tobias's grasp and he was knocked across the deck. Before Francesca could do anything to stop him, Timothy let go of the lifting rope and went to help Tobias. The A-frame twisted again, the mast-stub was pulled horizontal and the lifting rope was wrenched from the hands of Timothy's team before they had any chance of tie it off. The mast swung violently and the metal hoop pulled out of the wood, spraying sharp splinters everywhere.

To Francesca everything seemed to slow down. The mast started to fall, its jagged point downwards. 'Look out Timothy!' she yelled but it was too late. All the Apprentice had time to do was to turn. There was a horrible sound of splintering wood as the end of the mast hit the deck. Francesca was aware that he had tried to step aside and hoped the mast had missed him. But even as she thought this, a fountain of blood came from Timothy's chest and she screamed in horror as the boy staggered and fell on to his back.

Tobias ran forward to the prow, picked up the red flag, and waved and yelled at the teams on shore. Seeing what he was doing the Apprentices woke up from stunned horror and jumped down to the shore and shot off to help secure the long ropes.

Realising he had done as much as he could to stop the A-frame falling on them Tobias dropped the flag and came back to kneel next to Timothy. Three sharp pieces of mast had impaled the boy through his left arm and chest. Blood was pooling under his body and running in small, determined streams down the planking. He was delirious.

'Did I do it right, ma'am?' he said.

'He wants you,' Tobias said to Francesca. His words pulled her from frozen shock and she kneeled down.

'What do I say?' she whispered.

'Whatever gives him comfort.'

'Did I do it right, ma'am?'

'Yes,' she said. 'You got it just right. Not even a master carpenter could have done better.' He coughed and she could hear a gargling sound as his breath forced a passage past blood in his throat. His right hand started to meander towards the wounds in his chest. She took it and held it. She couldn't bare to see it touch the pieces of wood that were killing him.

'Is Master Tobias there? I can't seem to see clearly.'

'I'm here lad.' Tobias smoothed back the boy's hair.

'Did I do a good job?'

'Yes lad, a fine job.'

'That's good. Would you have a word with Peter to make sure I…' The voice faded and the face took on a subtly stony look. The Outlander gently stroked the boy's eyelids down so that Timothy would not look emptily at the grey sky.

★ ★ ★ ★

The Burial Ground was on the low hills on the other side of the valley from the Glasshouses. The site gave a fine view of the Gathering Hall and the other community buildings. They walked the Mourning Path in line behind Timothy's body sewn into its traditional winding-sheet, carried on a board by the members of his roundhouse. He had no partner, so no one walked in front of the body singing the traditional lament; singing, so many said, to warn the underworld that a son or daughter of the Heron Fleet was on their last journey. So the lament was sung by everyone in the cortège.

The sunlight is falling and the darkness approaches,
The need of the day dying hard on the hill,
For young or for old, the end of their story,
Their last has been gathered before falling still.

Francesca came first behind the body. Since Timothy was an Apprentice, tradition dictated that the Council send a Gatherer as their representative. Feeling responsible, Francesca had begged Peter to be sent. Behind her was Tobias and Timothy's Crèche Mother Judith. Then there were several of the members of the Apprentices who had helped on the tragic attempt to repair the mast. Last there were three Carpenters, including their Chief, his presence a measure of the respect for Timothy.

A soil that is fertile will welcome our comrade,
Though his voice may be stilled and not heard in the hall,
But we shall remember and tell tales that keep him
Alive in the memory of many and all.

They arrived at the Burial Ground. A new grave had already been dug next to that of Jacob the Gardener who had died in the spring. The soil on that grave still looked a naked rich brown, though some grass had started to encroach. Ready to be used by the mourners there were two passing-spades stuck into the top of the pile of soil next to Timothy's grave.

Now gentle earth accept of his offering,
Life that he gave may all celebrate now,
His last longest rest within sight of our haven,
Power to the field and to our gathered food.

They stopped at the edge of the grave and two of those who had carried the body jumped down as the others rested the board and lifted Timothy's body clear. Then they handed it down to open, kindly arms. When Timothy's body had been placed gently at the bottom of the grave, his friends were helped out and all the mourners gathered round.

'Friends,' said Francesca. She stood up as tall as she could and tried to look as grown up, though she didn't feel it. But there was a debt of honour to be paid here and she was willing to pay it as best as she could.

'Friends, we meet to say goodbye to someone who was a comrade. All of you knew him better than me. You played with him in the Crèche, he lived with you in your roundhouse, shared the hardbread with you at table, you trained him in the carpenter's shop. I admired him for his enthusiasm and dedication in the short time I worked with him. I admired the way he recruited many of you to do a job you were probably unsure of and moulded you into a team that attempted something that has not been done in Heron Fleet in many years. In losing Timothy the Apprentice, we lose Timothy the Gatherer: the buildings he would have designed and built, the many things he would have added to the community. As we bury him let us all resolve in what we do to make up for that loss.'

She took the nearest passing-spade and shovelled the first soil into the grave.

'Farewell, friend. Rest easy.' Tears were running down her face but she let them fall as she added a second and then a third spade of soil.

Tobias came next. Then the others in turn, saying their own farewells, spoken aloud or held within a personal silence. Each turned more of the soil into Timothy's resting place. Last came the Chief Carpenter. When he had spoken of how much he had looked forward to taking Timothy into the Carpenters' Guild, he joined with Tobias and they finished closing the grave. Then they all stood and repeated the evening blessing together.

Reaping and sowing,
sowing and reaping,
this is the world we have.
All we know is the cycle of life.
Power to the greenwood.
Power to the field.
Power to our gathered food.

As they finished the blessing, Francesca saw a figure running up the Mourning Path towards the graveyard. It was Caleb. They all turned towards him as he entered the Burial Ground. He stopped and spoke to Francesca.

'You must come quickly. Anya and Jonathan have been taken before a special meeting of the Council. Ruth has told Peter that they have a relationship which is in breach of the Rule.'

The Founder's Diary V

Day 96

... There was an eerie silence as I fumbled for the keys but they twisted and I couldn't get the grip I needed to turn them. 'Come on!' screamed Miriam. At last they turned. only for the engine to cough and refuse to start. 'Out Out! Take cover.' We threw ourselves out of the doors and crawled round to the back of the pickup. Bill grabbed his automatic rifle and jumped down to join us. We ducked down expecting a volley of shots.

'What are they waiting for?' said Miriam.

'Perhaps we surprised them,' I said.

'Can't be, they must have heard us coming,' said Bill but there was still no return of fire.

'Could you have killed them all?' asked Miriam.

'Doubt it.' Bill popped his head out and then ducked back. He took off his hat and put it on the barrel of the rifle. Then he poked it just a bit above the tailgate; not so far as to be obviously fake but enough to give a clear target to anyone on the barricade. I giggled with nerves as we played out a deadly parody of Cowboys and Indians; still nothing from the barricade.

'Miriam, there's a pillar to our right at about twenty metres. It gives good cover. Can you make it, gal?' She nodded. 'I'll bob up and fire a burst. Run like hell. Ready?'

'Yes.'

'Go!' The automatic rifle chattered. Miriam pelted for the cover and made it.

'Safe,' came Miriam's voice. Bill turned to me.

'Now you. Same routine.' I leant over to him and kissed him. 'You take care.' I stroked his cheek and he smiled.

'I will pet. I will.'

My heart raced and the blood hammered in my ears. Then I ran for it, trying not to take exactly the same line as Miriam, reasoning that any watchers would be ready for me. The rifle rattled behind me and then I was with Miriam behind the column. 'Safe,' I yelled back.

'What's he going to do?' said Miriam.

'I think he's going to charge the barricade,' I said.

We pulled out the two pistols that we had for personal protection and watched as Bill came out from behind the pickup, the rifle at his hip, firing continuously. He had a fixed bayonet which reflected the light and he was screaming at them. In his anger and wild courage he was like my man. I realised I could love him, that the kiss was not just a matter of the moment's emotion. We fired wildly round opposite sides of the pillar. He reached the barricade and in two strides was at the top, his figure a clear target. The barrel of the rifle started to fall and for a fraction of a second I thought he had been hit. His body turned and then he waved us over. We put away our pistols and walked across to him.

There was not a soul there. We started to laugh hysterically as relief mingled with stupidity and we hugged each other. After a few minutes, we pulled ourselves together. 'We better check properly,' said Bill.

There was a shelter hidden away at the back, deeper under the bridge. Inside there was the corpse of a man who might have been about thirty, fair-haired, with an old-fashioned rifle. On a couple of stacked-up packing cases there was a telephone. 'A guard post,' said Bill. He went over to the phone and picked it up. 'It's not connected,' he said. I knelt down by the body. The man was face down and I rolled him over. He'd been dead a long time and the skin has shrunk back from his lips. There was still dried blood on them, a smear on his cheek and a dark shadow I had seen once before. Miriam came over. 'Oh God.' There was a set of black swellings rising from his exposed collar bone up his neck, behind the ear and on into the hairline.

From the barricade down to the hospital we were quiet. We found the turn-off from the ring-road easily and from there the hospital was obvious, a set of low buildings with a couple of tall four-storey central blocks. The streets were empty. There was no one to stop us. We hid the pickup near a back door to one of the main blocks and broke in near some laboratories. We looked in a few but all were broken glass and dusty machines. We moved on.

A short corridor led us to the waiting room in the central atrium. It was a chaos of mattresses and makeshift beds. There were bodies in strange, stiffened poses with arms and legs at twisted, writhing angles. All had the swellings or other bruise-like marks on their skins. It was the same story in A & E, with dead bodies behind all the screens. Some showed signs of having died while being treated; empty drips, hanging from metal stands, connected to needles in desiccated arms.

Off a corridor, near some examination rooms, we found a store room. Its door was locked and so we forced it. The drugs were well-ordered and Miriam sorted out those she needed while we packed them into our backpacks. 'There aren't many phagocitics left,' she said. 'They must have used a lot of them in trying to treat the disease.' We moved on. Not far away there was another intact store with supplies of bandages, dressings and instruments. 'What's left on the shopping list?' said Bill.

'Mainly morphine and tetanus injections,' replied Miriam. 'We'll need the operating theatres or ICU for the morphine, and Outpatients for the tetanus.'

ICU was a shambles with desiccated bodies in the beds. Some seemed to have torn at their own flesh before dying. Some were still connected to machines by tubes and masks. There was a temporary dormitory in one area where the doctors and nurses had slept. They had died in the same way as their patients. 'Whatever this disease was, it took all these people very quickly,' said Miriam.

We searched the place and found enough morphine for our needs. 'I'm not going to risk taking equipment that's not in intact sterile packs. So a table's out,' said Miriam.

'What about the fridge?' said Bill.

'I'd love one but the risk is too high.'

151

The final stop was Outpatients where the chaos of death was complete. It had been wrecked by panicking people and though there were fewer bodies, one or two had gunshot wounds. 'Looks to me that someone forced their way in here.' said Bill. We found a large supply of tetanus vaccine and left by the front door.

Rather than go back through the buildings we went round the outside and came across a garden. It was a warm spot and plants were still growing. In the middle there was a half-dug grave next to three others. Bill went on guard, his rifle ready as his eyes searched the lines of the buildings. Out of the corner of my eye I caught the movement of a figure. I swung round. Realising he had been seen, the man, who had been running away, stopped and turned towards me. 'Go away. Go away. Haven't you done enough!' he screamed and then he disappeared.

'How come he's still alive?' said Bill.

'Who knows?' said Miriam.

I'm writing this in a bivouac about three miles from the hospital. At first light we'll get back to the fort and I'll be glad of its protection.

Day 99

I have avoided Bill while Miriam and I put the infirmary together. Even when he came in carrying the boxes and equipment from the pickup we avoided each other's glances. But it is only a matter of time before we have to talk and I fear that discussion because I do not know what I meant by the kiss. Was it a symbol of affection or an act of a momentary solidarity? I like Bill and it would be comforting, as the spectre of the plague grows in my mind and my sleep is haunted by images of the bodies in the hospital, to retreat into a comfortable relationship with him. To accept what the fort offers by way of safety and security; to no longer have any need to live for a wild, dangerous trek.

Then there are the children. Bill is brave, kind and vulnerable. The children need a father and they like Bill. Charlie spends as much time with him as me since he's become the unofficial message boy for the guards. I suspect that was Bill's idea, but a

152

kind one since it keeps the lad occupied as he grows. It would be logical for the children and good for them. And underneath there is the thing I won't admit even to myself: that I need love and companionship.

But in accepting the fort would I be giving up hope? Not just the hope of recreating Winter's Hill but something more elusive. I would be giving up the dream that people can be more than what they were. That people, me included, need not live in a way that leads to destruction and the death of nature. That we can live in a way that does not lead to plague, for where did that disease come from except from ourselves?

Day 101

It has finally happened. On the narrow path between two of the buildings I ran into Bill. Even then I tried to pass him by with a polite remark but we knew it was the moment and he stood his ground. 'Did you mean it?' he said.

'Mean what?'

'The kiss?' I didn't know what to say. 'Did it mean something to you?' he repeated.

I paused and stuttered, 'Yes.'

'Then why not come and join me?' I shook my head and ran past him into the infirmary.

Miriam was there and got me to sit down and brought me a drink as I sniffled away. She asked what was wrong and I told her about the kiss and Bill's offer and how I didn't know what to do about the children. I even told her about my own needs and how alone I felt. She did her best to comfort me and I was grateful but I was surprised by one remark. 'I thought you didn't like soldiers?' she said.

'You said Bill was a good man?' I countered.

'Not good enough,' she said.

Day 104

The infirmary was finished today and we are up and running,

starting on the tetanus jabs. Our first patient was the Commander followed by all the soldiers. Bill was tenth in line. Miriam was doing the injecting at that stage and so I was saved the embarrassment of what he might have said. I shall have to give him a proper answer soon. Tomorrow we'll start on the foragers, including the Winter's Hill group.

While I have been concerned about the infirmary I have heard little about how our plans for escape are going. It seems debate about transport continues but the stores are growing. I went to see James and he thinks we will be ready to go in a month's time if we decide to go in the winter. He wants me to start thinking about what medicines I will want to bring with us.

Day 105

The second day of the inoculations went well. Seeing all the foragers together emphasises that the Winter's Hill community still look in much better shape than the rest. But it's not all good news since our children are showing more signs of ill health than they did. They have nearly as many colds as the other children and some are listless and run down. But the civilian foragers are the worst off. In fact one woman collapsed after her injection and Miriam and I are taking it in turns overnight to keep an eye on her.

Day 106

Miriam and I are puzzled. Even after a day in the infirmary the forager, whose name is Joan, seems no better, in fact we think she is slightly worse. She had a reasonably good night and was bright enough this morning, even eating a bit of breakfast. We thought she would be up by midday but about mid-morning she dropped off into a restless doze in which she rambled and tossed about. Her temperature is up and after listening to her chest with a stethoscope Miriam says there is a wheezing deep in her lungs.

Day 107

Joan has a very high fever. She is still and not delirious anymore but you can now hear the wheezing clearly. Miriam has closed the infirmary and we have isolated ourselves inside it in case it is infectious.

Bill has volunteered to get our food in to us by poking it to us across a no-man's-land at our door on a makeshift trolley. He pulls the empty dishes back using a rope. It's comical but effective and we're glad of his cheerful encouragement.

We hold our breath that this is something ordinary; just a bad case of early winter flu.

Day 108

The horror has come. Joan woke up this morning. Her temperature fell rapidly towards the end of the night and then suddenly she was awake and lucid. She still wheezed but nowhere as badly as before. She said she felt fine and asked when we would let her out. We said we'd wait until the evening to be sure.

She got up for a midday meal and looked on the mend until she had a coughing fit. The coughing completely exhausted her and blood started to drool from the corner of her moputh. We got her back to bed and Miriam asked me to pull up her blouse at the back so that she could sound her chest from the back.

Running up her spine was a black line, like the bruise left by a blow from a stick. At the base of her spine there were the beginnings of swellings and the skin either side looked grey and brittle.

It took only four hours to kill her. Black tracks of swellings appeared in a sort of network across her body. They seemed to be following the lines of the major nerves and where they went the skin turned grey, dried up and died. We tried antibiotics and some of the phagacitics but nothing did any good. Eventually all her skin was dry and lifeless and it stayed that way even where the swellings went down. The last place to be affected was her head where the skin drew back from the lips exactly as we'd seen before in the city.

In the final phase the delirium returned and she clawed at her own skin ripping deep gashes in herself. I held her in my arms and tried to restrain her hands but she threw herself around, bucking and groaning with incredible strength. Then suddenly it was over. She relaxed and struggled to breathe. Then she sighed and rattled in her throat.

Day 109

Miriam and I were locked in with Joan's body overnight. We told Bill what had happened when he brought us breakfast this morning and he called the Commander and we talked through the open door.

We told the Commander that we must have brought the plague into the fort from the dead victims in the hospital. So we reckoned the incubation time must be roughly ten days. We said we would isolate ourselves to see if we developed symptoms and suggested Bill join us since he was likely to be a carrier. Before he joined us he should burn his own clothes, our clothes and Joan's body. Then he should put on clean clothes and bring us clean clothes as well.

They have just locked the door and the three of us are alone.

Day 112

The last two days have dragged past. We watched for every twinge or cough which might indicate the onset of the plague. We have been driven apart, each into our own corner of watching and waiting.

Food has been coming in as before but with the evening meal tonight came a bottle of whisky with a note from James. He'd said he'd found it earlier in the day and everyone had thought it should be used to cheer us up. It was a familiar bottle to me.

We drank a little of it with the food, still subdued but at least together. Bill finally put words to what we were all thinking, 'What do you think our chances are?'

'Hard to say,' said Miriam. 'We know from Joan what the stages are but that's all we know.'

Day 113

They let us out this morning. Three of the civilian foragers have what looks like the first signs of the plague. We have made them as comfortable as we can.

Chapter 12

'Where have they been taken, Caleb?'

'To the Gathering Hall. Two of the Gatekeepers came to the roundhouse and said that the Head of the Council needed Anya to go with them right away. Anya was willing to go without a fuss but Jerry and I thought they ought to explain to us why before they just carted her off. So we asked why she was wanted and finally they told us. At which point Jerry said very firmly that if they didn't have any objection he was going to go with Anya to help her if he could. So I came straight away to tell you.'

'Any sign they've called on Jonathan?'

'Yes, I met Mary trying to gather up the members of their roundhouse. Hamied has gone with him. She thought Hamied would be able to ask questions on Jonathan's behalf since he's still his partner. But as well as being Anya's partner, you're a Gatherer. I think they can't refuse to answer any questions you ask.'

'Well let's hope so.'

She was trying to stay calm, to find in herself the centre of confidence and balance that had got her through giving Timothy's eulogy. But as they got nearer and nearer to the Gathering Hall she felt that confidence leaking away. How would she deal with making a case in front of the whole council? She feared failing to stand up for Anya. So it was a great relief to find that all she faced was an informal group of three Council members, sitting around one of the larger tables, in a quiet corner.

Hamied sat across from Anya and Jonathan. With Peter were Sylvia and Thomas, a Gatherer from the kitchens who she did not know well. The Red Book was open on the table. Ruth sat at the far end facing Peter, with a very determined expression. Caleb, Jeremy, Mary and a couple of other Apprentices who were friends of Anya and Jonathan, watched from an adjacent table.

'Good, we can start these proceedings,' said Peter, beckoning Francesca to sit next to Hamied.

'Proceedings?' Anya burst out, getting up from her seat. 'Are we on trial?'

'This is an initial informal meeting, Anya, but in a sense it is a trial,' said Peter. 'It will be best for you if you try to stay calm. The Red Book lays down very clear instructions on how accusations of breaking the Rule are tested and they protect the rights of those accused.'

Jonathan took Anya's hand and gently pulled her back to her seat.

Peter continued. 'Let me explain. Anyone accused of a breach of the Rule has a right to hear that accusation from their accuser. If they admit the accusation is true then the Council meets in private and hands down an appropriate punishment.'

Anya, was immediately on her feet again. 'So punish us. It's true. We admit it.' Again Jonathan got her to sit.

'Anya, it is not as simple as that for Apprentices. The Founders did not consider children, and therefore Apprentices, old enough to plead for themselves. However we may feel about that, they were trying to be as fair as possible. Even if Apprentices agree with an accusation the Red Book makes it clear that any accused Apprentices must have their case put to the Council by a Gatherer before any punishment is given.'

'Waste of time is you ask me,' Anya interjected.

'It is to protect you,' said Peter. 'The Gatherer who argues the case for an Apprentice is there to make sure that inexperience or the misjudgements of youth don't lead to unfair punishments. Do you understand, Anya?' She nodded reluctantly.

'The purpose of this meeting is to hear the formal accusation and hear what you and Jonathan have to say in response.'

Francesca took a deep breath and interrupted Peter before he could continue. 'Excuse me, Peter, there is one thing I want to ask before we go any further.'

'Of course, Francesca.'

'What range of punishments can be set by the Council?'

'Compulsory separation of the couple or at worst banishment.'

'Tell her the whole truth, Peter, she deserves to know. People have been killed in this community for breaking the Rule.' It was Tobias. He had come in quietly and joined Caleb and the others watching the proceedings.

'As you well know that is not true. No member of the community can be lawfully killed by another.' There was relieved sigh from the watching Apprentices, but Peter had not finished. 'However, it is true that, very rarely, in the long past, being found responsible for a breach of the Rule has led to the deaths of the accused.'

'What!' It was Anya again. 'So we could be on trial for our lives.'

'It could work out that way,' said Tobias.

Peter was exasperated. 'Look, these are hypothetical issues. For the sake of everyone we need to proceed. Ruth, would you repeat your accusation, please?'

Ruth stood up. Her cheeks were white. 'I accuse Anya and Jonathan of having a relationship outside the provisions of the Rule. I have seen them three times near the river in recent weeks. Twice they were kissing and fondling each other. On the third occasion I believe they were having sex.' She sat down as if there was nothing else that could possibly be said.

'Are you willing, if necessary, to repeat that accusation in front of the whole community?'

'I am.'

'Anya and Jonathan. Do you agree or disagree with the accusation?' Jonathan began to speak but Anya cut him off.

'I've already said. We agree with the accusation. We have had a sexual relationship.'

'In that case, I only have to name a Gatherer to speak for both of you. I took the precaution of finding a volunteer before this meeting. Thomas is willing to stand in this capacity, though any Gatherer may volunteer for the job or be suggested by another Gatherer.'

'In which case I volunteer,' said Tobias. 'I believe I am still a Gatherer.'

'I think your status as a Gatherer would be a matter of intense debate,' replied Peter. 'Since you left the community under the shadow of the same accusation I hardly think you'd be a fit spokesperson or could pretend to be a Gatherer any longer.'

'But you've got to admit, Peter, looked at in one way there is hardly anyone more qualified to speak for Anya and Jonathan than Tobias,' interjected Sylvia. 'Let's assume that Tobias is still a Gatherer. What happens if there are two volunteers?'

Peter sighed. 'In the event of one of the accused having a partner who is a Gatherer, that Gatherer chooses.'

'So in this case, Francesca has the right to choose. Well girl?'

Francesca paused. Thomas might be a prudent choice but Anya needed an eloquent defence.

'I thank Thomas for his offer but I choose Tobias.'

★ ★ ★ ★

While Peter might have been caught off balance with Tobias's offer to act as Speaker for Anya and Jonathan, he quickly dealt with some of the other housekeeping issues needed to prepare for their Testing. Jonathan was placed under Thomas's care and went off to temporary quarters to Thomas's longhouse. Francesca was released from the Infirmary and given formal responsibility for Anya's conduct.

But Peter didn't get everything his own way. By one vote the Council endorsed Tobias's claim to be a Gatherer, so that he was recognised as Speaker.

While Francesca found all these things to her liking, she was still worried about what impact the news of Anya's pregnancy might have. She turned the problem over in her mind for a few days; Tobias had to know as soon as possible but it had to come from Anya. She concluded that all she could do was engineer the opportunity for disclosure and see what happened.

At the end of the next evening meal she got Anya and Tobias together on the excuse that she wanted to talk to them about things that were worrying her about her role in the Testing. After a few questions about what it would be like giving evidence and how things would be organised, she turned to the issue of punishment.

'There are still things I don't understand about punishments that might result from the Testing,' said Francesca.

'Peter was right; it's separation if you remain in the community, banishment for one or both of you if you don't,' replied Tobias.

'And that's the limit. Are there no other circumstances that could make a difference?'

'Not really. That's the limit. If you're thinking of what I said about people had being killed in the community in the past, that happened after banishment when people tried to come back. They then got killed by the community but they weren't members of Heron Fleet at the time, so technically no community member has ever killed another community member.'

Anya was looking uneasy. She took a deep breath. 'What would happen if there was a child conceived as a result of a relationship like mine and Jonathan's?'

'Well then the punishments would be the same but the community would claim the child as theirs. They would never let the baby go even if they banished the mother.' He paused and saw Anya's expression. 'Are you pregnant?'

'I think so.'

He groaned. 'It would have been better if that had been raised at the informal meeting.'

'I'm sorry,' interjected Francesca. 'I knew but I suppose I've been trying to ignore it.'

'Well there's no point in looking back,' he said. 'Do you know for sure you really are pregnant?'

Anya hesitated. 'I suppose I can't be absolutely sure.'

'Well then, the best thing to do is to make sure. You must go to the Crèche Nurses and ask that they test you. Francesca will have to ask for you since you're her responsibility.'

'I'll arrange it for tomorrow,' said Francesca.

'No, if you give it a day or two it'll look better, as if you've only just told Francesca. In fact it would look better still if Francesca went to Peter to ask what to do. It emphasises that Anya and Jonathan are obedient to the Rule.'

Francesca acted on Tobias's advice. The day after next she

went to find Peter and asked if she could have a word with him. She duly told him that Anya suspected she was pregnant.

Peter sighed. 'Then she must go to the Crèche Nurses for them to prove it. Thank you for telling me. I'm afraid this matter gets worse and worse and I am fearful of what it will do to the community.' Then he looked at her and smiled, 'I must thank you for your maturity in all this. As the one who must have been more hurt than anyone, you're setting an example to us all of how a Gatherer should shoulder their responsibility.'

'It is not as difficult as it might be,' she replied. 'Tobias is a great help and I still love Anya.'

After talking to Peter, Francesca went to find Anya straight away. Talking to Peter was easy; talking to Anya was going to be much more difficult. While Anya had not objected to going to see the Crèche Nurses originally, since then she had become more and more worried.

'What did he say?' she said to Francesca immediately.

'What we had expected, that you need to go to the Crèche Nurses to confirm you are pregnant.'

'That's easy for him to say,' said Anya. 'He's not the one who's going to get poked and pushed around.'

'It won't be that bad,' said Francesca, hoping to sound encouraging despite her own misgivings.

The fact was that the Crèche Nurses were a mysterious group. They had never been members of the Council and there were never more than six of them. In the normal way no Apprentice would have any dealings with them at all and a female Gatherer would only come into contact with them when she was told that she had been chosen to have a child.

Even that was shrouded in secrecy. It was said they came in the night and told the chosen women to report the following morning to start tests and inspections. Such was their authority: when you were called you went. The partners of those chosen were never consulted and never allowed to attend anything to do with the impregnation or the birth.

'I know Tobias thinks it is important, but I don't see the point,' Anya continued. 'What difference can it make? We are guilty. We did what we are accused of and more.' Francesca shuddered. Whilst she had come to terms with Anya having sex with Jonathan and had mostly suppressed her jealousy, she could still be taken unaware by Anya's remarks.

'But without a successful argument against punishment they'll banish you and you'll have to leave Heron Fleet.'

'Would that be so bad?' said Anya. 'I'd be together with Jonathan and when it is born we'd have the baby.'

Francesca was horrified. 'How could you leave Heron Fleet? It's our home; it's everything that keeps us safe and sound.'

'But it doesn't allow us to love freely or bring up our own children.'

Francesca floundered around for an argument but all she could come up with was, 'I think you should ask Tobias a bit more about what the world is like outside Heron Fleet before you decide to wander off into the wild.'

'Sorry,' said Anya. 'I know you're doing your best. I'll be a good girl and go with you tomorrow but I am very frightened about what it will be like.'

'Don't worry, no matter how bad it is I will not leave you on your own.'

★ ★ ★ ★

The Crèche Nurses had a separate building near to the Infirmary. The following morning Francesca and Anya made their way there and reported to the Head Crèche Nurse who looked Anya up and down, making no attempt to disguise her hostility.

'So having defied the Rule that binds us all together and has kept us safe for generations, you now need me to tell you if you and your lover have added insult to injury and conceived a rough child?' The Crèche Nurse emphasised *rough*.

Anya swallowed hard. 'Yes ma'am.'

Dealing with the Head Crèche Nurse was much worse than dealing with Peter or even Sylvia, thought Francesca. Partly it was her presence and physical appearance. She was old, possibly the oldest member of the Community, but unlike Sylvia tall and upright, with an added aura of arrogance that Sylvia, as bent and as formidable as she was, did not possess. Her grey hair was cropped tightly to her head, her skin was pale and tight across high cheekbones. Her complexion was sallow and her lips had vertical brown creases at their edges. Clean white nails, that Francesca thought were sharp, exact and could pinch unmercifully if required, were attached to bony hands, with pronounced blue veins on their backs.

'Well I suppose if I must, I must, though personally I would just make both you and him Outcast right now. See how you'd like to survive a winter without the shelter of the Rule. Come this way.'

Francesca squeezed Anya's hand as they were led through into a back room, in the middle of which was a wooden table. The Head Crèche Nurse looked at Francesca. 'You've no need to remain. You have done your duty by bringing me these soiled goods.' Anya flashed a frightened glance at Francesca

'I am responsible for her to the Council,' replied Francesca as calmly as she could, wondering what she would say or do if this woman ordered her to go.

'Yes, I suppose you are, but my dear, the Council's right runs weakly here.' There was no human feeling or sympathy in her voice. Francesca felt a spasm of hatred rise within her. The Head Crèche Nurse went on, 'Does that surprise you? Well the Rule makes the Council and its Head responsible for the survival of the community each year. They have to plan how to raise and gather the harvest and they settle differences in the community. But they are elected and they come and go.' She sounded bored and above influence by any ordinary Gatherer. 'On the other hand, we select our own. We serve for life and we are charged with the survival of the community over the long term, generation to generation, not merely year to year.'

She went over to a bench at the back of the room and took down from a cupboard above it three small clear glass bottles. One held what looked like water but was more viscous, the second a liquid the colour of blackberry juice and the third had pale green contents. Then she took an earthenware beaker of slivers of wood such as might be used to light a fire and a bowl of washed lamb's wool. She picked off a piece of the wool and carefully wound it on to the end of one of the spills so it formed a ball. Finally she took from the cupboard a bright metal object like a pair of blunt, flat shears made of silver-steel. The shears were hinged and when the handles of this instrument were squeezed the blades opened outwards.

'Take all your clothes off and stand over by the table,' she said over her shoulder to Anya. Slowly Anya began to strip until she was standing naked where she had been told. The Head Crèche Nurse turned and looked her up and down in the way one of the Shepherds would have looked at a good ewe but with less humanity and pride. 'Pity. Good breeding stock but after this you're no good to me.' She turned to Francesca. 'You don't need to be here, unless of course you want to stay.'

'As I said, she's my responsibility to the Council.'

'Do I sense a bit of revenge? Hoping I'll degrade her a bit? Would that serve as a reprisal for her daring to leave your loving bed?'

Francesca had never met anyone as cruel as the Head Crèche Nurse. She was cruel not in her words but in her exercise of power, though at that moment it was not the power over Anya that made Francesca angry, it was the power this woman had over her. Francesca did not know which was worse, the need to bite back her words because of the importance of establishing Anya's pregnancy or the travesty of her real feelings that this woman ascribed to her. She desired to claw at the Head Crèche Nurse's face. To make this unloved and unloving creature see what real love was and how fierce it could make even a lowly, inexperienced Gatherer.

'Well, what I have to do may be a bit degrading but from our point of view you're all just entries in our stock book.'

The Head Crèche Nurse walked over to Anya and placed her hands over her breasts, squeezing and pushing them first from the top, then the sides and from underneath. She picked up the bottle with the deep red liquid in it and splashed some on to Anya's nipples. Then she ran her thumbs across them and waited until they responded and became erect. As she did so a second, younger Crèche Nurse came in. 'Please, can you make notes for me, Rebecca?' said her superior.

'Of course, ma'am.' She was smaller and had a fresh face. Francesca looked at her in the hope of seeing more understanding but whilst she did not openly sneer at Francesca's glance, Francesca could see a common detached deadness in the young woman's expression similar to that of the Head Crèche Nurse.

Rebecca went to a second cupboard with a sloping top. She got out a large black book and placed it on the surface. Then she got out a small pot of black liquid and a small collection of bird's feathers that looked as though they had been cut and shaped at the end. Finally, she opened the book. 'Ready, ma'am.'

'You'll find her record about three pages in. Apprentice twenty-three: Anya.'

Rebecca turned the pages over. 'Found it, ma'am.'

'Start recording, please. Breasts firm and nodule-free. Nipples show some enlargement consistent with early pregnancy.' Francesca watched as Rebecca made a series of black marks on the pages of the book with what must have been a pen and ink.

The Head Crèche Nurse's hands moved down to Anya's waist and hips. 'No thickening of the muscles above the hips but we would not expect that at such an early stage.' Her left hand then went down to the base of Anya's abdomen. 'Neither is there any swelling above the pubis. Hand me a pan.'

Rebecca handed the Head Crèche Nurse a shallow earthenware bowl with a broad spoon-like extension. The Head Crèche Nurse handed it to Anya. 'Stick the end between your legs and piss into it.' Anya tried to do what she was told but at first couldn't manage anything. 'If you have any difficulty, think of the swimming lessons, or the feel of his prick,' the Head Crèche Nurse added.

Francesca started to feel sick. Anya's body was precious to her. To see the breasts she had so often caressed treated like meat was terrible, worse still to see Anya sexually abused by this grotesque woman. But she knew if she called out in protest or even showed emotion Anya too would lose control and that would be a victory for these persecutors. She must concentrate on establishing whether Anya was pregnant and nothing else.

When a sample of urine had been obtained, a small amount was poured into another bowl and Rebecca added some of the clear liquid. 'The test is positive, ma'am.'

'Well, if the mucus test is positive then we'll know for sure,' replied the Head Crèche Nurse. 'Get up on the table and put your feet in the harnesses,' she said to Anya. Rebecca swung out two supports with loops of cloth up at the sides of the table towards one end. Anya lay on the table and put one foot into each strap. The Head Crèche Nurse inserted her fingers into Anya and started to probe around.

'The hymen is completely broken and I can easily feel the cervix. It seems distended and firm.'

Francesca couldn't watch any more. She closed her eyes and turned way.

'Give me the speculum.' Francesca heard Anya groan slightly and Francesca guessed that the metal shears-like instrument was the speculum and that it had been inserted into her lover. The commentary went on.

'I think I have a sample.' Anya groaned again. 'Yes, that's it. You can get down now.' Francesca opened her eyes. Anya was quietly crying. Francesca helped Anya out of the slings and got her clothes. Clearly a spill with the wool had been inserted into Anya. It lay in another bowl and some of the green liquid had been poured on it. The Head Crèche Nurse and Rebecca were observing it carefully. Francesca could also see into the bowl. Thin swirls of red colour were beginning to form from what was coming from the wool.

'And this tallies with the record of her periods in the book?'

'Yes, ma'am.' Rebecca referred to the book where Francesca could see rows of marks and more writing. They were pointing at one row where there seemed to be a gap. 'Yes, she missed at the end of last month. She was probably at maximum fertility when she encountered the boy.'

'Well that settles it.' The Head Crèche Nurse went over to where Anya was trying to get dressed and hit her smartly across the face with an open palm. Francesca had to force her hands to remain at her sides.

'Slut! If it wasn't for the child inside you I'd poison you right here and now.'

Then she turned to Francesca. 'She's pregnant alright. Now get her out of my sight. I've better things to do with my time.'

Francesca supported Anya out into the open air. They walked a few steps but Anya's willpower gave way. She collapsed into Francesca's arms sobbing uncontrollably, while Francesca, through her own tears, tried to comfort her.

The Founder's Diary VI

Day 115

It has been two days since the new cases of plague were recognised. In that time the total number of infections has risen from three to nine and the infirmary is full. A temporary bed area has been set up in an adjacent room which wasn't previously connected through, but a door was knocked in the wall this afternoon and that will mean that we can take twenty more patients once extra beds have been improvised.

I have been briefing volunteers from the Winter's Hill group to act as nurses. The Commander was against us using any guards in case another fort got wind of our predicament and attacked us. But he's given us Bill since he knows most about what to do and might, like Miriam and me, still be infectious. We were against using the civilian foragers since Miriam thinks their poor health may make them susceptible to infection, so that left the Winter's Hill group.

Miriam and I have talked about the infection risks. We're not too worried about us having been the carriers now. If we infected Joan then we think we should have shown signs as soon as we got back. It looks as though Joan caught whatever it is from the outside, which would account for the rapid number of other cases and brings the frightening prospect that the infection is already well established in the fort. All the new cases have been from the civilian foragers.

Day 116

I am writing this on night duty. Miriam and I have decided to do every other night while the other one gets some proper rest. My job is to supervise the volunteers. We set up a corner where we can brew tea for everyone who's on duty. It's got a mattress for Miriam or me to get some sleep on.

We had our first death today, which was the same as Joan's. The man rallied in the morning but went down by mid-afternoon with the black tracks appearing very rapidly. The progress was terrible as his skin became dry and brittle. In some places it split and began to bleed as he writhed around in the last stages. He died fighting for breath and coughing up blood in the evening. Almost as soon as he was dead another patient, who had seemed to be better, totally collapsed and the first evidence of tracks were seen in his groin. I am expecting him to die before morning.

So as not to disturb the patients who aren't delirious the infirmary is dark and the volunteers are using oil lamps as they go from bed to bed. Miriam said it reminded her of pictures of Florence Nightingale's hospital at Scutari. 'You mean we all look like Ladies with a Lamp,' I said.

'Yes,' she said. 'And the fact we have just about the same level of treatment as she had to offer our infected patients.'

Day 117

Another twelve patients today: three civilian children, seven adult foragers and most worryingly three soldiers. Five more have died.

An orderly burial site has been arranged and along with it a ceremony of burial. The bodies are burned and then their ashes are collected in containers and placed in holes in a patch near to the inner fence. If the person had any particular friends they say something about them. Then the Commander says a few words and then the earth is filled in. It is decent and sombre. I think I know now what the man was doing at the hospital. He was burying his friends. I wonder who will be the last of us to bury anyone.

Day 118

All the three soldiers died in the night. The progress of the disease is increasing, ten soldiers, including the second-in-command and the Commander himself. Before he became delirious, he called for James and some of the more experienced soldiers that are left. They talked privately. When they had finished I noticed that the soldiers came to attention and saluted James. He came over to me when they had gone. 'The Commander has asked me to take over from him if he dies and his men have agreed. I don't know what I will do if I have to lead everyone who survives.' Then he walked away, his head hanging.

Day 119

Five more soldiers are dead and all the civilian population has now been infected except two: a teenager called Christie and Miriam. None who has shown symptoms has lived. The children seem more resistant but in the civilian group they have all succumbed slowly. Today the first of Winter's Hill showed symptoms. Catherine and her partner Geoff and their two children. They were the last people to join Winter's Hill. But this is not the worst blow for me and Miriam. Bill was brought to us delirious this afternoon. The soldiers who brought him said he'd stayed at his post when he must have had the fever.

Day 120

Bill died early this morning. I was able to speak to him in the brief respite before the swellings started. I made my peace with him. He told me how much he regretted that we couldn't be together and how he had fallen for me when he saw how brave I'd been when trying to treat his wound. I said I loved him, though in truth I don't know if I really did. When the swellings took hold it was almost as if you could see them grow as you watched. It took two of us to hold his hands away from his arms and face as he tried to claw at his own skin. Finally, he screamed out, arched his back and then relaxed, dead. I collapsed at his side sobbing. Miriam came and, with Charlie's help, pulled me away from Bill's corpse.

Day 121

Miriam must have given me a shot of something for I must have slept the clock round. I didn't wake up until earlier this evening. I was on the bed we'd set up for use when we are on duty. I realised immediately something was different but it took some time to realise what it was.

It was quiet. No one was moaning, no one yelling out in the last stages of the plague. I got up and walked through the infirmary. There were no patients and no volunteers. I was alone. Outside it was just as quiet and still I saw no one. I was suddenly very frightened. Was I the only person left? Had everyone else died? The picture of the bodies in the hospital came into my mind.

I walked down towards the gate. Coming round a corner of the main building I realised why it was so quiet. Winter's Hill people were digging a long trench. By the side of the trench there were thirty bodies ready for burial. I recognised all the patients who had been in the infirmary the night before. The bodies of the Commander and his second-in-command were there. I spotted Geoff and Catherine, their offspring and finally Bill. Miriam saw me. She came to me a put her arm round my shoulders.

When the trench was complete we buried them all. There are thirty-five of us left. Thirty-three from the Winter's Hill group plus Christie and Miriam. Everyone else is dead. But no one who is left has any symptoms of the plague.

Day 124

For the last three days we have all been in shock and in a quandary. Without the soldiers we cannot defend the fort. If any other forts find out, we will be attacked and massacred. So we must leave and run the risk of travelling towards the coast through the winter. On the other hand we cannot be certain that the plague has run its course in our group and there will be no more cases. Miriam thinks that it is possible that we are all immune from whatever it is that causes the plague but the only way we have of knowing is to wait for the ten days' incubation period to pass.

So over the last three days we have been debating this problem inside the council and outside, while we loaded all the stores we could find into the small group of lorries that we will use as transport.

Day 125

The loading was completed this morning. From now on we can go whenever we wish. At dawn James sent out scouts towards the forts we know of. They came back at about midday to say that only one still seems operational. But there were signs that there may be some sort of column of transport coming towards us from the other side of the city.

After all the scouts were back James called us together and we heard their reports. Then we voted. A majority were in favour of leaving as soon as possible.

Day 126

We started this morning at dawn, and have been going for about four hours as I write this. About an hour after we left we heard explosions and gunfire coming from the direction of the last remaining functioning fort in our part of the city. We think whatever the column was that was coming from the direction of the city centre had reached them. We may have got away only just in time. By this evening we will be out into the country to the west of the city.

Chapter 13

With a struggle Francesca got Anya back to their roundhouse and into bed. She waited until Anya had fallen asleep and then went down to the jetty where Tobias was still working on the repairs to his boat. She went on board, found him and asked if he had time to talk. They went down the steps into the cabin.

'Are you alright?' he said. 'You're as white as snow.'

'I'd be better for a drink of water.' Her hands were shaking.

'I think I can do better than that. Hang on a minute,' and he went forward into the main hold of the boat.

She looked round the cabin. It had a simple, wide bed that faced the door. On one side there was a lift-up flap below cupboards built into the wall. It was the same sort of flap that she had seen the Crèche Nurses use for writing in the stock book. On the other side of the bed was a set of shelves which held a collection of what she knew must be books. They were all tucked behind bars that would keep them in place even during the fiercest of storms. She went over to them and carefully took one down. She flicked through its pages, past writing she could not decipher and pictures of strange scenes: people in odd-looking clothes, enormous cities with things suspended in the air. Tobias came back.

He was carrying a large, plain glass bottle and two beakers, also made of glass. 'This is what you need,' he said cheerfully. He dropped the beakers onto the bed and then, pushing the bottle under his broken right arm, he pulled its stopper with his free hand.

'Hold the glasses for me,' he said to Francesca. She picked them up from the bed and held them out to him. He poured a little of the liquid from the bottle into each, re-stoppered the bottle and dropped it onto the bed. He took one of the glasses for himself.

'Try this.' He raised his glass to her. 'To life,' he said and swallowed the liquid in one satisfied gulp.

She tried to do the same, raising her glass and replying, 'To life,' but the smell of the liquid got up her nose. Before she could drink, it made her cough so all she managed was a large sip. The liquid burned her tongue and mouth, and made her lips go numb. Then her nose was full of the fragrance of a fruit she couldn't identify. Despite its sharpness, it was not unpleasant and she swallowed, feeling a thread of warmth as it went down inside her. She coughed again. 'What is it?' she said, sipping again.

'Where it came from they call it *aquavite*, the water of life. In other places it's called moonshine, brandy and many other names. This was made from a fruit called the damson. But wherever it comes from and whatever form it takes, it cheers the heart in times of trouble.' He paused. 'What happened this morning?'

Francesca sat on the bed. 'I went with Anya to see the Crèche Nurses. It was terrible. They humiliated her. They probed and assaulted her in all...' she hesitated, '...in all her most private places.' She looked away embarrassed and began to cry. Tobias laid his hand on her shoulder and squeezed reassuringly.

'Is she pregnant?'

The simple, firm question helped her composure. 'Yes she is,' but as soon as she had said it she remembered the picture of Anya on the table and it made her angry.

'You know more than anyone about the Rule,' she burst out, 'more than anyone except Peter. The Head Crèche Nurse said that Peter has no control over them. She said that while the Head of the Council comes and goes from year to year, the Rule gives them the responsibility of seeing that the community survives from generation to generation. We're powerless against them!'

Tobias sat next to her on the bed and topped up their glasses. 'I don't know exactly what power they have because they are not referred to in the Red Book.'

'What! How do you know?'

'I've read it.

'You've read the Red Book?'

'Yes. Soon after Peter, Sylvia and I became friends I started to teach Peter how to read. I had only one book then and so I had to use that. One evening we were going through it when we started to talk about what the Red Book might actually say. "I wonder what's actually in the Rule," said Peter. "It would be great fun to know whether, when Old Septimus," he was the Head of the Council then, "whether when Old Septimus says that such and such is in the Rule, whether it's actually there."

'"It would be very convenient if he could make it up as he went along," I added. "Why don't we borrow it, read it and then we'll know for sure?"

'From that remark grew a plan. I hadn't lost all my scavenger guile so finding where the Red Book was kept was not too difficult. One night, when Septimus was away visiting the herders on the northern boarder we got into his longhouse, I borrowed the Red Book for the night and read it. We returned it to its proper place before dawn and no one ever found out.'

Francesca laughed. The picture of Peter, of all people, stealing the Red Book from the Head of the Council and reading it in secret with Tobias was unbelievable.

'You're a remarkable man,' she said to Tobias. 'So what does it say?'

'Well it wasn't written by one person or at a single time; there are different parts to it. Some bits are about when to plant things. Some are about how to settle differences between Gatherers; Peter was using that part at the informal meeting. There are the words of the Founder's songs and other recitations used at different times of year. There are the rules about the Harvest Festival and Mayday but they come very late on in the book and must have been written well after the initial foundation of Heron Fleet.'

'What comes first?'

'The very first entry in the Red Book is the terms of the Pact. Next is the Rule which, as far as I can remember, only refers to the creation of the Council.'

'So the Head Crèche Nurse was wrong?'

'Perhaps. The Red Book doesn't mention them as such but the terms of the Pact, which centres on the commitment to have children under a single-sex partnership regime, implies that, even from the start, someone must have had to do the impregnation the Crèche Nurses do now.'

'So what Anya suffered this morning has always been part of Heron Fleet?'

'Well at least the potential for that sort of cruelty has been.'

'You know I think they even keep a record of every period every woman has.'

'Well that might make sense. You might need that information when you have to make the choice of who gets impregnated. It's got to have some bearing on who is the most fertile or predicting the best time to do it.'

'But to find that out they'd have to spy on us all, all the time. That's, that's…' she was lost for words.

'So calculating, so oppressive? Yes it is. But it doesn't surprise me. People with secret powers in any community can easily get as cruel as the Head Crèche Nurse was to Anya. I've seen what happens to people in the Scavenger Gangs; I know how casually cruel people can become. The big question is why the Pact was written at all? After all, the Pact is not strictly part of the Rule even if the community now treats it that way; even though it's the first document in the Red Book. In other communities and even in the Scavenger Gangs, a pact is something made between equals. It's an agreement and it dissolves if one of the parties to it ceases to agree to it. If the Pact has any of that nature then why shouldn't a couple refuse to be bound by it whilst remaining loyal to the Rule?'

'I'd like to see you get that argument past the Crèche Nurses.'

'Nonetheless it's an interesting thought. The most important thing at this moment is whether you feel better?'

'Yes thank you. You seem to put things into perspective for me.'

'In that case you should be getting back to Anya.' He stood up and collected her glass up with his. 'There's one thing you should know before you go but it's not good I'm afraid. I went to see Ruth.'

'What did she say?'

'She is adamant. She'll not withdraw the accusation. In fact, if she could, I think she'd personally throw Anya off a cliff.'

'Why is she so bitter?'

'Well I don't think it's about Anya or Jonathan, I think it's really about you. Because she still loves you, she wants to hurt you for hurting her. At the same time she thinks that if Anya is out of the way, she might get you back. Either way she will stick to her story. It may be irrelevant to the Testing anyway since Anya and Jonathan have already agreed it is true. She may have started the process but she can't stop it now even if she had a mind to. I wonder if she really knows what it means for her. The only effect of her withdrawing the accusation, or refusing to repeat it at the Testing, would have been to give us a bit of a moral advantage.'

★ ★ ★ ★

The next few days rather dragged for Francesca. Anya recovered physically, but remained uncharacteristically quiet and withdrawn. Francesca tried taking her down to the boat but Anya didn't know her way round well enough to be of help with the repairs. The only good news was that Tobias had his splints off and had been discharged from the Infirmary.

'They've let me come back and live on the boat,' he said, clearly happy to be back on board. 'But I'm to eat in the Gathering Hall, so if anything new comes up I can tell you about it in the evening.'

In the end Francesca, desperate to find something to occupy both Anya and herself, went back to as many of her duties in the Glasshouses as she could, taking Anya with her. This worked well. Sylvia set them easy things to do like dividing and planting out rhubarb plants. The simple physical effort lightened Anya's spirits. There was the extra advantage that the area of the Glasshouses they were working in was well away from some of the more curious and gossipy Gardeners.

After the evening meal Francesca, Anya and Jonathan all spoke to Tobias. 'Not much new to report,' he said. 'I've been trying to gauge how the community feels about all this. They seem divided.

The younger Gatherers seem to be on our side, the older ones against. Then there are the ones that remember me. They're dead against us. I think they see it as a way of settling old scores! Still, one thing's for sure, everyone is on Francesca's side. There's hardly a bad word being said about her.'

A big boost for Anya was a visit from her old Crèche Mother, Elizabeth, who came to find her and see how she was.

'The Crèche Nurses won't help you but you're still my Anya and I've learned a bit about having babies over the years, so what I know I'll share with you. When this lamb is born,' she said, patting Anya's stomach gently, 'he or she will need all the help they can get. Worst comes to the worst, it will have me and I don't care who knows it.'

Francesca left them alone and Elizabeth talked to Anya for a long time. At the end they hugged each other warmly before Elizabeth went back to her current charges.

'Is that better?' asked Francesca.

Anya smiled for the first time since the visit to the Crèche Nurses. 'Yes,' she said. 'Nice to know someone outside our immediate friends still cares about me and the child.'

But just as there seemed to be a breathing space in which they might all come to terms with what was happening, things changed again. That evening, at the end of the evening meal, Peter stood up and called for silence.

'The Council has conferred and has decided that the Testing of Anya and Jonathan will take place the day after tomorrow here in the Gathering Hall. All Gatherers and Apprentices who are not required for essential duties are welcome to attend.'

'So now we know,' said Francesca to Anya.

'Yes, at least the waiting is over,' Anya replied and she squeezed Francesca's hand, though she looked fearful again.

★ ★ ★ ★

It was Francesca's responsibility to get Anya to the Gathering Hall by mid-morning. When they got there, the Hall was almost completely full. One of the Gatekeepers showed them to their places in front of the Council Table. Two smaller tables had been set up. At one Thomas and Jonathan sat. Francesca and Anya were shown to the second. Tobias sat a little way to the right at a third table on which was a small pile of books.

The Council door opened and the oldest Gatekeeper came in. He carried a long black staff. He walked in front of the Council Table until he was in the middle. Then he turned and banged staff on the floor three times.

'All having business and interest in the Testing of these accused, should now present themselves. Please take your places and stand for the Council.' As everyone in the Hall stood he turned and faced Peter's chair. Then the Council filed in. When they were all present, the Gatekeeper turned his staff horizontal and placed it in front of Peter, bowed and withdrew. Peter held up the Red Book.

'See people of Heron Fleet. Here is the Rule we follow. It is in the name of this Rule that we meet today. It is the Rule that keeps us together and contains the Gatherer principles of community, identity and stability.' Then he put the Red Book down and the Council and people sat.

'I will start by explaining how this Testing will proceed. Those to be tested are at the front here with their sponsors. The purpose of the Testing is not to prove if the accusation is true or not, Jonathan and Anya have already agreed that it is, but to decide punishment in the light of Anya's and Jonathan's responsibility. Since both of those to be tested are Apprentices, Tobias the Outlander will speak on their behalf. Francesca as the Gatherer partner of Anya, and therefore the senior partner of either accused, has chosen Tobias and the Council have agreed that, though separated from Heron Fleet for many years, he still has the status of a Gatherer. Tobias the Outlander, do you accept this responsibility as Speaker?'

Tobias stood. 'I do, Peter, and I will exercise it in accordance with the Rule and the principles of justice common to all humankind.' Then he sat down again.

'The Speaker can call others to give evidence for the accused. All those called must respond. The Rule does not allow for excuses. The Council may ask questions of those called.

'According to the history of Heron Fleet, there has not been an accusation of this nature in many generations. Even disputes, which have to be settled formally before the Council, do not occur more than once in five seasons or so. As a result, this is a unique occasion in our generation. I have had to and will have to rely on the instructions in the Red Book about how to carry out this Testing. I hope all Gatherers will support me in that endeavour.' There was a murmur of endorsement.

'It is inevitable that this accusation will stir up strong feelings in many. Can I remind you all that it is the tradition in Heron Fleet to allow everyone a fair hearing? I hope that all will restrain their reactions to what they hear and allow this Testing to proceed without interruption.' There was a second murmur of agreement.

'There is one fact that was not known at the informal meeting. The Crèche Nurses have confirmed that Anya is pregnant.' There was a gasp from the gathering. 'This means that the future of the child born from Anya's and Jonathan's relationship will also have to be settled by this Testing.'

Anya was on her feet. 'It is mine and Jonathan's baby. You and the Council may settle whether we can remain members of Heron Fleet but what gives you the right to settle my baby's fate?'

'The Rule, girl, The Rule,' shouted back Peter. 'The Rule you and that boy have broken. This Testing takes place by the authority of that Rule and not by your selfish wish. Francesca, please make Anya understand that she must be calm during these proceedings.' Francesca took Anya by the shoulders and, having embraced her, got her to sit down quietly.

When everything became calm again Peter went on. 'In a moment I will call Tobias to speak for Anya and Jonathan but first, consistent with our tradition of openness, the community will hear the accusation that has been made. Please come forward, Ruth.'

Ruth made her way forward and stood between Peter and the tables at which Anya and Jonathan were sitting. She had clearly rehearsed what she had to say and did not need to be prompted to speak by Peter. To Francesca she looked much as she had at the informal hearing; white cheeks and determined looks.

'I accuse Anya and Jonathan of having a relationship outside the provisions of the Rule. I saw them three times near the river before the Harvest Festival when Anya was teaching Jonathan to swim after her dangerous assault on him on the bridge coming back from the fields.' Tobias was right about Ruth's hatred of Anya, thought Francesca. She would say anything to denigrate Anya's reputation.

Ruth continued. 'Twice they were kissing and fondling each other. On the third occasion I believe they were having sex.' As she finished she looked at Francesca. Francesca stared back at her. Quite quickly, Ruth looked away. She threaded her way back to her seat in the body of the Hall, her moment at the centre of the drama over. Francesca thought Ruth shrank as she walked up the Hall. She felt sad for her since in not being able to face her look, Ruth must have known that any hope she had of getting Francesca back was over.

'Thank you, Ruth,' said Peter. 'Please proceed, Tobias.'

'Thank you, Peter. I call Francesca, Anya's partner.'

Though she and Tobias had talked about some of the tactics of the Testing and Francesca had expected to be asked to speak, she had not expected that she would be first. She got up and came forward.

'Hold on,' said Peter, seeing she was uncertain where to stand, 'we'll get you a stool.' The Gatekeeper brought one and positioned it just in front of the tables so that Francesca could see Peter and Tobias and also would be heard clearly in the rest of the Hall.

Tobias got up and walked over to her. 'Francesca, when did you first know about the relationship between Anya and Jonathan?' he asked.

'The night of the Harvest Festival, Ruth told me.'

'Told you? How?'

'What do you mean?'

'Well, did she come straight up to you and say, "Anya is having an affair with Jonathan"?'

'No, she wasn't as clear as that, she said she'd seen them on the river bank together and then said something about it being a good job that they hadn't been seen by anyone in the Council.'

Francesca's voice was firm and confident but she was beginning to have doubts as to where Tobias's questions might lead.

'So at that point you were not sure. When were you certain?' She realised that he intended to take her far from the agreed plan but she had to go on, nothing but the truth was due to the Council and the community.

'When I saw the look he gave Anya when she came in to light the fire.'

'And what did you do in reaction to knowing that?'

'Well, I don't know exactly. Parts are still unclear to me because of the injury to my head but I know that I must have become hysterical with grief and ran out into the storm.'

'Were you trying to kill yourself?'

She looked at him wildly but his face was impassive. She would have to answer the question and confess what she had tried to do that night to the whole of the community. She took a deep breath. 'Yes I believe I was.' There was a quiet chatter of surprise in the Hall.

'Please everyone. Do not interrupt the proceedings,' said Peter. 'Please continue, Tobias.'

'Well, whatever you wanted to do, you still had the presence of mind to save my neck when you found me, for which I thank you. But let me go back to how you felt. Why did you think like that? You have a reputation of being sensible and reliable. The way you have coped with all this,' he waved his hand round at the Council and the whole Hall, 'has enhanced that reputation.'

Someone shouted 'Hear! Hear!' from the back and sporadic clapping broke out. As the noise died away, a voice that was clearly Elizabeth's shouted, 'Well said, Outlander. Well said,' which got a ripple of laughter.

Peter was on his feet again. 'Will the community please restrain its reactions.' Despite her own fears Francesca realised that Peter was nervous, perhaps more nervous than she was she thought. Then Tobias was speaking again.

'You're not a person known for outbursts of hysteria, are you?'

'I suppose not.'

'So what drove you to it that night?'

Despite her nerves, Francesca answered in the confident voice she had started with. 'Because I love Anya and I could not accept she had rejected me.'

'Many would find that a remarkable thing to say. Many would wonder how you can be so restrained and calm telling us something that must have caused you so much pain and grief.'

'I have come to accept things as they are.'

'If it were possible would you have Anya back even after all that has happened?'

'Yes,' she said without a pause.

'If there was no other way and there was a baby to care for, would you care with Anya for that baby?'

'Yes.' Again there was no hesitation.

'Why would you do that for someone who has hurt you so much?'

'Because I don't believe real love stops because a person in a partnership does something wrong, nor in the end is it about who you have sex with. In the future if Anya needs me back, well... I still love her.'

'And who do you think taught you that?'

Francesca was thrown by such a surprising question. 'What do you mean?'

'Did your Crèche Mothers teach you that?'

She thought for a moment. 'They were good examples of what love is, so is the Harvest time when the whole community works together, as are the friendships between the Apprentice but...' she paused again '...but I think the answer is no. I think it's inside me, somewhere inside here,' and she knocked gently against her chest with her hand.

'Thank you. Before I finish, I want to take you back to the matter of Anya and Jonathan's baby. What do you think should happen to it?'

'Until only a few days ago I would have said that the best place for the baby would be in the Crèche. The Crèche Mothers brought me up well and I believe most of us were happy as children.' There was another round of approving hear-hears. 'But

I've seen cruelty from the Crèche Nurses which I wouldn't have believed was possible. I've started to wonder if other women in the community have been shown the same sort of cruelty and disrespect that they showed Anya. That has given me doubts.' The Hall was silent, though there were many glances exchanged between mature women Gatherers.

She continued. 'More than that, I wonder how the safe and secure community of Heron Fleet, the community that I gave my allegiance to only a little while ago, and the community I have loved all my life could tolerate such cruelty. The Crèche Nurses make me wonder whether the community I love is somehow a sham.'

'Thank you. Now, I really have finished,' and Tobias smiled at her.

Francesca was just about to go when Peter spoke. ' I endorse what Tobias has said about your conduct and so I would not want to make this more painful than it has to be, but I want to be absolutely clear about what you said earlier in your answers to Tobias. If Anya wishes, you would resume your partnership with her?' Francesca nodded. 'Please say it so that all can hear and there can be no doubt.'

'Yes,' she said in a voice that carried clearly to the back of the Hall.

The Founder's Diary VII

Day 129

We have been going three days. Once clear of the city we turned southwest. Miriam suggested we could use the outskirts of a local forest to give us extra shelter if the weather got worse. We got to it two days ago. It was one of the forests that had been planted by the government before the cold had come when some of the city-folk were still trying to reverse the effects of the pollution. The trees on the edges had suffered badly in previous winters. The cold had killed all the broadleaved trees and even the majority of the pine trees. Their dead, leafless skeletons were either grey where all the bark had been stripped off or mottled with red and orange welts of fungus eating what was left of the wood. But there were more living trees further in, though the gloom deepened.

Day 130

We ran out on the top of a ridge today at the forest centre. We've decided to camp for the night in a clearing so we could see the sky rather than the dark canopy of the trees under which we have camped for the last few nights. Miriam and I were getting our tent sorted out when suddenly Charlie and Alison came charging in. Charlie's eyes were wide with astonishment and Alison hid her face in my dress. 'What's wrong?' I said.

'There's a giant over there!' Alison whimpered and pointed across to another ridge running parallel to ours. 'It will eat us.' she sobbed.

'What is she talking about, Charlie?' I said as I comforted her.

'It's not a giant but I've never seen anything like it before. Come and look.' Poking up above the trees, looking away from us, was indeed a giant, his arms outstretched to the sky. But there was no movement, no life in him. James and a few others were looking at his wreck. Charlie went over and put his hand in James's. 'What is it?' he said.

'It's a wind turbine Charlie. It was used to make electricity from the wind for the cities. It's a very big version of the windmill we had a Winter's Hill. Do you want to have a closer look?' Charlie nodded. So we gathered up anyone who was interested and climbed down to the stream between the ridges and then up the other side, where we picked up a track that seemed to be going in the direction of the turbine. When we got to the top of the second ridge we could see that the giant wasn't alone. There were fifty to a hundred others set on the ridge and on the ridges beyond. A couple were still revolving slowly but the rest were still, some with broken sails. We forced open the rusting door at the bottom of the tower of the one Alison and Charlie had seen. Inside there was what James said was the switching gear that directed the electricity generated to the cities. He pointed up at the long staircase that went round the inside of the tower. 'The generator was up there,' he said to Charlie. 'It was mounted behind the blades themselves to maximise efficiency so that the most electricity could be generated from the wind.' Charlie was obviously fascinated, which worried me. It seems to me that all technology is dangerous. All of it leads to death and plague in the end.

Day 135

It is getting colder. For the last few days the sky has been clearing and this morning it was clear blue but the night-time temperatures have been dropping and the frost in the morning is harder. We cleared the forest the day before yesterday and are trying to travel southeast now. We will have to cross a big river in a day or two on a road bridge but it's out in the country so we hope it will not be dangerous. After that, according the maps we salvaged from the fort, it looks as though the route should be fairly easy.

Day 136

The weather broke today. We woke up to find the sky was overcast and flurries of snow were falling. As the day went on the snow got heavier, by evening there was a good four centimetres on the ground and the wind was getting up. We found a sheltered valley to camp in. In the night the wind started to gust badly. One of our tents was blown down and three of the men had to stop it blowing away. We have a good collection of tents from the fort but we can't afford to lose any of them.

Day 137

The wind has dropped and it has stopped snowing. Proper cloud has been replaced by a white haze through which the sun filters. The surface that has been left by the snow is treacherous. In places the snow must have melted as it hit the ground and underneath there is layer of ice. In others the wind has produced drifts which might conceal rocks capable of damaging the lorry wheels. At the very least the drifts make it difficult to see the edge of the green lanes and tracks we are using. At one point the sun broke through the haze and we could see a sort of circular rainbow form. There were four separate rings, orange ones interspersed with blue. There was also some sort of secondary ring reflected from the snow on the ground. Then the haze cleared and it disappeared. An hour later the sky was covered with a think layer of high cloud which came quickly from the south. By the time we camped, a light fall of rough snow crystals was beginning.

Day 144

The blizzard has been blowing for a week and though there has been the time to write I have not had the will, finding it difficult to concentrate in the cold. The temperature plummeted the night after we saw the halo ring. Wind howled through the tent ropes and round the lorries. The tent material flapped and made sleeping difficult. We made it through that night OK but in the morning you couldn't see more than few metres. It was like looking though thick fog but this fog was made up of snowflakes and ice crystals that were flung about by a sharp, gusty wind. The crystals bit your face if you went out with any area of skin uncovered. The lorries were moved to circle the tents and provide some extra shelter and all the winter clothing we have has been given out. We just have to sit it out. Two days ago we saw our first medical case due to the cold. Two of the children were brought to us with uncontrollable shivering. They didn't seem to know where they were and the skin was cold to the touch. Their temperatures were low. We made them hot drinks and wrapped them in as many blankets as we could find. Gradually they recovered, but it gave Miriam and me a fright. It was clearly hypothermia, happening even when people were in the tents and sheltered from the snow and cold.

Day 145

The temperature has stabilised at minus ten degrees but the snow has stopped. The camp is one huge snowdrift. We can just see the tops of the lorries but the pickup is completely covered. We had started to dig the vehicles out when Chloe cried out and clutched at her chest. She had been helping dig out one of the tucks. Miriam and I ran over but it was too late. She had had some kind of heart attack and was dead in the snow where she had fallen. It must have been the exertion of the digging.

Day 146

We buried Chloe under a cairn of stones, the earth was already too frozen to work. She and Christopher had been two of the first members of Winter's Hill. Her death has hit James almost as hard as it has Christopher, who seems to have aged overnight.

Day 147

We finished digging out the vehicles this morning but none of them will start. The water systems are frozen and it's quite possible that, since they are diesel-powered the fuel may be too thick to work. One of the lorries has had a small fire lit under it to see if that will thaw out the engine.

Day 148

Mercifully the weather is still holding, though it remains bitterly cold. We have started two of the lorries and people are still working on the third, but the pickup is irreparable. They say the cylinder head has cracked, whatever that means.

Day 149

On our way again. We have put together a rota of who rides and who walks. All the children will ride wrapped in blankets. Christine and Charlie are taking turns minding a camp stove in the middle lorry. The stove has been set so that there can be regular hot drinks for all those coming off walking shift and the children. People will spend two hours walking and one hour riding.

Day 150

New system working well; it seems that it has even improved our speed. James thinks we have covered about half the distance from the city to the sea.

Day 152

I was walking with Miriam behind the last lorry. The weather was better, the temperature had risen and it felt warmer even though it was still just below freezing. The sky was clear again and the sun was hot enough that the snow was melting in some places and water was running down the track. We were coming down from a range of hills we had just crossed, down into a plain where we hopped it was going to be warmer or at least a little less windy. Below us, about five metres down a steep bank, was a stream.

Miriam and I were talking about whether we needed the rota to be used when I heard a shout. 'Careful!'

In front the first lorry had come to a sharp turn. As they turned their back wheels started to skid left. Skidding like this on the sort of tracks we have been using have become commonplace so neither Miriam nor I paid much attention. Then there was a more urgent shout. 'Look out! The bank is giving way.' I watched as the back wheels of the first lorry slid steadily towards the edge of the track above the stream. A rain of stones, snow, mud and boulders was falling from the edge of the track down into the stream. The back wheels of the lorry spun and the driver crashed the gearbox as they changed down to try to get more grip. Slowly the lorry got the grip it needed but as it pulled itself to safety, behind it the track gave way. The front wheels of the second lorry fell into the developing hole. The cab dipped and lurched over the edge. The cloth side of the back of the lorry quivered. Then the back toppled left and the lorry rolled down the bank. It came to rest upside down. We could see the driver struggling to get the door open. He seemed alright. People were already clambering down, responding to shouts from the adults taking a cold break in the back and the weeping of the children. It happened suddenly from then. There was a flicker of yellow at the edge of the one of the canvas sides. The flame took hold, nothing large or too bad, I thought. Then there was an explosion as this innocuous flame reached one of the drums of diesel the lorry was carrying. Alison and Charlie were on the lorry. I skidded and tumbled down the slope as the flames roared. I found Charlie knocked about but still alive. He had been thrown clear as the lorry had tumbled over the edge and rolled down the bank. I left him where he was and tried to get as close as I could to the lorry but the flames beat me back. Miriam caught up with me and pulled me away. Alison and three other children, two adults in the cab and one other, have been killed.

Chapter 14

After Francesca had answered questions, there was a break for people to stretch their legs. As soon as the Council had gone Tobias came straight over and gave Francesca a huge hug.

'Your answers were wonderful, you know that don't you?'

'I'm too confused to judge,' she replied. 'I certainly wasn't ready to confess to the whole of the community that I had tried to kill myself.'

'I'm sorry I put you in that position but it emphasises how truthful and honest you are. If you're in doubt about the foundations of Heron Fleet and the legitimacy of the Rule, then that must give everyone pause for thought.'

Jonathan came up to them. 'I agree with Tobias,' he said. 'You were very brave to say what you said and it was very moving. I'm sorry to have caused you so much hurt.' He turned to Tobias. 'Hasn't it simply opened the way for the Council to separate Anya and me?'

'I don't think Francesca's answers have increased that risk significantly.'

Anya had been standing listening. 'I don't see it that way. I think it has improved the chances of them putting the baby safely into the Crèche where nice Aunty Francesca will be there to take care of it.'

Francesca was shocked. Before she could stop herself, she turned on Anya. 'How could you say that? It's not like that!'

'No? Look me in the eye and say the thought had never crossed your mind. If you can't have me, well perhaps you'd be prepared to settle for a more unorthodox relationship.'

'It's not me who wanted a baby! If I repeated all the things you said to me when you told me that Ruth's accusation was true, other people might think you used Jonathan as well as me just to get the baby you wanted!' Jonathan and Tobias looked on incredulously. 'But I'll tell you this, no matter what happens I'm going to spend all the time I can playing with the children in the Crèches. I'm going to teach them to sing and recite and I'm going to make sure that if those Crèche Nurse witches try to control their lives they'll have to get past me first. If they end up calling me Aunty Francesca then I'll be honoured.'

The Hall was filling again. 'I think we should be getting back to our places,' said Tobias in the awkward silence. They started to sit down.

As soon as the Council was back in and Peter had called for order, Tobias stood. 'I am aware, Peter, that Heron Fleet has no library of books and that very few of even the senior Gatherers can read. In my travels and by trading in the cities I have come across books that record some principles other people have used in governing communities.' He walked over to his table and pointed to its small pile of texts. 'I would like to offer these three as evidence of what people in the past have thought were the correct principles that might be used to govern a community like Heron Fleet.'

'I hope this is going somewhere, Tobias,' interjected Peter. 'The account you gave of the world outside Heron Fleet when you first came to us doesn't suggest that what they might contain would be likely to offer us a good example.' There was some muffled laughter from those who knew those stories.

Tobias smiled. 'It is true that the Scavenger Gangs offer no examples of civilisation to Heron Fleet. But not everything known about how to govern a community comes from the Scavenger Gangs or even the Rule. What's in two of these books show that the founding principles of Heron Fleet were thought of long before the Founders passed them to us in the Red Book.'

'Oh yes,' shouted a voice from the back. 'So what do we owe them then, Outcast?'

Tobias took up the challenge. 'Good question, what do we owe them? Well, take the principle of voting for a council as a way of settling differences in a community. We owe that to people in a city called Athens in a country called Greece, thousands of years before the Founders.' He held up one of the books and carried it over to Peter. 'That principle is in here. That part of the Rule was not invented from scratch by the Founders, they used examples they knew.

'And it doesn't stop there.' He walked back to the table and took up the second book. 'This one contains the idea of a community working together to grow its own food. The author maintains living together was the way humankind lived when we first began. It makes the argument that the only way to stop human beings destroying the earth is to go back to that original way of living. The author called the principle self-sufficiency and without it the book predicts catastrophes of famine, disease and disastrous changes in the weather. It advocates the principles by which Heron Fleet lives. The principles that every Apprentice swears to honour: community, identity and stability.' He placed the second book in front of Peter.

'But it is this book that is the most interest to us at this Testing. You might ask what principle from the book did the Founders adopt? Well they didn't adopt anything from this book. Maybe they had never read it, who can say?'

'So why is it interesting?' shouted the heckler.

'Because the principles it contains argue against the central guiding principle in the Red Book, that the needs of the community are more important than the needs of the individual. This book says that the really important things that define human beings, things that no one should ever be allowed to take from us, are ours not because we earn them by what we do for a community but are ours simply because we are human.'

The intensity of noise in the Hall had grown steadily as Tobias had been talking about the books. It increased again, making it difficult for Tobias to be heard, but he was not going to be deprived of his dramatic climax.

'I agree with this book. It implies that the Rule is both unjust and in error because it does not accept the idea that we all have what the book calls rights. Those rights include the right to justice as in this Testing, the right to a say in how we are governed as in electing a Council, the right to our own beliefs even if they differ from those of our neighbours, the right to protection from violence. This book says that when some of those rights were omitted from the Rule it fell short of what each one of us can legitimately expect as our human heritage. A heritage we have from the moment we are born to the moment we die. Francesca gave a wonderful description of the basis of one of those rights, to love who we choose. This book says that if that principle had been laid out in the Rule by the Founders then there would be no Testing of Anya and Jonathan today because they would have the right to love who they choose and to bring up their own child!'

The uproar was immediate. Peter shot to his feet shouting for order but he was too late. There was open arguing in the Hall as Gatherer shouted at Gatherer. All he could do was adjourn the Testing.

★ ★ ★ ★

It was clear that the Testing could not resume that day. The best that could be hoped was that tempers would cool enough for the evening meal to be held as normal. To help calm things down Tobias volunteered not to eat in the Hall that evening and suggested that Francesca, Anya and Jonathan also stay away. Peter accepted this and said that he would announce that the Testing would resume the following morning.

'Why don't you eat on the boat?' he suggested.

'Provided you promise not to have us towed out to sea?' replied Tobias tartly.

'Interesting idea,' Peter replied with little if any irony. 'I'd be very tempted if I thought I could get the boat round into the river mouth without you noticing.' He stalked off.

Thomas agreed to bring the food for the meal to the boat so they could go immediately and be away from any argumentative Gatherers who might be hanging around after the meeting.

'Thank you,' said Tobias to him. 'You have been courtesy itself.'

'I feel it is my duty as a Gatherer to enable the Testing to take place fairly and openly,' Thomas replied. He paused. 'I thought what you said about the three books was very interesting. I too often think of the Rule as being something that we should never debate or change. I would be grateful if, at sometime, I could read those books.'

'You can read?' said Anya.

'Don't be too surprised. When I was younger I obtained two books from an Outlander Trader who came to Heron Fleet with some fresh meat to sell. We got on well and he gave me the books as a parting gift. So I learned to read. There are not many books in Heron Fleet but there are a few like mine and those of us who have them pass them round. We teach those who can find us to read if they ask.'

They started to make their way to the jetty. As it turned out there were very few people about so they did not have to hurry.

'Well that was a turn-up,' said Jonathan.

'Umm,' said Tobias thoughtfully. 'Makes me wonder how backward-looking some of the senior members of Heron Fleet really are.'

'What do you mean?' said Anya.

'I had never really considered how many quietly-acquired books there might be in Heron Fleet. There would have been many occasions over the years when interested members of the community like Thomas would have had the opportunity to obtain a few books here or there. With books comes the incentive to read, with reading come new ideas.'

'What is the good of new ideas here?' said Jonathan. 'No one would ever let you use them.'

'I'm sure they would if they could see a good reason for using them,' said Francesca. 'For instance, if new inventions offered an increase in the harvest. After all, Tobias was allowed to build the central domes of the Glasshouses using methods he learned in the cities.' Anya and Jonathan were astonished.

'You built the domes?' said Anya.

'Only the first three,' said Tobias. 'I'd always been interested in the things the people of the cities made using methods that had been lost.'

'That's understating it. You have curiosity for curiosity's sake,' said Francesca.

'Yes, you're right,' said Tobias. 'Cutting out reading suppresses curiosity and it is one of the reasons Heron Fleet has stopped developing and growing. That makes it vulnerable. It is possible the weather is getting more stable. "Good," says comfortable old Heron Fleet, "I can take it easy, when really it may be just the time to make more communities like Heron Fleet and for Heron Fleet to increase its size. Even if the weather isn't getting more stable and the cold that brought the Founders here comes again, only the communities that have some of knowledge the City builders used will stand any chance of surviving.'

They had got to the boat and Tobias led them on board.

'How are the repairs going?' Francesca said to him.

'We still need to raise the new mast as you can see. We found some damage to the steering gear we didn't know was there, which is a complication, and some damage below the waterline isn't completely repaired. We've done what we can from inside the hull and it's watertight, but to finish it off properly she'll have to come out of the water in the spring. Peter will have the pleasure of my company until Mayday at least.'

They followed him down the cabin steps. It was twilight and below deck it was almost pitch-dark.

'Hold on,' he said. They heard him rummaging about. 'Got it.' There was a click and a beam of blue-tinged light illuminated the bottom of the steps.'

'What on earth is that?' exclaimed Jonathan.

'Oh, sorry, I take it for granted. This is an electric torch.' Tobias weighed it in his hand with pride and pleasure. Then he tossed it to Francesca. 'Imagine what a whole set of big versions of those would do for the work in your beloved Glasshouses,' he said to her. 'How much more might you do in the growing season? How much extra might you grow? Perhaps you could make ones that helped plants grow in the dark parts of the year.' Francesca passed the torch to Anya. 'Imagine a whole row of big versions of those set in the roof of the Gathering Hall so people could work with more than the light from the fire and a few burning torches in the winter.'

They passed the electric torch around. After a few minutes it started to get faint. Tobias wound it up so that the light recovered.

'You might even use the river to generate the electricity from some sort of water-powered winder. Surprising what a good idea might do?'

There was a voice from the deck. It was Thomas. 'I've got the food and the tagines are going cold. So if you want it hot you better show yourselves.'

It didn't take long to set the food out on the cover of the deck and start on the meal. By the time Peter arrived an hour or so later they had eaten well and Tobias had passed round the *aquavite* at least twice. Their spirits were high and they were in the process of persuading Francesca to sing or at least recite one of her poems. But Peter didn't seem to look kindly on what he found. He surveyed the scene with evident distaste.

'Come on, Peter, sit down,' said Tobias, offering him a glass. 'You never objected in the past.'

'I don't think I will,' Peter replied. 'It won't take me long to deliver my message. I will not allow the three books you quoted this afternoon to be admitted as evidence. This Testing is not an excuse for a challenge to the validity of the Rule. Rather the accusation must be judged only in the context of the Rule and against the code that has kept this community safe for generations. Anya and Jonathan acted in the knowledge of the Rule. It seems only just and fair that they are tested in the context of what they defied.'

Tobias stood up. 'And that is your final word?' he said.

'Yes, that is my final word. The community as a whole will hear it tomorrow when we resume.'

'So any arguments that are to be put for the Council to consider before pronouncing punishment must be put in the context of what is in the Rule and only what is in the Rule?'

'I think that is what I said. Though I suppose more precisely I mean all those parts of the Red Book that govern how Heron Fleet behaves.'

Peter began to go, but just before he stepped down onto the jetty he turned. 'Tobias, I've used one more of my rights under the Rule this evening. Because of the excitable feelings that your final statement this afternoon created, I have imposed an evening curfew. Thomas and Francesca, you should be getting your charges back to their quarters. Goodnight.' He stepped on to the jetty and disappeared into the darkness.

★ ★ ★ ★

The Gathering Hall was even more crowded than the day before. Francesca thought that it was unlikely there were any Gatherers anywhere else. She even spotted the Crèche Nurses sitting discreetly at one side. It was unheard of that they should attend an open community meeting. The Council filed in and after calling for order Peter addressed them.

'There are just two things I want to say to everyone. The arguments raised at the end of yesterday's proceedings led to fierce disagreement between members of the community, which made it impossible to conclude this Testing in a single day.

'Friends, however we feel about what is said, it is the Gatherer way to hear all arguments with quiet respect. I hope there will be no more outbursts such as those of yesterday. I must warn you that I have arranged with the Gatekeepers that, if I order it, they will eject any members who cannot discipline themselves.

'The second thing is to announce my decision not to accept the books that Tobias quoted yesterday as evidence.' Despite his previous warning, there was a buzz of talking around the Hall. He paused to see if the noise would develop into anything more but it died away and he went on. 'Tobias, you may continue.'

Tobias stood up. 'I thank the Head of the Council and I call him to answer questions.'

This time there was a gasp from the onlookers. Peter pushed back his chair and stood up, raising his hand in a gesture of quiet. 'This is in order, as Speaker, Tobias has the right to ask any Gatherer to answer questions.' He made his way round to the other side of the Table and sat on the witness stool.

Tobias approached him. 'Last night, when we were discussing the matter of including the books in evidence…'

Peter cut in, 'I hope that does not mean you intend to challenge my decision.'

'No, I just want it to be clear. I will not challenge it but I want you to confirm what you said to me then.'

'I said that arguments would have to be put in the context of what is in the Rule and only what is in the Rule.'

'You also gave me a definition of what that meant.'

'I said it meant all those parts of the Red Book that govern Heron Fleet.'

'Could I sum up your attitude as being that the Rule is perfect and could not possibly need changing?'

'I would not say perfect but I am certain that it is all that we need here in Heron Fleet.'

'On what do you base that belief?'

'On the fact we are here and have survived. That we have prospered for many generations in the face of uncertain weather.'

'But the Rule cannot control the weather?'

'No, but it has given us a successful way of dealing with the dangers we face. It has enabled us to prosper because it has cemented the relationships of the community and enabled us to work as one. What you suggested yesterday would give every member of the community the right to choose their own way irrespective of the effect those choices would have on what the community needs to do to survive.'

'Can you give us an example?'

'Well take the jobs within the community that are given to Apprentices when they become Gatherers. Sometimes the desire of the individual coincides with the need of the community, as in Francesca's case, but that cannot be true for everyone. Someone has to do the jobs few people would choose. The discipline of the Rule allows that balance to be maintained. It also allows those who are not chosen for the role they want, to take comfort in the fact that others are in the same situation. That makes people feel better.'

'A fellowship of misery?'

'A fellowship in which none starve and in which all are valued for their work.'

'Yesterday, Francesca told us all that she felt that loving Anya came from within herself and not something that she had been taught by the community. Don't feelings like that make people individuals, whereas your view of the ideal Gatherer denies people meaning except as members of the community?'

Peter looked sadly at Tobias. 'Years ago I loved someone the way Francesca loves Anya but I found out that feelings betray, whereas being a member of the community is always reliable.'

'So all the people are to be denied their individuality, because a few get hurt in the process of sorting out the conflicts of freedom?'

Peter was clearly angered. 'No! It's not just that. Think what it would be like in a community where everyone chose what they wanted to do so one year we had too many Fishers and not enough Gardeners. The Head Fisher would take the best for the jobs that needed to be done, the rest would have to become Gardeners anyway. So people might not find roles at all and would have to leave the community. It's doubtful if the community could afford to feed someone who didn't contribute to the communal effort. Either way they would know they had failed and feel rejected. There is a fellowship of misery if you want one, and one that would not be redeemed by any sense of doing your duty to a community, which is your family.'

'And the rule on single-sex partnerships, where does that fit in?'

'It's a part of the Rule. You can't agree to some bits of the Rule and ditch others.'

'But it's not part of the Rule at all, is it?'

Peter looked cautiously at Tobias. 'What do you mean?'

'Well, it's not part of the Rule. It's actually a separate document in the Red Book, as you and I know. It's even celebrated as such in the ceremonial songs of the community. It's the Pact that made single-sex partnerships the norm in Heron Fleet, not the Rule. That's the truth, isn't it?'

Peter hesitated. 'Yes, it is, but we have always treated it as part of the Rule.'

'Always? How can you know that? I remember that when you and I borrowed the Red Book when we were Apprentices and read it from cover to cover, the Rule follows the Pact. Isn't that right?'

Peter said nothing in reply, so Tobias continued. 'If you open the cover of that book which sits there now in front of your central place on the Council Table, isn't it true that the first thing in it is not the Rule but the Pact?'

'Yes, it is. Which must mean, that when the Founders wrote the Rule, they included the Pact.'

'Does the Rule say that?'

'Explain.'

'Does it say something like. "We the Founders recognise the Pact as the part of the Rule"?'

'No.'

'Something like, "The Pact is the foundation of all that will keep us safe in Heron Fleet"?'

'No.'

As Tobias had been questioning Peter he had been moving slowly backwards and forwards between the Head of Council and his table. He was now close to Peter. It crossed Francesca's mind that their debate was now more like a personal conversation which she and the rest of the community were overhearing.

'Is it your view that the Rule, which includes the Pact, is the perfect, complete and only source of authority by which to govern Heron Fleet?'

'Yes.'

'Then how did the Crèche Nurses get the power to spy on every woman in the community? What in the Rule gives them the right to keep a secret record of what they find?'

'They don't,' said Peter.

'Head of Council, you know they do. Francesca has seen that book. I suspect a number of women Gatherers here now have also seen it. So don't lie to us. It's beneath you, as well as being against the Rule. Tell us what in the Rule gives those women...' he pointed directly at them so everyone could see the growing anger on the Head Crèche Nurse's face. '...power. How can any Crèche Nurse say to even the most junior Gatherer of the community that her *power* exceeds that of you as Head of the Council because she is charged with protecting the community from generation to generation whereas it is only given to you to get the Harvest in from year to year?' Tobias picked up the Red Book from the Council Table and gave it to Peter. 'Show us where they,' he stabbed his finger at the Crèche Nurses again, 'were given such powers.'

'It was necessary. It wasn't possible to control the birth rate without someone who controlled the gift of pregnancy.'

'So they were introduced outside the Rule.'

'No, they were an outcome of the Rule.'

'But they were something that the Founders didn't anticipate?'

'No!' Peter was getting desperate.

'How do you know that the Crèche Nurses became necessary to the functioning of Heron Fleet? There can only be one source of how things happened as Heron Fleet developed. You have it in your hands. You and I have read that book and though there's lots of interesting information in it, it doesn't mention the Crèche Nurses at all.' Peter was squirming like a fish on a hook. 'If they are not sanctioned by the only book Heron Fleet officially owns, how do you know they were necessary?'

'It's a tradition passed down from Head of Council to Head of Council!'

'But you found your own faith on the rightness of the Rule on the fact that it has always maintained Heron Fleet and kept it alive. That requires precision of knowledge. No set of traditions would be enough for you.'

'But that is the truth of it,' said Peter. 'I rely only on the Red Book.'

'Do you remember, at the beginning of this Testing you said, according to the history of Heron Fleet, there has not been an accusation of this nature in the community in over a generation. Where did you find the history of Heron Fleet to confirm that?'

'It's just the oral traditions!'

'But it's so precise, coming from someone who is normally so precise. Head of Council, may I remind you that all Gatherers must speak the truth at a Testing according to the provisions of the Rule. I will ask you clearly. Is there a hidden written history of Heron Fleet beyond the Red Book?'

'No,' said Peter.

'Remember, the Rule you serve requires truth from all Gatherers. I ask again, is there a written hidden history of Heron Fleet beyond the Red Book?

'No,' insisted Peter, but everyone could see the struggle on his face.

Tobias put his hand gently on the shoulder of his former lover. 'Peter in the name of all we once were to each other, do not betray your true self. Where is the history?'

Peter was cornered. He looked across the Hall to the Crèche Nurses but led by their Head, they all stood up and left. Finally, he spoke. 'It is called the Founder's Diary. It is in safe-keeping in my longhouse in the same place I keep the Red Book.'

'And does this Founder's Diary record why the Pact was made?'

'Yes, it does.'

'So we can see what the Founders intended the Pact to mean and judge for ourselves whether they thought it should be part of the Rule or is still relevant to Heron Fleet as it is today?'

Peter swallowed hard. 'Yes.'

'Then is it not time that the people of Heron Fleet heard what the Founders intended?'

'Yes,' Peter whispered.

The Founder's Diary VIII

I have lost track of date, day, in fact of time itself...

The cold and the snow have returned. We are down on the plain but I do not know how we got here. I have no memory of detail, not even of how she was buried. The temperature is falling again and the sky is full of snow.

...

We are in the middle of another blizzard. Charlie and Miriam are taking care of me. I think they are fearful I will give up hope and die. But I will not die while Charlie lives, though I wish to die; I wish to not have to bear any of the world's sadness anymore.

...

There is only one lorry now. The blizzard wrecked the other one. What cannot go on the one that is left we have to haul behind us on improvised sledges. It is minus fourteen degrees. James has spoken with me. I have promised him I will go on.

...

Today I saw one of the children fall. I went over to her but it was not Alison. I left her in the snow. She was dead. When I look out from the secret places behind my eyes I see we are all in hell. We all left her in the snow. We no longer have the energy to bury our dead.

...

I wake up in the tent with Miriam. The wind flaps the sides and there is a hissing of ice crystals across the material. Charlie sees I am awake, he hugs me and starts to cry. He wakes Miriam. I have been asleep for two days. They feed me and tell me that there are only two children left now: Charlie and one other whose name I once knew but now means nothing to me.

...

I saw Naomi die today. Her speech seems to me to have been

slow recently, though I do not remember how I know. She collapsed in front of me. I went to her and pulled her up on her feet. She thanked me and took a few more steps. She had no gloves and her hands were frostbitten. I hold her hands. They are ice cold and feel waxy. She takes another step and falls on her back. She has a wild look in her eyes. I wake up in the tent again. Miriam tells me Naomi is dead when I ask.

...

Where is the lorry? All I can see are the others. I try to count them. I only get to twenty-three. Charlie helps me over the soft top snow. There are ridges in the snow. Grooves as if some great sledge like the one I pull has been drawn across this landscape. The ruts are dusted with drifting ice crystals. It reminds me of sand on a beach and I start to laugh. But it is the wind and the snow that have carved these lines. It goes dark again.

...

Miriam shakes me awake. I must come and see. She drags me away from the dead tree I am propped up against. I stumble over the snow and ice. My feet are sore and swollen. I do not think I will live long. We stop at the edge of a small bank. 'There,' she says. 'We are here.' I look out. There is a flat part of stony something. There are rocks with blue ice on their tops and further out waves breaking on more ice. But the wind is warmer. It does not bite at my face. I pull down my scarf and laugh. Charlie is next to me. 'It's the sea,' I say to him. 'We are at the sea.'

'Yes mum,' he says. He hugs and kisses me.

Day 180

I know the date again. The nightmare has gone, leaving only the sadness. It is twenty-eight days since Alison died, and we are at the sea. As James thought, it is warmer, at least in the part we have found. We have made camp in a cave above a river. The wind here is less and the ice is kept out of the river mouth where it meets the sea by a broad shingle bar. Behind us is old woodland. But this is not dead like much of the forest we went through when we left the city. Here the trees are damaged but still alive. Even better there are a few sheep and goats taking shelter in the wood and the soil is not frozen. We are surviving on roots we can find and we have killed one or two of the weaker goats for food. A heron flew over us today. James believes that this means there are fish in the river. He is taking Charlie with him tomorrow to see if he can catch any.

Day 181

There are fish in the river. James and Charlie are making a fish trap to place in the channel where the water comes into the river at high tide. They will put it in the river at low tide. They've seen the heron fishing there.

Day 182

James and Charlie brought back twenty fish from the river yesterday afternoon. We toasted them over the fire in the cave. They say they are going back tomorrow. Dare I hope we can survive here? That Charlie will have a future?

Day 189

The last calamity: James and Charlie are dead. They went out as they have done for the last week to catch fish but they did not come back. We searched for them. We found James's body upstream, trapped in some dead reeds. Charlie's body was a bit further on. They must have fallen in while fishing. The water is so cold they would not have survived long.

Day 190

There will be no more grief, no more attachment of mothers and fathers to children. We have lost so many. We have lost them all; all the bright ones who would have carried on our ideals. There must be others to carry on the community we will build here but they will not know their parents and we shall not acknowledge them. We will breed as we will breed our sheep, making the best of all the variety we have by insemination. We will not risk having attachments through natural affection so we will only live and love those of the same sex. This is our bargain. This is our pact and we will write it down. This we swear and sign to, for as long as it is necessary, for the good of all.

Chapter 15

Francesca sat on the end of the jetty. She looked into the clear water of the river as it flowed beneath her feet on the incoming tide. Occasionally, she would see a medium-sized fish swim past as it came into the river. They were the sort of fish that liked the boundary between the salt and fresh water; they would return to the sea on the ebb.

The Pact was born out of grief, not principle or argument; born out of the sorrow of the few who survived. It was never meant to be permanent in the way Heron Fleet had made it. The Founders agreed to it because they could not bear any more sorrow. Its validity was as the final words of the diary said: 'as long as it is necessary for the good of all'.

'Penny for them?' It was Tobias. He sat down next to her.

'Pardon?'

'It's an old saying – a penny for your thoughts. I think it has something to do with money in the cities but I've never really worked how money worked. I can only get as far as thinking of it as some sort of bartering. Though whatever a penny was it must have been very valuable because what can be worth more than a person's thoughts?'

'I was just thinking about why the Founders wrote the Pact.'

'They had a terrible journey.'

'What do you think they would tell us to do if they were here now? If they could see what division it was creating in the community?'

There was a noise from behind them. Someone had yelled something and there were raised voices. Tobias turned round and gasped. As Francesca turned she saw Anya, Jonathan and Thomas running towards them down the slope. There was a group of about twelve shouting and screaming people, chasing them. She and Tobias got to their feet. They saw Thomas slow and then stop. He waved Anya and Jonathan to go on while he turned to face the crowd. Seeing Thomas, his hands outstretched in a calming gesture, they stopped. It gave enough time for Anya and Jonathan to reach the jetty. For a moment it seemed that whatever Thomas was saying to them was having an effect but then a burly Gatherer with a staff stepped forward. Francesca recognised him as the one who had heckled Tobias during the Testing. In horror she watched as he raised his staff and struck Thomas across the face, knocking him down to the ground. The crowd ran on towards them.

'Thomas!' screamed Anya and started to run back to help him.

'Stop her Jonathan.' It was Tobias. 'Better to make a stand here where we can retreat to the boat or swim, than fight on their ground.'

Jonathan grabbed Anya, who turned on him and boxed his ears. But he persisted, swallowed her in a bear hug and held her tight no matter how hard she struggled.

Tobias pushed Francesca forward. 'Move down the jetty, you two,' he shouted at Jonathan and Anya as he ran past them. 'Get on board. It's the safest place. Francesca, guard the gang-plank while I get some things from below.'

The crowd were nearly on the jetty. Francesca ran past Jonathan struggling with Anya to get her on to the boat and stopped in front of the crowd, who had not yet set foot on the jetty. The crowd edged forward. Again the burly Gatherer, a herder Francesca thought, stepped forward.

'We don't want to do you any harm missy.' His words seemed sincere but the way his big hands held his staff suggested something very different.

'If you don't mean me any harm then you best turn round and go away.'

'All we want is to get rid once and for all of that Outlander scum and the shame those two whores have brought to Heron Fleet.'

'I don't believe the Council have said what they will do yet. Are you saying you know better than the Council?'

'If need be.' He shifted his weight and moved the grip on the staff to a position from which he could strike at her.

'You great big bully!' It was Anya from behind her. 'You great flabby oaf.' A staff came flying though the air and landed at Francesca's feet. 'Go while you can, before my Francesca breaks your head.'

'I'll not take that from a wench who's with rough child.' The man started to move. He was only three paces from Francesca but was not that quick in the sprint. She had just enough time to pick up the thrown staff and whack him a sharp blow on the back of the head as she dodged left. He tripped and sprawled face-down on the planks, loosing his grip on his stave. Francesca kicked it into the river, put her foot in the small of his back and the tip of her own staff over his shoulder in his face.

'That's enough.' It was Tobias. 'Most of you know what I've got in my hands.' Francesca glanced up, he had a crossbow to his shoulder and there was a bolt in place. 'The first one of you that takes a step forward I will shoot. I'm a good shot and that person will die on the spot.'

The crowd hesitated. 'It won't stop there, I've armed both Jonathan and Anya. Just remember how fiercely a mother will fight for her unborn child. You face them if you can get past me and Francesca, and that, I think, is a very big if.'

He was next to her now. As he had been speaking he must have worked his way round onto the jetty from the boat. With the crossbow in their faces the crowd looked far more uncertain. One or two at the back turned and sloped off.

'That's it, nice and slowly, just back off,' Tobias took a step forward. Francesca turned to face them as well, brandishing her staff while at the same time putting more pressure onto the herder's back in case he decided to try to move.

The crowd looked down at their feet and backed away. Francesca poked the herder sharply in the back. 'Your friends have gone. Get up slowly and you can join them.' She stepped back and he got heavily to his feet. He rubbed the back of his head with his hand. Francesca saw, with some satisfaction, that there was blood on his hand from the blow she had given him.

All that remained was to help Thomas. When they were certain the crowd had really dispersed, Francesca and Jonathan went to get him. He had been knocked out but by the time they got to him he was coming round. He was a bit bruised and stiff but easy enough to help back to the boat, where Francesca bandaged his forehead.

★ ★ ★ ★

They did not report the attempted attack to the Council, agreeing that to do so might make it even more difficult for tempers to cool in the community. While no one had definitely said that the Testing had finished, not even Peter, it was impossible to think how it could go any further without inflaming more ill feeling or further polarising opinion after the reading of the Founder's Diary. Everyone simply waited for the Council to decide on what had been established. In turn the Council waited for Peter to be in a fit state of mind to continue. The official line was that he was sick but Francesca thought *gone to ground* would have been a better description. In the meantime Sylvia presided at the evening meal, which was eaten in a subdued and watchful mood for the next week.

The only other change was that the weather started to break in earnest. The wind backed and started to blow steadily from the northwest. The weather turned colder and wetter, and after three preliminary thundery squalls, a fully fledged winter storm blew in with driving snow and hail.

The change in weather brought a change at the Council Table: Peter reappeared at evening meal. Though Sylvia still presided, he was back and everyone was waiting for what would happen next.

Two days later the Council met. That evening the mood was the tensest it had been. When the Council filed in, Peter resumed the Head of Council's seat. When it came time to offer the evening incantation he stood up but did not take up the hardbread.

'He looks awfully strained,' said Caleb in Francesca's ear as the Hall became quiet. Francesca held her breath. Without thinking she reached out for the hand of Anya who was standing next to her.

'Fellow Gatherers,' said Peter. His voice trembled. 'Friends.'

Francesca looked over at Tobias. Gone was his normal air of truculence. His whole attention was on Peter. For the first time Francesca saw on Tobias's face the expression of the caring lover he must have once been to Peter.

'Friends. I do not know how each of you feels about what happened in the Testing and what has been revealed about our life here at Heron Fleet. I can only speak for myself and say that for me nothing can ever be quite the same again. I still believe in the Rule as the best guide to how the community should behave but there will have to be much re-examination of whether that is still true for the majority of us. As a result I have decided that I am not the right person to guide the community through that process. I will be standing down as Head of the Council from the end of this evening's meal. The Council have elected Sylvia to take my place for the rest of the year until a new Head of the Council can be elected at Harvest.'

'Wow,' said Jeremy. 'Has a Head of the Council ever stood down before?'

'I don't think so,' replied Christine.

'Other than to bless the hardbread one last time, I have only one thing left to do. For the sake of the whole of the community and the sake of the individuals involved in the Testing a decision must be given. Would Anya and Jonathan please stand forward.'

Anya let go of Francesca's hand and stepped forward, followed by Jonathan. Francesca went round the table and stood with Tobias. He put his arm round her shoulders and she put hers round his waist. There were tears in his eyes. She could see Thomas a little way down the table from Peter. His face was stern but he did not look troubled. A good sign perhaps, she thought. Standing next to Peter was Sylvia. Her expression was resolute and unreadable. Whatever was to come was not quite to Francesca's mentor's mind.

'Anya and Jonathan. You have admitted that you have acted in contravention of the Pact and hence the Rule. If you are to remain in the community after admitting as much you would have to relinquish each other. Will you do that?'

Anya and Jonathan looked at each other, then Anya spoke. 'No. We love each other and will not be parted.'

'We had expected as much,' said Peter. 'Some of us would have thought less of you had you said yes. As a result the Council has no choice but to have you declared outcast.'

'No,' cried Jeremy. 'Caleb, say something.' His voice was joined by several other cries of *no* and other groans from across the hall.

Peter lifted his hands. 'Friends, please hear the whole of the decision.' The hall went quiet again. 'Bearing in mind Anya's condition the Council will not carry out this punishment until Mayday so that your journey will be as safe as it can be for the child you will have with you.'

'What did he say?' said Susan.

'He's throwing them out into the world with a child,' said Jeremy in high dudgeon. 'Shame on him.'

'No, you don't get it, Jeremy. If the child is going with them then the Council aren't claiming the child. Anya will keep the baby!'

'The Council have taken into account what is now public about the circumstances of how the Pact was made. They have decided that in the light of story of the Diary, that the Founders may not have intended the Pact to separate a child from its mother under the circumstances of this case. Anya and Jonathan, you will keep your child.' People started to clap in a wave of noisy approval. Peter went to pick up the hardbread but he was prevented from starting the incantation once more. Standing in front of him was Tobias.

'May I say something, Peter?'

'I think you're a pretty difficult man to shut up at the best of times.'

'Thank you. I see within this judgement a moderation that is fair and I thank you and the Council for it. I will match that moderation with an offer of my own if I may. I have thought for some time that more communities like Heron Fleet should be established to complement the others that I trade with. I cannot sail until Mayday myself, the day Anya and Jonathan will be declared outcast. They are welcome, with their child, to come with me on that day to found a new community. Any who wish to come with us will be welcome.'

Chapter 16

The winter's wind whistled in the thatch of the Gathering Hall and the main wooden members of the roof creaked, making drifts of dust and some snowflakes tumble into the body of the Hall. Winter had laid its hands on Heron Fleet and it would not loosening its grip until near to Mayday. The ground outside was hard with frost and slippery with ice. The morning's wash was a chilly affair and clothes were put on as quickly as possible. The dash to the warmth of the Gathering Hall for breakfast was treacherous and the Infirmary was busy treating a long line of sprained ankles and bruised hips, elbows or knees.

Francesca was doing her duty as part of the skeleton crew of Gardeners looking after the Glasshouses. There were a few herbs to be taken for the kitchen and fresh winter greens in the upper houses to be harvested but in general the plants were gathering their strength for the warmth and light to come. So for only two days a week was she Francesca the Gardener, the rest of her time she was carding, weaving or sewing, around the great fire in the Gathering Hall with everyone else.

She looked up from the summer shift she was assembling from the cut and shaped pieces of wool-cloth she had been given that morning and considered the Hall. It was quiet. People had fallen into a rhythm of work that might have been called placid, even drowsy. There was some weaving going on and its clackerty-clack set something of a musical rhythm that might, on other occasions, have imposed a more urgent pace to the work or roused a shanty or reaping song in the Hall. But not this morning. Only in a circle of tables between her and the west window was there any sign of animation. That was the workgroup that included Tobias, and he was telling them stories from his days as a Trader, as he had done practically every day since ice on the river had prevented him doing any more work on his boat and he had shut her up to endure the winter without him.

At the beginning of the winter, Francesca had enjoyed being a part of his circle but after a while she had withdrawn. His stories were always entertaining but she felt she needed some sort of peace and quiet in which to think her own thoughts. Sewing in her own corner, mostly on her own, gave her that space.

She was also beginning to understand his technique, to anticipate just when in a story he would raise the tempo of the words or drop his voice or employ another of his tricks to heighten the drama and effect. While she admired his storytelling skills, they did not help her in the choice she had to make. She did not wish to be swayed by emotion or charmed by his rhetoric. She wanted to work out coolly within herself whether she would stay at Heron Fleet or go with him when Mayday came.

'Very eloquent isn't he?' A tall figure lowered herself painfully on to the bench opposite and propped up a beautiful ash staff against the table. 'He always was very plausible.'

'You make it sound like that's all you think he is ma'am.'

'I don't think he's all wind and no weather as the Fishers say. On the whole he accomplishes what he sets out to do and what he attempts is driven by principle.'

'But what?'

'But he gets carried away. That's what happened when he took Lucia for his mate. He didn't just live with her and the child, he wanted the community to admit he was right and they were wrong.'

'So you think this new community of his will fail?'

'Certainly not. He is right about the improvement in the weather. I've thought for a little while the good weather we've had in the past few years might be permanent. I've seen signs of it in our harvests. Plants and trees that only gave fruit once in five years now give regular crops. Also they are putting on growth that is meant for use several years hence. The trees know and are reacting. Besides, what all the upheaval of the Testing proved was that Heron Fleet has been backward-looking for too long. A bit of transplantation may well be no bad thing. A sister community that does things differently to us but comes from our stock may be just what we need to get us out of our rut. I think he will succeed but where that will leave those he leaves behind here, that is the question I have to answer. As Head of the Council, they are my care until my old bones can't manage it anymore.'

'I'm thinking about going with him.'

'I understand that. If I were your age I'd think very hard about it as well. But Mayday is a fair way off yet. You've no need rush the decision, as if you will. Francesca the level-headed is what they call you behind your back. But have you thought about how you might feel working alongside Anya and Jonathan when he is her partner and not you?'

Someone got up from the group and came over. It was Tobias. He sat down beside Sylvia.

'Are you working on Francesca to get her to stay here?' he teased.

'No she wasn't,' Francesca interjected. While Tobias had been appreciative of what Sylvia had done, the tension between them about her part in hiding his daughter was always there in the background. Francesca hated hearing them spar over issues that were no more than surrogates for his central bone of contention. She loved and respected them equally. Sometimes she felt that the choice she would have to make was really a choice between the two of them as much as between the promise of a new community and her loyalty to Heron Fleet.

'I presume if you were prepared to forgo the pleasure of showing off to the Apprentices that you want to talk to me,' said Sylvia.

Tobias started to frame a witticism in reply but saw the expression on Francesca's face and thought better of it.

'Perceptive as ever Sylvia. I wondered if you'd let me teach any who wanted to read and write?'

'I don't object in principle,' Sylvia replied. 'But are you sure that it won't stir up ill feeling again?'

'I haven't had anyone say anything derogatory to me for, ooh, two days at least,' he replied. Sylvia glared at him. 'Two weeks really. More importantly there's nothing bad been said to either Anya or Jonathan for ages.'

The western door opened and as if on queue Anya came in out of the snow accompanied by Elizabeth. One of those who had barracked Tobias at the Testing was on his way out. Francesca watched as he stopped and spoke to Anya, who smiled. Even the most violent of opponents of Anya and Jonathan had been mellowed by having an expectant mother walking round the community instead of being hidden away by the Crèche Nurses. Many had become well-wishers to Anya's unborn child and then its mother, eager for nothing to go wrong for the baby.

'I'd like to see anyone dare say anything bad to Anya and live while her watchdog is around,' commented Sylvia, nodding towards Elizabeth. 'What do you think, Francesca? How would you advise I respond to this Gatherer's request?'

Francesca was taken unawares. She blushed, realising that she was being asked for advice by the Head of the Council in much the same way that Sylvia might have asked another Member of the Council, even though it seemed like a casual chat between friends.

She had her own reasons for hoping Sylvia would say yes. She wanted to learn to read and write and if Sylvia gave her permission she would be Tobias's first pupil like a shot. Things were much calmer than they had been after the Testing. But it might well be seen as a step too far by some of the staunch traditionalists. Reactions might be bad.

'I'd allow Tobias to teach just one or two people, discreetly but not in secret, to see how it went. If there's no reaction then he should be allowed to increase the group gradually, ma'am.'

'Well that's a bit...' Francesca just knew Tobias was going to say *timid* and frowned at him along with Sylvia who, it seemed, had had the same thought. As a result Tobias saw both women frowning at him and changed his mind. '...But I suppose it's a sensible move.'

'Do you have anyone in mind as a start?' asked Sylvia.

'Well, Caleb and Jeremy would like to learn and then there's...' again he paused. 'I wondered if Francesca would be allowed?'

'Yes I think so,' said Sylvia after apparently thinking carefully about it. 'A Gardener who could read and write might be very handy at keeping records from year to year as well as picking up some new tips from any books on gardening you might have or come across in your travels. I think Francesca should join your class.'

★ ★ ★ ★

The classes went well. They started work with Tobias for an hour each evening before the community meal. That way they could not be accused of shirking work but everyone who came into the Hall early were sure to see what was happening so the word would get round gradually. They started and waited for any bad comments but none came. The biggest reaction was mild curiosity from a few who came and looked on some evenings; perhaps wondering if it might be for them.

It only took them a few days to learn the sounds of the letters and then another few days to be able to write them reasonably clearly. Rather than waste precious paper from the store he had on the boat, Tobias used some seed trays from the Glasshouses and part-filled them with sand normally used for potting-on seedlings. Then his pupils could write the letters in the sand with their fingers and when all the space was taken up with their attempts the tray could be shaken and reused.

Three weeks after Tobias's class started, Thomas stood up at the end of the evening meal and announced that he would take on three students who might have acquired the basics of reading and would like to improve. From then on there were two classes each evening: Tobias's beginners and Thomas's improvers.

Then one night it looked as if all the arrangement was about to come to an abrupt end. Francesca was the first to spot him. People were starting to come into the hall for the evening meal when he lumbered in from the eastern door. It was the Herder whom Francesca had knocked down on the jetty. Whilst he had been apparently friendly, since he was headed determinedly in their direction and he didn't look friendly at all. She nudged

Tobias and he stood up. The herder stood in front of them. Francesca looked at his size and bulk and wondered how on earth she had had the courage, let alone the strength, to knock this big fellow down.

'What can we do for you friend?' said Tobias. The Herder swayed slightly backwards and forwards but didn't reply. From out of the corner of her eye Francesca saw Enoch the Head Blacksmith ease his way through the small crowd at the door that was watching what was going to happen. To Francesca's relief, he sat down quietly about three tables back and watched.

'What can we do for you friend?' Tobias asked again.

'Well it like this master Outlander,' the Herder's voice trembled. 'I wondered...' His voice faded away.

'Yes,' said Tobias in an encouraging tone. 'You're among friends here; if you need help then we'll do what we can.'

'Well master, I wondered if you could teach me to count and do my sums.' There was an audible release of breath which confused the man. 'You see I have a really bad memory and I'm always getting the number of the sheep wrong. Jem told me that you might be able to teach me how to make notes like and count them up so I'd be able to do me job better. If I've got the word wrong I'm sorry, it was Jem who called them sums.'

It took a bit of organising but in the end Simon, solved the problem of providing a basic arithmetic class. Francesca wondered if Sylvia had nudged him into it but Simon never gave any indication that he was anything less than delighted to do the job. The Herder started a few days after his request and was rapidly joined by several others, all of whom had realised they could do their jobs better if they could count and do their sums on paper or even on a piece of bark stuck to the side of a sheep-pen.

Gradually the classes became part of the pattern of winter life. People joined and stayed, some took what they wanted and moved on, to be replaced by new students. Some, notably Jeremy, Caleb and Francesca, developed enough competency and love of reading that Tobias lent them books to read outside the class, using any suitable time in the class or out of it to help with passages they found difficult.

One evening Tobias's three star pupils were sitting near the fire, well after evening meal, going through a passage from Jeremy's book. He was getting impatient with what he was reading; impatience which had become frustration.

'Oh tear it!' he said. 'What are these people doing? I just don't get what is going on in their heads! How can anyone behave like they are? If they love each other why don't they declare their partnership? Where are the rules that tell them how to behave?'

'I think I understand it,' said Caleb. Their Rule about how they have to behave is not written down. It's not like our Rule, it's contained in how they behave towards each other. If they are impolite then they suffer the disapproval of the other members of their community. That's their Rule.'

'Fine,' said Jeremy, tossing the argument back at his partner. 'But it's so wasteful of time and words and...' his impatience blew up. 'Oh just everything. Haven't they got anything better to do, like gathering and planting?'

'No as far as I've ever been able to work out they haven't,' said Tobias.

'So this story isn't just made up?' said Francesca. 'Elizabeth Elliott really existed? People in the cities really lived as the book says?'

'I think someone made up the story. But the world it describes that was once real.'

'So they had music and sang songs just as we do?' asked Francesca.

'Yes,' replied Tobias.

'So what were their songs like?'

'Can't we get back to the book?' pleaded Jeremy.

'Yes,' said Francesca. 'But only if Tobias promises to show me what their songs were like.'

'Deal,' said Tobias. 'Now, can we get on?'

Several nights later Tobias placed a green book in front of Francesca at the evening meal. The book had golden letters embossed into its leather covers. Slowly she read the title on the spine; *Bloomfield's Poetical Works*. She looked up at him.

'They're the nearest thing I have to songs, they're poems and they called them ballads which is another word for songs.'

'Thank you,' she said, tears in her eyes. She stood up, embraced him and kissed him on the cheek. 'Thank you.'

★ ★ ★ ★

Through the next few weeks she was never without the green book. Every minute she could spare she read it. She struggled with the some of words, often having to check their meanings with Tobias but even before she could understand the words, very often she could understand what a poem was about through its pace and swing. Pretty soon she had learned several of them by heart and had started to compose tunes to make them into songs of her own.

One evening an informal choir was formed. As usual Francesca was asked to sing, which she did. Towards the end of the songs she offered to sing one she had made from the poems in the book. It was about a ghost in a wood that terrifies a woman walking home but turns out to be nothing but a stray donkey. She had devised an accompaniment on the lute that included the sounds of the donkey's bray and the whole song was very funny, unlike so many of the rather wistful and formal songs of the community.

'Excellent,' said Tobias after she had finished an encore for everyone. 'I never thought you would put that collection to work so quickly. Keep the book. I think she would have approved of having it passed on to you.'

'Whose book was it?' asked Francesca.

'It was The Lady's book. She was the woman who died when I marooned the Scavenger Gang and escaped here, the night you saved my life. She reminded me of Lucia. That's why I fell in love with her.'

'Thank you. I'll always treasure it. What was she like, this Lady?'

'Sad and lonely. It was her favourite book. I found it hidden away on the boat when I was working on it. She must have left it there so I would find it. Perhaps she knew she was going to die. Who knows? Make happy songs out of it like the one you just sang, rather than remember the sad story of how it got here.'

'Do you have a favourite poem from it I could make into a song to say thank you?' said Francesca.

'Not from that book, no.'

'From another?'

'I have a favourite poem I used to share with another, yes.' He reached into a pocket in his jacket and pulled out a small book, nowhere near as grand as The Lady's.

'Would you read it to me?' said Francesca. She sat down on the bench and he sat next to next to her. The Hall was almost completely empty. The fire was dying down and the Gatekeepers were extinguishing the torches. Their last job would be to bank up the fire for the night so that it did not go out.

The poem was written on a piece of stained, folded paper, kept in the small book. As he opened it to take out the paper, a lock of fair hair dropped out on to the table. Francesca picked it up and without thinking rolled it between her finger and her thumb feeling its fine texture and then held it to her nose; its smell was comforting. He unfolded the paper and started to read.

Let not my love be called idolatry,
Nor my beloved as an idol show,
Since all alike my songs and praises be
To one, of one, still such, and ever so.
Kind is my love to-day, to-morrow kind,
Still constant in a wondrous excellence;
Therefore my verse to constancy confined,
One thing expressing, leaves out difference.
Fair, kind, and true, is all my argument,
Fair, kind, and true, varying to other words;
And in this change is my invention spent,
Three themes in one, which wondrous scope affords.
Fair, kind, and true, have often lived alone,
Which three till now, never kept seat in one.

As he read she began to recite, covering up the parts which she mis-remembered. At the edges of her memory there was a woman's voice saying this poem to her. The voice was associated in memory with hair as fair as the lock she held in her hand.

When he had finished and was wrapped in the sad thoughts of his Lucia she placed her hand on his. 'Father,' she said.

Chapter 17

The following morning Francesca was determined to find Sylvia. She missed her at breakfast and after calling at Sylvia's longhouse, where she had just missed her again, she was directed towards the Kitchens. Fortunately, half-way there she ran into Simon coming back from the Smithy. He told her that Sylvia was headed in the direction of the Glasshouses.

'She wants to check on the stocks of potatoes and how the brassicas are doing. You'll have to be quick. She won't be there long, she's got a Council meeting at noon.'

Not wanting to be on another fool's errand Francesca hurried. She could see Sylvia from the moment she entered the upper house. As Simon had said she was examining the kale and sprouts growing there. Francesca ran down the path, making enough noise so that Sylvia turned towards her before Francesca had got to her. All decorum forgotten she stopped abruptly on the path facing the Head Gardener.

'I know,' she said.

'My dear girl, you know more than you think you do, so it's not much of a surprise that you know. Know what?'

'I know who I am.'

'Again an easy question to answer. You are Francesca, Gatherer of Heron Fleet, Gardener.'

'I found out last night. Tobias showed me his favourite poem. I already knew it. My mother used to read it to me when I was little and somehow the words went in. I was composing a song based on as much of the words as I had remembered for Anya weeks before he got here. When he read it I knew or I thought I knew I was his and Lucia's daughter. Now in the morning I'm not as sure as I was. Tell me the truth. Am I right?'

Sylvia sighed. 'This is what I've feared from the moment he

226

came back and I saw him in the Infirmary. I knew I could stop him asking the Council directly and the Crèche Nurses would never tell him in any case but I always feared an accident like this, a coincidence. Yes it is true you are Tobias's daughter but it may not prove to be as important as you think.'

'How can you say that? We all need to know who we are.'

'I've already told you the most important things: you're Francesca, Gatherer of Heron Fleet, Gardener. The most promising Gardener of any generation I've seen. Help me down to the main dome and we'll talk about it.'

A few minutes later Francesca and Sylvia were sitting on a bench drinking herbal tea at the hub of their common world. Francesca had made the tea using the Head Gardener's private charcoal heater and she felt calmer.

'You know most of the story already,' said Sylvia.

'So couldn't I just be imagining it? Have I imagined I knew the poem and he's just gone along with me?'

'Would you want it not to be true?'

'I'm not sure. I need to know who I am. I'm not sure it matters whether it's Francesca or ...or...'

'Philipa. Your name was Philipa.'

'That's what he told me. Then it's true?'

'Yes, it's true.'

'If it is true, why can't I remember something else? Something about when I lived with my... parents... in the roundhouse?'

'You were very young.'

'But not too young to remember the poem. Why that and nothing else?'

'Well you've always had special a gift for songs and words so I suppose that it was just that coming out early. But I know that in your head there's more than just a half-remembered poem.'

'How do you know?'

'Remember I sat by your bed after you nearly died in the storm. You talked in your delirium. You went back again and again to talking about the storm and saving Tobias but gradually I realised that you were also talking of another stormy night when you'd run for your life.'

Francesca though about the dream she had had in the Infirmary and the parts she had been unable to fit into Tobias's story.

'I dreamt about the wind breaking into a roundhouse. A man leading me down the bridge as the water broke over it. He talked to me and held on to me tightly. There was lightning so strong you could see it through the thatch. A man and a woman helping me up to safety out of the water. They gave me to a woman with yellow hair who kissed me.'

'I was the woman who helped you up out of the water. Peter was the man. You already know, I think, who the woman with the blond hair was, that was your mother, my friend. The man whose hand you held was Tobias. You have a memory that is all your own of something only four other people in the world could know anything about and only you see it from your angle.'

★ ★ ★ ★

The confirmation that she was Lucia's and Tobias's daughter did not make things easier in the next few days. In fact Francesca started to admit to herself that Sylvia may have been right when she'd suggested that knowing might create more problems than it would solve.

Initially with Tobias it had been wonderful. He filled in all the details of the story. Best of all he told her about her mother. But he assumed too much. Most seriously he started to assume that she would go with him to help found the new community rather than stay at Heron Fleet. This was also assumed by the rest of the community.

A less important but more awkward effect was that he immediately went over to calling her Philipa and tried to persuade other people to do the same. But she did not feel like Philipa. To herself she was Francesca.

The debate came to a head at one evening meal. Tobias had been referring to Francesca as Philipa all through the meal. Jeremy and Caleb had been valiantly trying to adjust but Elizabeth had simply been ploughing on with Francesca, oblivious to

Tobias's feelings. They were just finishing when he decided to challenge her.

'Elizabeth, why don't you call Francesca Philipa?'

'She was Francesca when she was in the Crèche and to me she'll always be Francesca no matter what.'

'But her first name was Philipa. Doesn't that take precedence?'

'Not in my book it doesn't'

'I bet Francesca prefers it,' added Anya. 'I bet it gives her a feeling of importance.' Anya was expected to give birth any day. She was uncomfortable and short-tempered. As a result she had been digging at Francesca in minor ways for days, revealing that the doubts she had had about Francesca's motives at the Testing had not gone entirely away.

Tobias went on talking to Elizabeth. 'So you're saying that even if your Francesca asked you to call her Philipa you'd ignore her request and just go on calling her Francesca come what may?'

'I'll tell you when she asks me,' and she laughed as she finished off the last of the hardbread she was eating.

'So there's a challenge, Francesca. Which will you choose?'

'Bound to be Philipa,' chipped in Anya. 'Like I said, makes her more important.' There was a pause and all of them looked at Francesca.

'Philipa is a nice name. My mother, who I never knew, gave me that name and I honour it for that reason if no other. It doesn't make me feel more important, it just makes me feel separated from things I love here and now. Francesca is the name I've had for all the life I can remember. Francesca is my Gatherer name and that's the name I feel comfortable with. Please call me by that name, even you, Father.' Then she got up and left the hall. After that everyone called her Francesca, even Tobias though she could see that it gave him some pain.

It was about three days after the debate about her name that what everyone in the community had been waiting for happened. She had been doing one of her shifts in the Glasshouses and had come directly to the meal from there. As soon as she came in Thomas waved to her and came over urgently.

'Anya went into labour this afternoon. Jonathan and Elizabeth are with her and one of the Shepherdesses who know most about lambing, but it's not going well. They want you to go across in case the worst happens. They're in the Infirmary.'

Fear made her feet swift. Before she got through the door she could hear Anya's cries; she was sweating and in pain, gripping tightly to Jonathan's hand as what seemed like waves crashed over her. Elizabeth was on her knees looking into Anya.

'I think I can see the top of the head but it stopped moving when the contractions came. Could it be stuck?'

'It could be. Use two fingers to feel round the head between contractions,' said Hermione, the Shepherdess who was helping.

Elizabeth waited until Anya's next bout of crying died away and then did what Hermione had suggested. 'I think there's something caught round the shoulder,' said Elizabeth. 'What do we do?'

'I'm not sure,' said Hermione. She beckoned to Francesca. 'It's very serious,' she said quietly. 'The sheep give birth much quicker than this. When something like this happens the sheep and the lamb usually die if nothing is done. Usually we sacrifice the lamb to save the sheep by cutting off the head and delivering the bits or any other lambs behind the one that's stuck, before clearing out the womb. But this is a baby and Anya is a not any old ewe.'

'Stop talking among yourselves and tell me what I can do. Would that I knew what the Crèche Nurses know,' said a despairing Elizabeth.

It took only a few strides for Francesca to be out of the door and running across to the Crèche Nurses' house. No one had seen any of the Crèche Nurses since they had withdrawn from the Testing. It was assumed that they had gone to ground in disgrace in their house. Francesca hammered on the door but there was no answer, not even a sign of any movement in the house. She hammered again. Finally, in frustration, she yelled at the door.

'Does it not matter to you that a child of Heron Fleet is dying in need of your skills?'

Someone rattled the catch of the door and it opened. It was Rebecca, the young Nurse who had taken notes when Anya had been examined.

'She has gone into labour and it is not going well. One of the experienced Shepherdesses thinks that both Anya and the child will die. Come now if you have the skills to help the baby, even if you won't help Anya.'

'What do they think is wrong?' said Rebecca

'They think something is caught across the baby's shoulder.'

'What is it, Rebecca?' The Head Crèche Nurse appeared behind her junior. 'It's you,' she said, seeing Francesca. 'Is that slut in labour? There's nothing we can or will do about it. Come away, Rebecca.'

'But ma'am, the baby will die.'

'None of our affair. When more have died then they'll give us back our rightful place, come away.'

'The mother I know has done wrong but the child is innocent and is a child of the community. Let me go at least.'

'No! Go and you can never come back to us. Do you hear me?'

Rebecca looked at her chief. 'I can't let a community child die without trying.' She turned to Francesca. 'Take me to them.'

Back in the Infirmary it was clear that Anya was in more pain and Elizabeth more desperate. Immediately Rebecca took charge. She inspected how far the baby had come and probed round the baby's head as Elizabeth had done.

'You were right,' she said to Elizabeth. 'The cord that connects the baby to the mother is caught up. The baby is too closely wedged in the birth canal for us to release it and the pulling the contractions produce on the baby will soon damage the cord to the mother if it hasn't already done so, cutting off the blood supply to the baby.'

'Can you do anything?' said a fearful Elizabeth.

'Yes, but it will be difficult and I'm going to need everyone's help. Is there any poppy juice and suspension of valerian in the Infirmary?'

'Yes,' said Hermione. 'I got the steward to make sure that we had access to all the drugs the Infirmary had and a complete set of surgical instruments in case we needed them.'

'Good. Well done. But we may need something that only the Crèche Nurses normally are allowed to have. Jonathan, will you run to Sylvia and ask her for the some tincture of hemlock. She will not be willing to give it you but you must convince her that I am the one asking for it. Tell her it's for the baby and I cannot go back and beg some from the Crèche Nurses. Go quickly; Francesca will take over helping Anya while you're gone.'

As soon as Jonathan was off on his errand Rebecca told them all, including Anya, what they were going to do. 'We're going to slow the force of the contractions down and help Anya not push as hard as she has been when they come. That will be painful so I'm going to give her a large dose of both the poppy juice and the valerian to help her. With things a little less stormy we'll see if we can free the cord, in which case the baby will come quickly and easily. There is a risk that Anya will start to become too drowsy and her breathing will get shallow. Francesca, it will be your job to see that that doesn't happen. You must tell me the minute Anya starts to fall deeply asleep or her breathing becomes shallow. If she doesn't breathe properly then the baby will die soon after and I'll have to act very quickly to save it. If that happens then you all must do what I tell you without question.'

Hermione passed two beakers of valerian suspension and poppy juice to Rebecca. 'Hold her head up, Francesca.' In turn she pressed the beakers to Anya's lips to drink. 'Anya, just swallow slowly. I know that you've no reason to trust me considering how we first met but I'll not let a community child die or its mother if I can help it. Francesca, is here and she'll look after you. I know how much she loves you and she'd stop me doing anything bad even if I'd a mind to.'

Anya was so weakened that the herbs took effect quickly. In minutes her contractions were diminished, or at least they didn't seem as painful, and Anya was more relaxed so that Rebecca and Elizabeth could get to work. Francesca stroked Anya's hair and talked to her.

'Just keep breathing steadily.' Anya held her hand tightly.

'I want to say something in case I never get another chance,' Anya said.

'Shush. Don't think like that. Rebecca knows what she is doing. It will be alright.'

'I'm sorry I did all this to you. I still love you. If the baby lives, and I don't, please take care of it.' As Anya said this, Francesca realised that her voice was getting weaker.

'We think we've moved the cord. Can you ask her to bear down when the next contraction comes?' It was Rebecca.

'Did you hear that?' said Francesca

'Yes. I'll try.'

Rebecca started to count. 'Your muscles are tightening, I can feel them. One…two…three…four…five Go' Anya contorted her face as she strained at her stomach muscles.

'Good. Was there any movement Elizabeth?'

'A bit I think.'

'Right. Same again Anya. Here it comes One…two…three…four…five. Go'

Anya tried harder this time and she squeezed Francesca's hand more tightly as she strained. But as the contraction passed, Francesca could see that the effort had weakened her. The pupils of her eyes were tiny and her face was even paler than it had been before. She tried to say something but her eyes rolled and her head drooped to one side.

Francesca felt the pit of her stomach fall. 'Can you hear me Anya?' But there was no reply. 'Rebecca, she is unconscious.'

'It she still breathing?'

Francesca looked across her chest and tried to judge if it was rising and falling. 'Yes but very shallowly.'

'There's a lot of blood coming from round the baby's head, Rebecca.' As Elizabeth spoke Francesca heard a door open.

'Just in time, Jonathan,' said Rebecca.

A bottle was thrust into Francesca's hand. 'Pour as much of this into her mouth as you can and get her to swallow it by stroking. Elizabeth, is she still bleeding?'

'Yes! I can't stop it.'

'Try to make sure that the blood runs away and doesn't drown the baby.'

Francesca looked up as the last of what she realised must have been the hemlock left Anya's mouth. The current contraction had stopped and she saw Rebecca, a sharp surgical knife in hand, cut a deep line across Anya's exposed stomach.

'Don't mind the blood everyone. If she's bleeding then her heart's beating and she's still alive but we must get the baby out. Jonathan, Hermione, pull back the muscle below and above the incision I've made. How hard doesn't matter even if it tears at the edges. I must be able to see what I'm doing.'

Jonathan and Hermione pulled, tears running down Jonathan's face as he did what was needed despite the fact that it would hurt Anya. Rebecca struggled to feel and to see inside Anya.

'I can see the womb.' She picked up the knife again.

Francesca realised Rebecca was picking the right place for a second decisive cut. Anya gulped in air with one great breath as the knife went home and was suddenly awake. The knife rattled on the floor as Rebecca dropped it and thrust her hands into Anya's stomach. A second later she was holding up a blood-soaked but crying baby boy. Seeing Anya was awake she pushed the child into her arms. 'There you are. He'll do. Francesca, see she holds him as much as she can and clean him up as best you can.' Then, as Francesca watched, the young Crèche Nurse sank back exhausted, to be enfolded in the bloody embrace of Elizabeth, as one of the Infirmary staff stepped forward to staunch the bleeding, clean the wounds and stitch Anya back together.

Chapter 18

It was Mayday dawn and Francesca was standing with all the rest of the community on the hills above the burial ground to see the first rays of the sun come over the eastern horizon.

Though officially the start of the growing season, much had been done well before this Mayday. As winter had released Heron Fleet and outside work became possible, furious activity had started.

Tobias's boat was pulled up on shore so that the damage below the waterline could be properly repaired. The steering gear had been inspected in detail, damaged parts replaced, and everything greased and maintained. The second attempt at setting the new mast, the one that Timothy had built, was successful. But there was no cheering when it finally went home, just relief that it had not cost any more lives.

Once the boat was fit for sea Tobias and Sylvia could be caught in conversation about what Heron Fleet could give to help the new community get a good start. Seeds were obvious and enough was packed aboard the boat to set a reasonable first harvest.

'The Shepherds tell me we can spare the basis of a herd. Can you take a tup and half a dozen ewes?' Sylvia asked him.

'You're very kind,' Tobias said. 'But I don't know how long it will take us to find a suitable place. If you'll let me come back when we've found the site, it might be better to take them then.'

'That might be a problem. All who go might well be considered banished when they leave. The Council have not yet finally voted on that.'

Plants in the Glasshouses started to shoot on their own well before time and the Gardeners were suddenly stretched to the limit with clearing beds to make sure there was room for all the plants which demanded space to grow. Francesca was busier than most in the propagation chamber, sowing early marrows and squashes for the curcubit house, and chitting early onions and potatoes.

Anya was up and about, though still sore after the difficulties of the birth. She had stayed about a week in the Infirmary and after that had needed rest in the roundhouse but she had been walking round with the baby for a fortnight and everyone had been able to see the boy who had been named David.

Francesca had accompanied Rebecca back to the Crèche Nurse house to see if the Nurses would have her back after the help that she had given Anya. But the Head Crèche Nurse turned Rebecca away with several curses that made Francesca very angry. She was amazed how well Rebecca took the rejection and when Anya moved out with Jonathan onto the boat, as head of the roundhouse, she invited Rebecca to join them, at least until it could be agreed what she would do.

In many ways Francesca allowed all the activity and excitement to bury the decision that was coming. But now the morning was clear and there could be no more evasion.

As they all watched, over the distant island of the great bay, the sun rose, its golden top curving and shimmering. The river cliffs emerged out of a pallid, grey mist, immediately resolving into purple and dark red. At the same time the fields between where she stood and the river turned gold and Francesca could feel the warmth of the sun on her face cut through the cold of winter. The children with the Crèche Mothers cheered, and the Apprentices and Gatherers applauded. Quickly the sun's disc rose clear of the island towards a clear sky and the warmth increased.

'A fine day for a fine year,' said a voice at her shoulder. It was Tobias. 'Isn't that how the saying goes?'

'Yes, that is how it goes,' replied Francesca. 'If the sun is clear on Mayday morning, as it is today, there will be no typhoons, the harvest will be good and all the children born will be straight and true.'

'But where will you celebrate the next Mayday, here or in a new community that your skill has brought safely through a harvest and a winter?'

'Whichever it is, I will celebrate that I have done no more than my duty.'

'Is there nothing that I can say that will sway you? Will you not trust me and come with me? I know I have no right to ask. I deserted you and your mother. I will understand if you desert me now.'

'It's not a matter of desertion. I trust you not because you are my father but because of what you did to comfort me when I remembered about what Anya had done. I respect you for how you fought for Anya and Jonathan during the Testing. I love you because you gave me the courage to stop being frightened of every difficulty or threat to the community, even typhoons and autumn storms. I would follow you willingly for how you behaved when Timothy was killed and I blamed myself. Heron Fleet gave me the responsibility of being a Gatherer but you showed me what it was to be one.'

'So you'll come with us tomorrow? When Sylvia asks who will stand with Anya, Jonathan, David and me you will be with us?'

'The truth is I don't yet know.'

'But if what you've just said is true, isn't your decision obvious?'

'Just because what I said is true is the very reason that the answer is not obvious. When you told me how Heron Fleet tore Lucia and you apart, you said you betrayed her and me because you had a choice to come back for us and not sail away when you got free.'

'That I did. But you won't betray anyone by going, it's the opposite. You'll betray people if you don't go.'

'You mean I'll betray you. That's the trouble with you. You see things too easily through only your own eyes. It gives you courage and clear-sightedness on many occasions but it makes you stubborn and selfish as well. I am caught between two things I love, you and Heron Fleet. If I stay I betray you and many of those who will go with you who are my friends. If I go I betray not simply the Heron Fleet as an idea but all those who trusted my example during the Testing. Worst of all I will throw my own words back in my own teeth; the promise I made when I was made a Gatherer last Harvest. Father, you will have to wait until this evening when Sylvia calls for those who will go with you to stand forward. Before then I doubt if I shall know myself.'

★ ★ ★ ★

Francesca started the day visiting places around the community that meant something special to her, the Glasshouses, Timothy's grave. But it was difficult to find quiet to think the thoughts she needed to think.

Mayday was a day of rest, a day for friends to count blessings, a day for partnerships to be suggested and love to be considered. But she wanted to be alone not to see images of herself reflected from anyone else's eyes no matter how precious those eyes might be to her.

Intending to visit the fields where she had planted and tended the millet before last year's harvest, she crossed the river bridge. But when she got to the bottom of the combe where the path to the beach branched to the right, she stopped and considered whether even in the fields she might be too easily disturbed. The beach would certainly not be quiet. Down there she would find many groups lighting fires and reminiscing about the past year. So she struck out from the path and started to follow the edge of the wood upstream.

The further she went the higher the river cliffs got and the higher she had to climb. She had been walking for about three hours when she found her way blocked by the cliffs on her left and by a high line of rock running down from an overhanging crag above her. She realised that she must now be beyond the limits of Heron Fleet, for although along the river the pasture the community claimed and used went on further than where she was, the northern edge of the wood was not of any interest to the community and they did not claim it.

She stood on the edge of the cliff and looked down. Perhaps there was a third way of dealing with the problem of her choice, the one she had sought the night of the storm. If she fell from here, even if they found her body they would think it a terrible tragic accident, not an act of deliberate cowardice. She was looking at the drop and wondered what it would feel like to fall, when an irregularity on the cliff face caught her eye.

Almost directly below her there was a roughly semicircular ledge. It poked out of the cliff and there was more undergrowth on it than on any other of the small ledges on the otherwise sheer rock. It seemed to be an extension of a spur of rock from the wall that had barred her way. Curiosity about what the view would be like from that platform seized her and she wondered whether using the spur of rock she might be able to get down to it. After a few minutes she located the place where the spur joined the larger wall and after scrambling over some boulders found she could follow the smaller spur downwards. She slipped and nearly went over the edge at the point where the spur went abruptly over the cliff edge but found that afterwards climbing down got easier as the spur traversed the cliff face. At the end where it reached out for the ledge, part of it had fallen away and she had to do a bit of rock-climbing across the gap. *If I ever come back here I'll bring a rope,* she thought to herself. But one last effort and she was on the ledge.

It was bigger than it had seemed from above. A good eight metres across, it was only thinly covered in dead brambles and other scrub. She realised that had it been later in the year then it would have been camouflaged with thick, growing undergrowth. In fact the ledge was likely to be visible and accessible only in the spring or winter.

She smashed down the brambles and pushed through sprouting creepers and bracken. At the edge of the platform was an irregular rim of boulders that made a convenient low parapet. She pulled back some of the undergrowth over them to get a better look at what was underneath. There was indeed a low line of stones, some placed neatly on top of others. It was remarkable how regular nature could be. How, having rolled off the cliff face, these boulders had stopped in these positions, making an effective marker of the dangerous edge of the platform.

She turned her attention to the back of the ledge. The more she looked, the more convinced she was that there was an entrance of some kind at the back. She pulled down some of the creepers growing down from above. She was right. Some more steady work cleared enough to let the late afternoon light into a cave about four metres deep.

There had been many roof falls and there were irregular piles of chippings and boulders of various sizes in several places. On the oldest parts of the roof there were signs of what might have been soot from fires. Two piles of boulders and chippings stood out from the others. They were regular rectangles and faced the cave opening. At the far end of each were two larger stones. Into these stones someone had hammered letters which had not been well made in the first place and were now badly worn. She traced them with her fingers. They were names: James and Charlie.

She went out into the full sunlight and sat on the parapet. From the river far below a tall grey bird shrugged itself into the air. Tucking its long legs up and neck back, its sharp bill cut the air, pointing its way. It looped downriver a few steady wingbeats until it turned left and started to climb. It rose towards her. As it passed no more than two metres over her head its great wings blocked the sun so that she was in shade. Then its shadow passed and she was back in glorious sunlight as if the bird had brought the warmth and light back specifically for her. She too would make her pact as long as it was necessary for the good of all.

★ ★ ★ ★

As Francesca came in to the Gathering Hall she was given a beaker of water. She looked at it solemnly and then carried it over to her roundhouse table at which Jeremy and Caleb were sitting. She sat down and set the beaker in front of her.

'Hallo stranger,' said Jeremy. 'We thought we'd see you down on the beach earlier today.'

'I had a lot to think about,' she replied.

Caleb put his arm round her and gave her a hug round the shoulders. 'This can't be easy for you. You must feel pulled in two.'

'Something like that,' she said.

Rebecca came up with her beaker and sat next to her. She had left off her Crèche Nurse scarf and robe and was now indistinguishable from any other of the older Apprentices. Generally she looked younger, but at that moment she too was deep in her own thoughts.

Jeremy decided it was down to him to try to make conversation. 'Have the Council decided if you're a Gatherer or an Apprentice yet?' he said to Rebecca.

'Oh Jerry, don't be so tactless,' said Caleb. But fortunately Rebecca was so deep in her own thoughts she didn't seem to notice the question's inappropriateness.

'No, not yet. I was chosen so early for the Nurses I would still be expecting to do another year or so before becoming a Gatherer but I have so much experience and have seen so much, it seems a bit silly not to make me a Gatherer right away. The problem is what can I do. Perhaps I'll know a bit more by the end of this evening, who knows.'

Susan and Christine joined them. 'Have you decided?' said Jeremy as soon as they had sat down.

The girls shot a glance at Francesca. 'Yes Jeremy, but now's not the time to talk about it. Everyone will know soon enough.'

The Hall was nearly full but three places were left to fill round their table. Then Francesca saw Anya, Jonathan and Tobias come in. They walked through the Hall, Anya carrying David, Jonathan carrying his and Anya's beakers. Quietly they sat in the last three places at the table.

The Council door opened and the oldest gatekeeper came in. He walked down the length of the Hall to where the rope for the calling bell, the one rung each evening to announce that the evening meal, hung in the middle of the window ready for use, not pulled aside as it would be at any other evening meal. He grasped it and pulled. The calling bell mounted on the Hall roof rang. He rang it slowly, much more slowly than the calling ring. At the same time the council door opened and the Council filed in. Each Council member carried their own beaker except Sylvia. When they were in position at table the ringing stopped. Everyone in the Hall stood and Sylvia spoke.

'This is Mayday. We have again come through a winter and there is no need of the fire at the centre of this Hall that we lit at Harvest to keep this hall warm. We will light it again at Harvest this year but now we will extinguish it as a mark of our hope in the coming season.'

As she finished, the children came forward to the fire with the Crèche Mothers. Those that could threw the water from their beakers on the fire. It spat and hissed, and some steam went up to the roof, but the fire was still alight. Then starting with the tables nearest the Council people filed past the fire making their contribution to extinguishing both the fire and the winter. As they did so the cloud of steam in the rafters grew as the fire faded. But when all the Community other than the Council had done their part, it was still alight.

'How do they know that there'll still be some fire for the Head of the Council to put out? That's the bit I can never work out,' said Christine.

'Sometimes there isn't and the fire goes out before it gets that far. So they light a torch at the start which is still alight at the end so that there's always some flame to extinguish,' said Caleb.

'On the other hand, if the fire's still alight at the end of that the Gatekeepers have to cover up by racking out the flames after the Head of Council has had a go,' said Susan.

'But if they get it right so it really is the Head of Council who puts it out then those years are reckoned to be the best years, the lucky years,' added Tobias.

'So for the sake of us and the new community, I hope everyone gets it right this year,' said Anya.

The Council had nearly finished filing past and there was only a small patch of flame left in the hearth. Sylvia came forward and gave her ash staff to the oldest Gatekeeper. In return she was handed something nearer to a jug of water than a beaker. Another Gatekeeper stepped forward with the torch. Sylvia nodded and he placed the torch in the extant patch of flame. Then she poured her water out and the final flames of last Harvest's fire, the fire that Anya had lighted, was extinguished.

The Community sat and Sylvia made her way back to her place at the centre of the table where the evening's hardbread was ready for the first blessing of the growing season. But before she blessed and broke it she paused.

'So another growing season begins. But this evening is also the beginning of a unique venture for Heron Fleet. Come forward, Tobias.'

A nervous-looking Tobias got up and went and stood in front of Sylvia.

'Master Tobias, at the end of the Testing of Jonathan and Anya you challenged those that were willing to join you and them, in starting a new community, a scion of Heron Fleet. Do you hold to that challenge?'

'I do. I will take as many as will come. We will make our own Rule as the Founders made Heron Fleet's Rule. And while how we behave inside the new community will be different from Heron Fleet, we will still take the best of Heron Fleet with us as our example.'

'The Council has set no bar on people joining you in this endeavour. However, we have decided that each who do go with you will be banished from Heron Fleet, as has been the custom in the past.'

The community gasped. This was unexpected, considering the practical support Sylvia had offered to Tobias in stores and repairs to his boat.

She raised her hand. 'This is not vindictive on our part. The banishment will be qualified and people may return for a limited time to Heron Fleet for trade or help and those from Heron Fleet will be allowed to go to the new community for limited periods without their membership of Heron Fleet being called into question. We decree it to ensure that those who follow Tobias are truly committed. Do you accept this condition on those who will stand with you?'

'I do. But I hope in time that it will be a ruling we will not need to remember,' replied Tobias.

'Only time will see if that is the case and neither I nor you are likely to see if that part of what you wish comes to pass. Formally then, will all those who are determined to stand with Master Tobias come forward to signify their commitment.'

Anya and Jonathan immediately stood up and joined Tobias. Then there was a pause.

'Who will be the first?' murmured Jeremy. He did not have long to wait. There was a stirring in the tables of the Crèches and Elizabeth moved forward. She had not gone far when a little boy and girl intercepted her. Both carried small bunches of flowers. Francesca wondered where they had managed to find them so early in the season. Elizabeth stooped to talk to them, and having stroked their hair and kissed them, they ran back to their tables and she made her way down the Hall. Anya gave David to Jonathan and embraced her old Crèche Mother as she honoured the promise made long before David was born.

Francesca felt Rebecca turn towards her. 'Thank you for your kindness. You had more reason than most to hate me but you have stood by me. This new community will have need of my skills. I will go with them.' She stood and went forward.

'Wow!' It was Christine who saw her first. 'What on earth does she think she's doing?' Ruth was moving towards the group. 'After all she's done to try to destroy Anya – the cheek!'

'But she has no place here so why not?' said Caleb.

Two couples were next. 'Look at that,' said Jeremy. The first were Hermione and another Herder who Francesca thought was called Richard. The second couple were two Apprentice Smiths, Jean and Charles. Both couples were hand in hand.

'So someone has taken Tobias's commitment to a new Rule seriously,' said Caleb. 'Good for them.'

'Is that Simon and his partner?' noticed Susan.

'Yes,' said a surprised Francesca. 'How will Sylvia manage without him? Why would he take the risk?'

'It seems to me it's the young looking for adventure and older ones looking for a new challenge who are most likely to go,' observed Caleb.

'It looks as if one member of the Council is going to confirm that idea.' Thomas had stood up, shaken hands with Sylvia and started to move forward.

'Well, Master Tobias, did you think you would get out so easily of discussing those books of yours with me?' Francesca heard him say.

'You're doubly welcome for all that,' said Tobias as he laughed and clapped the Council man on the back and Anya kissed him.

But there was another stirring in the ranks of the Council. Since resigning as Head of the Council Peter had taken his seat in the most junior seat at the Council Table, right at the far end. As Francesca watched he shyly got up and came forward and stood in front of Tobias.

'Will you have me, Master Tobias, after all I've said and done?'

'Gladly friend, gladly,' and the former partners hugged each other.

'Sixteen,' said Susan. 'It would have been fitting if it had been twenty, as when the Founders set out.'

'In that case we'd better do something about it,' said Christine and stood up. 'Are we ready?'

'As we will ever be,' said Jeremy. The four friends from Francesca's roundhouse stood together.

'Will you be coming with us, Francesca our leader and our guide?' asked Caleb.

With the eyes of the all the community on her Francesca stood and held them to her as each hugged each other.

Then she stood back and shook her head. 'No, I will bide here. There are things I need to do.'

'So be it,' said Sylvia from the Council Table as she raised the hardbread in front of her.

Reaping and sowing,
sowing and reaping,
this is the world we have.
All we know is the cycle of life.
Power to the greenwood.
Power to the field.
Power to our gathered food.

Coda

A deeply grained, smooth ash staff leaned against a table set in front of a chair. The gnarled fingers of a left hand moved up and down the top of the staff, tracing the line of the grain in a way that was thoughtful and absent minded at the same time. The owner's right hand wrote in a book in front of her.

A boy of about twelve turned to his Crèche Mother in a worried way. 'Will she have time to hear my song?' he said.

'I'm sure she will Nathaniel. When do you ever remember when she did not have time to hear you?'

'Never,' said the boy, smiling.

'There's always a first time boy,' said a sharp voice, as sharp as the speaker's features, grey hair, hands and fingers. She put down the pen she had been using and shut the inkwell top with a click.

'It's done,' she said half to herself, half to the boy and his carer. 'Now Nathaniel, let's hear this new song you've prepared.'

The boy sang for her. His voice was fresh and pure; the words about the river and the woods. It reminded her of other times, other voices and the finality of what she was about to do. But the only things she could contribute lay elsewhere and what point in grief, sadness or regret of the past was there when there was still a present to respond to. The boy stopped and all those who had paused to hear him clapped.

'That was very good,' she said. 'The best I've heard in Heron Fleet for many years.'

'Probably not since one young woman many years ago, so I've been told.' The voice belonged to a man of forty or so years old. Dark haired, short, with powerful shoulders he was dressed in a dark brown tunic and leggings, with an ochre coloured cape.

'I always thought her skill was greatly exaggerated and since I am the only one here who actually heard her, I am the only one who can possibly judge.'

The man came over and stroked her hair. She pulled his hand down and kissed it. 'I take it we are ready, David?'

'Yes Aunt. I need to get the outgoing tide if we are to get to her before the end.'

'Is she so bad?'

'She should live for a few more days but I don't want to take the chance of you being late.'

'I'll be along right now then. All we have to do is collect my things from the longhouse.'

'I thought you'd say that so I've asked the Gatekeepers to take them down to the boat already.'

The grey lady pulled herself painfully to her feet using her staff. 'So well organised! If I hadn't been there I would never take you for your impetuous mother's son. Where's your spontaneity, lad? Perhaps I should take you on a little detour to the rope bridge, trip you up with my staff and give you a dipping. There's precedence in the family you know.'

She shut the book and called Nathaniel over. 'Natt I have a reward for your song, a gift, unfortunately it's the sort of gift that comes with responsibilities.' She picked up the book and handed it to him. 'I've finished this and it's time to pass it on to someone. I've chosen you.'

'Thank you, ma'am.' The boy looked stunned.

'Are you sure, ma'am?' said a rather confused Crèche Mother.

'Yes Miriam, I am sure. With your help he'll be a worthy custodian,' and she kissed the boy.

'Now David, it's time we went. Though I'm convinced she'll not go without seeing me, it is time and like you I don't want to take the risk. There are things to say before we finally part.'

With staff in hand and once her joints had warmed up, Francesca could move deceptively fast. Since they did not have to go to collect anything from the longhouse, she insisted they went the slightly longer way past her old roundhouse. Further on the eastern doors of the Gathering Hall were open and she paused. The sun was still high in the sky but there was sufficient light to come through the western window and illuminate the stained glass sun above the Council Table.

They moved on. 'Have you had time to see the new Greenhouses?' she asked David.

'Yes, they're very fine.'

'We've doubled the size and more than tripled the productivity.'

'Proud?'

'Perhaps a little,' she grinned.

'The Gardeners told me an odd story about you. That earlier in the year you were away as an ambassador?'

'Hardly an ambassador. I think the Council sent me because if it went wrong I would be the least loss. It sounds a bit more exciting than it really was.'

'Well it sounds exciting to me. You can tell me all about it as we walk.'

'Oh very well,' she said tartly. 'I was with some of the children in the Gathering Hall rehearsing some songs when I heard a great kafuffle outside the eastern doors. There were some raised voices and then in strides a tall man. He'd got striking blond hair, long down his back. He was carrying a long spear, well worked in the haft and with a silversteel tip. He stopped in front of me, bowed slightly and said, "Yen come in peace lady. Yen Dewy clan speaker. Me seek talk with yen leader. I seek the people who gather for the leader of me clan."'

'He was an Outlander and spoke the patois of the Scavenger Gangs?'

'Yes, and he bore the symbol of the office of a leader or a messenger, the spear. I got up and stood holding my staff as nobly and authoritatively as I could. "If you come in peace you are welcome here, I said. It seems to me you have travelled a long way. I am not any longer this community's leader, though I once was, but I can tell you that if you seek the people who gather you have found us for good or ill." He laid the spear on a table and sank down exhausted onto a bench. "Thank yen sky and water." he said. "At last."'

'The Gardeners said he'd come from the remnant of a Scavenger Gang that have left their city and are trying to farm.'

'That was right. They had realised that if they did not change their ways they would starve in the cities. They had contact with a few traders who had heard about some of the communities so they decided to try farming. They did reasonably well for a few seasons and they didn't starve but they knew they needed to improve to flourish. They heard vaguely about us being the greatest growers of food anyone knew of so the clan leader chose four of his best riders and sent them out, each with a ceremonial spear to show their authority to treat with the People Who Gather if they found us and ask for our aid in growing more food.'

'And you ended up going to see for yourself?'

'Yes. There's no way I could give them advice without seeing their position. So I said I would go if they could get me there given the state of my bones. They built me a carriage to fetch me and sent an armed guard. As fine a group of young men and women as I have seen in many days. You may have seen a couple of the type around the community, young men and girls with blond hair. They are here to learn some of our ways, especially the herding, while we have sent them some of our seed grain to improve their wheat. I also got some jolly good songs and ballads out of my visit and a not unpleasant acquaintance with some excellent beer. Important in company like that to hold your drink, lad. It's a matter of respect.'

They passed through the outer ditch. The oldest Gatekeeper was on duty. 'Looks like it should be a fine evening for a stroll. Travel well this evening if you travel far ma'am.'

'Thank you keeper,' she replied.

Around the jetty she could see a large crowd of people.

'David, I told you no fuss!'

'Sorry, but it's not my doing Aunt.'

The boat was head-on to the land. Its name, the *Tobias*, stood out clear and bright as did the figure head of the man himself.

'You never told me what he said when he gave you the boat and you promptly named it after him?'

'He reminded me that it was the tradition to give boats girls' names, since they could be capricious.'

'So he liked it then?'

'Yes, I think so. He was quite well aware how capricious he could be himself and that the joke just might be on him. He

249

would have certainly been pleased with that…' David pointed upstream to where a waterwheel turned and a second race, wheel and tailgate were being constructed.

'He saw the millwheel in operation, the last time he came,' said Francesca. 'The electric wheel next to it was his design but it wasn't until the end of last growing season that we had enough electric floodlights to make it worth trying to illuminate two of the domes to see if we could extend the growing season even further. Not that any of us are worried about the length of the growing season, as we were when you were born. Even the herons are coming back in numbers. In the spring they fly over going north or stop off to fish the river and then disappear upstream. Each year fewer fly south on the way back and there are more up-country if you go that way.'

As they made their way forward there were small cheers, some clapping and multitude of travel-wells. At the head of the jetty was the Council and its Head. He stepped forward and hugged her. 'Travel far and travel well,' he said. 'And return to us.'

'I'll do my best, Jason,' she replied.

She went on board. David had brought with him two extra adult crew to make the passages to and from Heron Fleet easier and quicker. 'I think you know Ruth and Keith,' he said.

The two paused in their preparations for sea. 'Mistress Francesca,' they said and then went back to work.

'But there's one crew member you've never met.' David called a young girl over. Francesca caught her breath. She was about the same age as Nathaniel but the likeness to Anya was uncanny. 'The introductions are unusual. Both of you can meet your namesake.'

'Ma'am,' said the girl.

'So you're Anya's grand-daughter?'

'Yes, ma'am.'

'Ma'am nothing, Francesca for preference, Great-aunt if you insist on being formal.'

'I've put your things down in the cabin, ma… Great-aunt. Father said it would be alright if I unpacked some of it.' She looked round and came close to Francesca. 'It's there safe and sound. Grand Nan said I should make sure to look after it especially carefully if I saw it.'

'Did she tell you what it would mean if I had it with me?' said Francesca.

'Yes. It would mean you would not be coming back to Heron Fleet since it would have to be buried with you when you died.'

'Does your father know?'

'No, Grand Nan only told me. She thought I should know since when she is gone she hopes that you will help me, since Dad is on his own now.'

'She was right.'

'It's very beautiful. I was thinking I might be a Gardener one day. I would be proud to have one of my own.'

'We'll see, we'll see,' and Francesca hugged the girl to herself and kissed the top of her head.

Their conversation was interrupted by a group of children on the jetty beginning to sing. The group included Nathaniel. He must have waited until she had gone and then rushed down here. The singing was a signal that the ropes on the *Tobias* were being loosened and the gang-plank taken in. Two of the fisher boats pulled her backwards. As the bow cleared the jetty, the prow downstream as the tide flowing out to sea took hold of it. Once the *Tobias* was midstream the smaller boats cast off their lines and David hoisted a small amount of sail. With Ruth and Keith on one pair of oars, the sail gave just enough way to allow steering.

They picked up speed and moved down the Fleet. She made the turn out to sea to sounds of cheering from people on the beach and rose easily to the swell as she set a westerly course. As she pulled out into deeper water Francesca could look back and see the two lines of Glasshouses tumbling over the headland. She watched them with the child until she could no longer make them out and even the top of the Gathering Hall had become invisible to her unnecessarily wet eyes.